Only Good Girls...

Mary Jenkins

Chapter 1

Mami's Voice in my head

This is always my favorite part of the day. Walking into Mami's house, smelling her home cooking, and watching Matthew run into her arms.

"Gramma, Gramma," my mom's face always lights up at the sight of her grandchild.

"Hola, Papi," I kiss my Dad on the head as I pass him in his usual position on the recliner in the living room. He gives me his usual nod of acknowledgment.

My cell phone beeps and as I pull it out of my purse to check, I can hear my mom in the background.

"Ay, Laurita, you just walked in, can you put work away at least while you are here." I see her look of disapproval and I can't help but smile.

"Si, Mami, I'm all yours." I read my message as I'm telling her this "It's just that we have this big merger, transition thing going on at work tomorrow and Eric was texting some of the details." I smile at my mom, and her head tilts weirdly before she starts studying my face. I sit up wondering what my mother, slash reader of minds is reading in mine?

"Laurita? It's been a while since we've been to church to light candles. I think we should go soon. God knows you are in need of some prayer." I feel my eyes rolling to the back of my head when I hear Mami's voice again. "I just want you to find a nice man, Mija. One who can take care of you…" Mami pauses and moves the hair out of my face and behind my ear "and who can help you raise Matthew." I know this is one battle I cannot win, so I don't even try.

"Is dinner ready?" I ask her, trying to change the subject. "I really can't stay too long. I have an early day tomorrow."

"You work too much if you ask me," Mami says as she turns back to check on the food. "Another reason you need a good man!" she yells from the kitchen, as I make my way into the dining room.

"Papi, where did Mami get the idea that if I get married, I'm not going to work?" I ask my Dad laughing as we both walk into the dining room and take our seats. Papi is very quiet and doesn't say much. Once in a while, I get a word or two.

Dinner is the same as always. Mami talks about her friends and their SONS and how just maybe I should think about going out with them.

"Laurita, I just want what is best for you, Mija."

"You are not going to be young forever. Soon, it will be too late, and all the single men will be gone!"

"Only Good Girls find nice boys."

Leave it to Mami to make everything seem so dramatic. All her little sayings…I can't help but listen, you know? It stays in my head. Like a constant reminder of what I should do or be doing. I don't always listen, but maybe that's why I find myself in trouble sometimes.

Maybe, I should Listen to Mami.

Chapter 2

REWIND - 14 Months Ago

O h shit, this hurts. I thought I was ready for this, but I never expected pain like this! Why didn't someone warn me?! I look over at Mami. Upset. She knew about this. Why didn't she tell me?!

"Mom, did you call Christine?" Mami is looking at me like she wants to cry, I need someone to be in here that can support me. Not someone who is crying because they can't see me like this.

"Yes, but don't you want me to call Jake?" Mami still doesn't want to accept that Jake and I are over. Oh, God, here comes another contraction. Why does she have to do this now?! This is hard enough!

"MOM!!! Jake doesn't care!" I'm screaming at her in the middle of my contraction. "I haven't heard from him in three months! Why would he want to be here *now?!*" I clench to the sides of the hospital bed hoping they can hold my weight and don't give way.

Mami looks at me, why can't she understand? She has hopes Jake and I will get back together. I just wish she would open her eyes and see that I'm in the middle of having a baby and maybe it's not a good time to be talking about Jake!

Where is Christine? I need her. Christine and I have been best friends for as long as I can remember. She promised she would be with me as soon as she found out Jake was out of the picture.

My contractions are about ten minutes apart. The nurse that was just here, brutally violated me and said I was only dilated to a five. All I know is I need to get to ten. I should have paid more attention in those birthing classes.

"Laurita, don't yell at me" Mami scolds me. "I just think he should know in case he wants to be here." She's looking down. She's afraid of what I'm going to come back with. Mami knows I'm stubborn, I don't give up a fight that easy.

"Mom, he left me," I tell her as calmly as possible while still counting the minutes to the next contraction.

Why do they torture us with clocks in our labor room? I mean, we lay here, and we stare at that clock. We *know* when it's almost time for that next contraction. It's a horrible mind game.

I see Mami's eyes tearing up. Why is *she* crying? Jake left *me*. "Don't cry, Mami. I need you right now." Oh my God, why is it coming on again? It's only been five minutes. The clock says five minutes!

"AGGHHHHH!!!!!" I feel the most excruciating pain ever! But I can do this. No drugs. I promised myself.

Why am I always making rules and promises? I need the drugs! I need the drugs!

The nurse is back. Surely, to violate me again.

She tells me I'm now dilated to a seven. She's calling the Doc.

I fight the urge to ask for painkillers. I've spent the last nine months watching my diet, making sure I wasn't hurting my baby. Why would I expose him to drugs now? The nurse comments how brave I am for doing this fully natural, but I don't feel very brave.

Be strong, Laura. Just be strong!

"Mami, please, stay with me." Fear is coming over me. Maybe I can't do this alone. "Mami, please, Mami, I'm scared" I grab her hand and hold it tight. She still has tears in her eyes.

Geez, I'm the one who should be crying! I'm the one who is being turned inside out! Somebody, please, get that damn clock out of here!

"Heeelllloooo, Is someone having a baby in here?" Christine is here. She looks over at me "Damn, Lo, you look like Shit." She has a disgusted look on her face, but she quickly replaces it with a smile and takes her place by my side.

"Gee, Thanks…AAAAGGGHHHH!!!" I'm full into another contraction. Three minutes apart now. Throw away that Stupid Clock!

Baby's coming. Whether I'm ready or not.

*****

"Lori, look at him! He's perfect!" Christine sees my baby in my arms for the first time. I'm utterly exhausted.

"Mom, you want to hold your Grandson?" Mom is still in tears but now they are tears of joy.

"Oh, yes, Laurita, let me hold him," She takes him and now the tears are streaming down her face. "What are you going to name him?"

I have thought about this a lot and never knew just how big of a decision this is. I'm naming a little human being. "Matthew John," I tell my mom.

She smiles and looks down "Well, hello, Matthew John, welcome to the family."

I guess Dad is still upset over the whole *I'm having a baby on my own thing* because he is nowhere to be found. He'll come around, once he sees Matthew.

I have no doubt.

Sadness sets in when the reality of the situation hits me. I never imagined my first birth experience to be with my mother and best friend. Growing up, as a little girl, you dream of your Prince Charming. Life doesn't prepare you for moments such as these.

"Ay, Mrs. Sanchez, quit hogging the baby, let me carry him" Christine walks over to my mom and puts out her arms. My mom has always seen Christine as a bad influence, but she won't say anything. She kisses Matthew on the head and gently hands him over.

I feel the tears in my eyes starting to fall. This is my baby. I have a son.

I. Have. A. Son.

God help us. We have a tough road ahead.

Maybe I should have let my mom call Jake. I wish he *was* here. I lie on my side, I'm still sore. The tears are starting to fall. Why am I so emotional? I asked my mom *not* to call him. My tears start gushing. My emotions are completely out of control.

"Ummm….Mrs. Sanchez, can you take Matthew for a bit. I have to go talk to someone." Christine walks over handing Matthew back to Mami and makes her way out of the room.

I turn back around to sit up. "Mami, give him back to me. I want to hold him." My mom walks over and lays him in my arms. I see the worry in her eyes. "Mom, what's wrong?" I ask her.

Just then I hear Christine yelling "You really have some fucken nerve! Don't you dare go in there!" the door to my room swings open.

I see the familiar hazel eyes staring back at me.

Jake.

"How…" I look at him and can't even get the words out. All of the sudden, I am very emotional. "How did you know I was here?" I ask him, my voice cracking and tears starting to form.

"Can I see him?" He steps toward my bed. I look over at my mother and wonder if she *did* call him.

"Why don't you get the hell out of here?!" Christine says angrily. "You're good at just walking away!" Christine is so mad, she is turning red.

"Christine, why don't you and I go downstairs and get something to drink," My mom says as she pushes Christine out of the room. "Let's leave Jake and Laura to talk." Christine stops at the door. Mami still trying to push her out.

"Are you ok, Lori?!" She looks over at my Mom. I know she will get Jake out of here if I ask her to. She will find a way.

"I'm fine, Chris." And my mom pushes her out the door.

Jake is standing here, next to my bed. I still haven't let him see the baby? There are so many things going thru my mind right now. Didn't I just wish for him to be here? Now, I don't know if I do. I'm so hurt and upset with him. As usual, he looks good, but I am *really* not in the mood to let his looks sway me today.

"Laura," he moves in even closer "I really would like to see him." My eyes begin to water. I am so emotional.

I turn Matthew and place his head on the opposite arm, so he is now facing Jake.

Jake stares at him. I wonder what he's thinking. He isn't making any moves to touch him, and he hasn't asked to carry him.

"What's his name?" he finally says after what seems like forever.

"Matthew John," I tell him, coldly. I really want to know why he came if he's just going to stand there. "Jake, why are you here?"

"I can be here, can't I," He says smugly, shrugging his shoulders. "I mean, I *am* his Daddy, right?" What does he mean by that? Jake knows I don't sleep around.

"Jake, yes, you are his *FATHER*," I tell him firmly. "But being a *Daddy*, that's something very different." Honestly, there is a difference!

"So, are you going to give him my last name?" He seems nervous. He's starting to pace around the room like he's uncomfortable being here.

"I haven't thought about that yet. Besides, I would need your signature to be able to give him your last name." I look at him trying to get some kind of hint as to what he is thinking. He's sitting now with his hands on his head.

"Yea, sure. I'll sign" he isn't looking at me in the eye. Jake does this when he's nervous or lying. I can read him, by looking into his eyes.

"Really? Or are you just saying that because I put you on the spot?" The sarcasm is dripping in my voice. "I can call down to Records to come up here right now and we can take care of it here." He puts his head down into his arms once again.

"Yea, sure, I said yes," He's nervous. I think I see the sweat on his brow. "Laura, I don't doubt you. I know he's mine." If he knows Matthew is his son, why is he acting like this? Why did he leave me? Or if he wanted nothing to do with us, why is he here now?

I ring the nurse and ask her to call the Records Department so that we can arrange for the Father's signature.

In the meantime, Jake sits in the chairs across from my bed.

"Did everything go ok?" he asks me nervously, "you know, with the delivery?" I wonder if he is really interested or just making small talk.

"Fine." He hasn't made a move to get closer to us. Even as Matthew lets out a slight cry, he doesn't seem the least bit curious about his son.

After 15 minutes, a woman comes to my room with what looks like legal contracts for Jake to sign. They all look very *'lawful'.*

She advises me Jake's name will officially be on the Birth Certificate and my baby *will* have his last name.

Matthew John Lakewood.

She gathers all the paperwork and leaves.

Jake is still fidgety. He's making me uncomfortable. "Well, ok, then. I have to go"

What? He's leaving? Just like that?

"Don't you even want to hold your son?" My expression is confused, fierce. I can't understand why he came here only to leave now.

"I don't know how to hold babies." He gets closer to the door. "Besides, I have to get to work." He opens the door. He looks back at me, then looks down. He can't even make eye contact. "I will call you, I guess."

I watch as he walks out.

I guess??? That's it?

I feel the tears form in my eyes. This time, they start to fall. I kiss my baby's forehead and can't help but think that the best part of Jake Lakewood is sleeping in my arms.

The door stays open and a nurse is walking in with a huge bouquet of roses.

"Someone is happy for you!" the nurse says as she places them on the table next to me.

They are at least two dozen long stem red roses, maybe even three dozen, and there is an extremely enormous teddy bear-shaped balloon that says, 'It's a Boy', I mean this thing is big, and tied around the vase is the cutest stuffed animal. A little monkey.

I reach for the card.

To the Most Beautiful Mother in the World
and her brand new Baby Boy.
        Love, Eric

Of course, Eric would do this. It's the jerks that we are always wasting our time on.

How could I ever think Jake would want anything more? He's cold and just plain mean. We always like the bad boys and Jake was just that, a Bad Boy.

Mami's voice is in my head again.

'If you are a good girl, Laurita, you will meet a nice boy'

The problem is, I *was* a good girl, I *am* a good girl, and here I am. Without a nice boy! My emotions get the best of me. Tears start to fall once again.

My Mom and Christine walk back in.

"Holy Shit, Lori, Who sent that?" Christine is looking over at the huge display of red roses and the life-size balloon. Mami, too, is shocked at the size.

"My boss," I say and Mami looks over at me curiously. Her mind-reading eyes gazing upon me, but I don't have time for that right now. Matthew starts to cry.

They don't ask about Jake at all. They see the tears on my face.

My new adventure is about to begin.

****

Chapter 3

A New Beginning?

Matthew is three months old now. He's growing so fast. I have found him a great daycare where he seems happy and I finally weaned him off breastfeeding. I kind of miss my larger boobs but not the pain that came with it. My Friday nights are not the same anymore. I go out but maybe once a month IF I'm lucky. This Friday night, it's just Matthew and me, he's in bed and I'm snuggling up on the couch getting ready to watch a movie.

I hear my cell phone ring, but the number is not familiar so, I send it to voicemail. I'm not in the mood to entertain telemarketers.

Christine is at Benny's, our favorite watering hole. About this time, she's on her third margarita talking to some unsuspecting young guy who thinks he's picking her up when it is the other way around.

It's about halfway thru the movie when the doorbell rings. I get up lazily and make my way to the door. I have no idea who could be coming over at this hour? Maybe Christine got bored or couldn't find anyone interesting. As I peek thru the peep hole. "What the?!" I whisper to myself.

Oh my God. I can't believe it!

First, my heart sinks but then I feel it start to race. Suddenly, I start to feel sick to my stomach.

It's Jake. I have a million emotions going thru my body all at the same time.

I don't want to answer. I stand behind the door for a moment, frozen. He rings the doorbell again. This time, he knocks as well.

"Lori! I know you're there. I see your car in the driveway." He's yelling thru the door. How dare he make assumptions. What if I'm on a date? Someone could have picked me up. I mean, I could be dating again. I'm not, but I could be.

Maybe, I should answer.

Why is he here?

Why is this so hard?

Just answer the door already, Laura!

I frantically fix my hair, as much as is possible. I gently turn the knob and open the door only ten inches. Keeping my body between the door and wall so he can't see inside.

"Yes…" I look at him up and down. Oh My, he does look good. But Jake always looks good. Tonight, he looks especially yummy. It might be my overactive hormones and the fact that I haven't had sex in like forever, but I felt my heart skip a beat just looking at him.

"Laura, Babe, um, I know you're probably mad at me." He looks at me with his beautiful hazel eyes, I am melting inside.

Me? Mad at you, Jake? You left me while I was pregnant! Why ever would I be mad at you? I think to myself, but I'm quickly distracted by his eyes. These hormones are making me see double!

"I want to talk." He stretches out his arms, like a salesman with a pitch, "I've wanted to talk for some time. I just didn't know how to go about it." He looks down as if he's ashamed.

Oh, no, the poor puppy dog approach.

I roll my eyes, trying to seem somewhat cool and collected but literally, my insides are aching. I want to take him in my arms, I want us to be the way we were as a couple. Before it got complicated.

"Jake, I..." I'm having trouble figuring out what I'm going to say, I move in front of the door now, clenching my hands together, nervous, speechless, and... *excited*? Jake still has this effect on me. My attraction to him, as strong as ever. Even after everything he has done, my heart still wants, longs for him. Or is it just my hormones...it's hard to tell at this point.

"So much has happened. Things that cannot be taken back." *Good, Laura, that's a good way to start.* So far the words are coming out like I want them to.

"I know, Babe, I left you when you needed me the most." He looks so good. I miss him so much. And he smells so good. "I know it's stupid to say that I wasn't ready but it's the truth, I ran because I was scared." He looks down again. "I never had a Dad." He looks up at me. Is that a tear in his eye? "I didn't know if I could be one with no one to base it on." He's nervous, I can tell.

"I understand you didn't have a Dad" I can't look at him, he makes me melt and I want him even more. "But if anything, that means you know what it feels like to grow up without a Daddy. Why would you want to do that to our baby?" I'm looking at him now but he's still looking down.

"I know, I know!" He says with shame, looking down again shaking his head. "Please, Lori, forgive me" He grabs one of my hands. Very few people call me Lori. Only those closest to me and he knows it.

Just like that, his touch goes thru me like a jolt of electricity. Why does he have this power over me?

"Can I come in?" he's closer now, He smells absolutely delectable. It's useless to say no. He knows he has me right where he wants me. I was the moment I answered the door.

"Ok," I say quietly. "But just to talk!" I say firmly.

Yea, right! I tell myself as we go in. I already know this familiar scene. My heart has won once again. My head is yelling at me to stop but I can't.

I love this man.

Jake walks in quickly making his way to Matthew's room. Matthew is sleeping but that doesn't stop him from picking him up and waking him. Matthew stares at him, and to my surprise, he doesn't cry at this stranger holding him.

"You don't know how long I've been waiting to hold him," he tells me as he cradles his son. I can't help but get emotional. I'm fighting back the tears. Matthew seems to be absolutely at ease, falling asleep in Jake's arms.

He stands there rocking him until Matthew is fully asleep. It almost seems like he knows what he is doing.

He places him back into the crib and kisses his forehead. He has a smile from ear to ear, one I rarely see on Jake and I'm happy. *This* is what I want!

"So, what movie are we watching?" he looks over at me. "I hope it's not Titanic again." He knows me so well.

I start walking towards the living room laughing. "We can put on another movie if you like," I tell him. "or we can just sit and talk about things" I turn and look at him.

I walk over to the kitchen and fill two glasses of water. I hand Jake his glass and he places it gently on the coffee table. He then proceeds to take my glass, placing it next to his.

I don't think Jake has "talking" on his mind.

He grabs my hand and pulls me to him. His arms are around me, holding me tight. I miss this. I miss him, his touch, and his smell. My heart is racing. My hormones, completely out of control.

"I missed you, Lori" he gently kisses my lips, biting my lower lip.

He leans in and whispers in my ear "you are so beautiful".

"No, Jake." I pull away. "It's not that easy, you know?" It really is. If he only knew just how bad I wanted to jump his bones right now, but I have to think of Matthew. I can't let him play with me like this, because it's not just me anymore. It's us now! He has to understand that!

"Lori, I know. I know you're hurt." He pulls in closer. "Let me make it up to you." He puts his arm around my waist again, "to Matthew. I want to be part of his life." He flashes one of his mil-lion-dollar smiles. "I want us to be a family." He knows exactly what he is doing. He kisses my neck as his hands grasp my waist firmly. "C'mon" he whispers in my ear. "You know we belong together." I don't pull away this time. He knows I'm still in love with him. He starts to lead me to the bedroom. I feel the rush. My heart is pounding so fast, it's been so long. I let him lead me. I for-get at that moment all that Jake has done to me.

Once again, I was his. He was mine. We were together. The way it was always supposed to be. Matthew's Daddy is home.

Chapter 4

Jake

I wake up and look over. There he is. It wasn't a dream. I feel happy. Jake is lying next to me, staring at me.

"Good Morning, Beautiful," he says as he runs his finger down the center of my face. "Would you like some breakfast?"

I look back at him. In my mind, I answer him. *'I would like to lie here forever, Thank you, and never have to live in the real world again.'* Of course, I can't say this to Jake. He seems to spook easily.

"Sure, I tell him, but I'd like to take a shower first." After last night's activities, I feel a shower is in order.

He looks at me with those beautiful, hazel eyes. "Ok, then, let's shower then we'll have breakfast."

Let's? Did I just hear that correctly? I smile.

Oh, Jake, please don't play with me. I think to myself.

After our shower, Jake and I manage to make a nice breakfast. We sit across from each other at the table, staring at each other like teenagers in love.

"How is work going?" he asks breaking the silence and tension between us. "Is Corey still giving you a hard time?" I can't help but make a face.

I look at Jake, puzzled. A hard time? I don't think I've ever told Jake that Corey, my supervisor, gave me a hard time.

"No, not really, Corey is just Corey," I tell him plainly. "It looks like it's getting better. I see a lot more work coming thru." I pour us some orange juice thinking to myself how nice this feels, sitting here having breakfast with my son's father.

I look over at him. He's so hot. I mean, Jake is super gorgeous. Imagine those men on Calendars. That's Jake. His body is chiseled; his arms are defined and strong. He is HAWT Hot!

"Do you think you can make some calls and get me some interviews?" I look at Jake curiously; I thought he was still working at the auto shop. "Jerry and I had a falling out and I kinda quit." Jerry is or *was* Jake's supervisor at the auto body shop.

"Ummm, yea, sure," I tell him. "I know a few places that are hiring. I could put in a word." I smile at him, and he smiles back his perfect smile.

I am so happy. Jake makes me happy.

Maybe, after he starts working, we could get a bigger place. God knows this little house is way too small for the three of us. Maybe I'm getting ahead of myself, but he wouldn't come back just to leave again, right?

Matthew starts to cry, taking me out of my daydream.

"I'll get him!" Jake gets up right away.

"Are you sure?" I tell him as he runs across the living room.

"Of course, I've been waiting to do this, remember?" I'm sitting here in awe. In the moment. The moment that I want to last forever. The moment that I have wanted to happen for so long. Matthew has a Daddy. A tear starts to form when Jake comes back into the living area with Matthew in his arms.

"What's wrong?" he tells me, seeing my emotion.

"Nothing. I just…" now the tears are really pouring down. "I have wanted to see you two together for so long and I can't believe this moment is finally here," I tell him through my sobs. I walk towards my baby and his Daddy.

He takes me in his arms and I feel his body against mine. He is still holding Matthew. "This is my family," he says in a whisper. "I was stupid not to see it before." Oh, God did someone give him a *say all the right things* serum before coming here. Is this really my Jake? The same Jake who left me when I was pregnant? The same Jake who couldn't hold his baby the day he was born because he had to get to work?

Please, let this be real. Let this be real. I feel like Dorothy tapping her Ruby slippers.

My heart is filled, and I want to believe this is true, but my mind is still telling me to wait. Be careful. We know Jake, remember?

****

It's been three wonderful months.

Jake is working in the Oilfield.

Work seems to be getting better for me and Matthew is almost six months old.

Life is good.

Jake and I have had our moments but nothing major. He seems happy, I'm happy and my Mom well, she's definitely happy. She's probably already planning the wedding.

This weekend Jake and I are going to shop for a bigger place. Possibly a house. We are still looking at renting, but a house is a strong possibility. I'm really excited.

"Miss S, Jake is on line 1" Casey, our receptionist snaps me back to reality.

"Oh, OK, Thank you, Casey," I tell her.

"Laura Sanchez," I'm like a school girl getting a call from the cool guy in school. I can't help but smile when I hear Jake's voice.

"Hey, Babe, I'm not bothering you, am I?" Oh, Jake, even if I was busy, I would drop everything for you, is what I want to say, but of course, I don't. I hold back.

"No, I'm working on some stuff, but I can take a small break, what's up?" I tell him, trying to act calm and cool.

"I just thought maybe you and I could go out tonight. Somewhere nice" he says.

What? Did I just hear that correctly? Does Jake want to go somewhere nice? That's a change.

"Okay?? Tonight? I'll need to ask my mom to babysit, but sure." I'm kind of excited. Jake has never really taken me out. We usually just go to a run-of-the-mill restaurant and then a bar for a couple of drinks. That's Jake's idea of a date. I might get to dress up this time.

"Okay, I'll see you at home, Love you," he says quickly.

"Love you, too" I hang on to the phone until I hear him hang up.

Wow, a real date with Jake. I can't wait.

I rush home from work thinking about what I'm going to wear. It's been so long since I've dressed up.

I look in my closet and for once, don't even know where to start.

I take out four dresses and place them on my bed when my doorbell rings.

My mom lets herself in, "Laurita, I'm here" she yells as she comes in.

"I'm in my room" I yell back. "I'll be right there." I'm so glad she didn't give me any problems about the last-minute babysitting gig.

I walk into the living room, Mami is already holding Matthew. I've tried on one of the four dresses and she looks at me up and down. The dress is an electric blue, form-fitting dress. Her pursed lips tell me she doesn't approve.

"Ay, Laurita, you're not wearing that are you?" my mom never approves of my clothes. "you need to wear something more youthful." She says, "you look old in that dress." If it were up to my mom, I'd still be wearing petticoats and flowers.

"This is just one of many that I'm trying on, Mom" She purses her lips again.

"Well, keep trying on. That one is no good for your shape." I love my mom but sometimes I don't need her honesty.

"Mom, I put extra clothes and his pajamas in here in case it gets late." I look at my mom to see her reaction as I hand her Matthew's diaper bag. "There are extra bottles and formula here and I was thinking that if it did get too late that maybe… he could stay at your place?" I look again at my mom. She makes a face, but her expression quickly softens.

"Yes, Okay…" she says. "He can stay with us. There's no reason to wake him up if he's already sleeping." I'm lucky I have such supportive parents.

"Thank you, Mom" I kiss her on the cheek. "this is the first time Jake takes me on a real date. I'm so excited." I tell her.

"I can tell," she says. "you never have trouble picking out what you're going to wear." She points at my room where she can see the dresses on my bed. "Well, you all have fun and I'll see you tomorrow." She kisses me on the cheek "and Por Dios, put on another dress, Laurita." I roll my eyes and I say bye to Matthew and kiss his forehead. My mom. Always the supportive one. I think to myself sarcastically.

Now, to pick my outfit.

Jake gets home at 7:30 and heads straight to the shower. I'm almost ready and have decided on a black, David Meister dress. Classy, simple, and beautiful. Jake's shower is short, as usual, and he puts on his best pair of jeans and to my surprise, he owns a button-up shirt. I have butterflies in my stomach.

As we drive, I notice we are going towards downtown. Wow. There are so many nice restaurants downtown. Jake parks and we make our way down to the River Walk.

"Jake, where are we going?" I ask him. So curious, I can't stand it anymore.

"Well, now that we're here, I guess I can tell you," he says smiling. "I know you have always liked this place and we don't get to come here often." My mind wanders, there aren't very many places on the River Walk that we've been to.

"We're going to the Hard Rock Café," He says excitedly. I almost stop in my tracks.

Really? He said we were going somewhere nice and we are going to the Hard Rock Café? I put on this dress and we are going to the Hard Rock Café? I can't believe it!

I guess Jake sees the expression on my face because his expression quickly changes. "I thought you liked the Hard Rock?" he asks me, concern filling his voice. This is Jake trying to do something nice and I'm making him feel bad.

"I do, but" my voice filled with discontent, "when you said we were going somewhere nice, I kind of figured it would be somewhere, I don't know… *romantic*" I look at him and see that I've hurt his feelings. "It's fine. If we sit in the right place, the Hard Rock can be romantic." I feel the disappointment inside me, but I don't want to hurt Jake's feelings any more than I already have.

We ask to be seated somewhere with some privacy. It's still very loud with the music but the booth is away from other patrons. It's just Jake and I and we are having a good time.

After dinner, Jake orders some drinks for both of us.

"Lori, I wanted to have this dinner today for a reason." He starts to tell me. He's looking down and seems nervous, "The last three months with you and Matthew have been a wake-up call for me." He's starting to fidget. Something is up. I've never seen Jake like this.

"I know you and I don't have the perfect relationship," He starts to say.

Wait. What? I thought our relationship was pretty good.

I hear Jake continue, "but I am ready to spend the rest of my life trying to make our relationship perfect" he goes on and reaches in his pocket and pulls out a box.

Holy Shit! I'm floored! I start to look around. I don't know what I'm looking for exactly but I'm shaking.

"Jake..." is all I can say as I finally look back at him.

I am speechless. I don't know what to do. Do I want this? Am I ready for this? I mean, I know I love this man but marriage? Really? That's a big step. A HUGE step.

Jake holds out his hand with the ring. I'd say it's about a half-carat solitaire. White Gold. He did good. It's beautiful and I smile.

"Did you think about this?" I sound nervous and I press my hands together "I mean, this is a HUGE step" I look at Jake's eyes. His eyes always tell me what Jake is thinking. Only he is not looking at me, he is looking down.

Why am I acting like this? You would think that I'd be happy that my Baby Daddy wants to marry me. Why, then, am I so scared?

Remember, Laura, Prince Charming?

Maybe yours just arrived a little late?

"Laura, I kind of thought you wanted this" Jake says under his breath, almost embarrassed. I'm making him feel bad again.

Twice in one night. Oh, no, that's not what I want to do. I'm just *scared*. I'm so nervous right now. Like I've never been before. I don't even think I was this nervous when I told my parents I was pregnant!

"It's not that I don't" I start to tell him, "It's just that we never talked about it." I think I'm going to hyperventilate. Really, like, I need some air. "You just took me by surprise, that's all." I smile at him. Trying to put both him and me at ease. But mostly me.

Breathe, Laura, just breathe. Live in the moment.

"We're talking about it now." He says again thru his teeth, and he puts the ring on the table in front of me. He looks me straight in the eye.

"Laura Sanchez, will you marry me?" Oh, yes, this *is* actually happening. Jake is proposing.

In a million years, I never expected this day would come.

"Yes" I whisper, this is the only word I can find, that makes any sense and manages to escape my lips. I'm sitting here, stunned and speechless. Happy, excited, and emotional.

Jake Lakewood just asked me to marry him.

My poison will now be *my Husband?*

****

I have been showing off my ring for the past two weeks. I still can't believe it. I look down and look at my left hand and just get lost in my daydreams, my fantasies of the wonderful life Jake and I are going to have.

Eric tried to tell me that he was happy for me, but I could see the disappointment on his face. Even now, it always seems like he has something to tell me, but he's holding back. I'm sure it's just a pride thing. My engagement has finally kept him from persistently asking me out.

Jake is in the field and won't be back for another week. We're supposed to set a date when he gets back. I'm so excited. Mami has called the whole family, people we haven't talked to in years, to let them know.

"Miss S, you have a call on line 1, she says she a friend of Jake's" Casey, as always snaps me out of my own mind.

"Thank you, Casey," I tell her.

"Laura Sanchez" I answer the line. No one answers. "Hello?" I say again.

"Hi," she sounds young "are you Jake's girlfriend?" she asks me. Girlfriend? I think to myself. I'm his fiancée and I smile to myself.

"Who am I speaking with?" I ask the person on the other end.

"This is Gina. Are you Jake's girlfriend?" She says quickly. She has a slight East Texas twang in her voice. Very subtle.

"Ok… Gina… I'm sorry, How can I help you?" I don't really like giving strangers information about me or my personal life.

"Well, you need to know Jake is a liar and he hasn't told you everything." She is being vague and although she has my attention, I'm really getting annoyed with this conversation.

"Gina, I'm a busy person. I don't have time to beat around the bush or play mind games. "Honestly, I don't. "So, just tell me how it is I can be of assistance to you."

"Laura, Jake has another family. He has a baby with me. A little girl. She's 3 years old. Her name is Blake." I literally feel the pain in my heart as it breaks. What? Did I hear that right? Jake has another baby. Is she telling the truth? My jaw drops, leaving my mouth hanging wide open. Can I believe her? "Where do you think he goes when he's not with you?" She has to be lying. She must be some vengeful ex who found out Jake was getting married. She is just trying to get back at him and will say anything to break us up.

"Gina, you must have heard that Jake asked *me* to marry him," I tell her flatly. "That's why you are doing whatever you need to, to try to stop that from happening. I understand. Jake is a catch. But he's mine. He's with me and he's asked *me* to marry him." I know what jealousy can do to a person and I'm hoping it has driven her to lie about her and Jake and their child. Please, God, make it all an act of jealousy.

"So, really, quit trying to pull at strings to keep him within your reach or to get me to call it off. It's not going to happen. I don't need to hear your lies," That should about do it. I hate drama.

"Really?!" she yells at me "Why don't you ask him where he's been for the last week?" she tells me as she hangs up.

I can't believe what I just heard. Jake told me he was out in the field. Could he have been with her? This is absurd. She can't be telling the truth. I need to get to the bottom of this. I can just call Jake and he will clear all of this up. Or maybe, I can just call her back. I want to know how much Gina knows about Jake.

I call Casey. "Casey, can you get me the number for the person that just called me, please?"

"Sure thing, Miss S," she says.

About a minute later, Casey is in my doorway with a yellow sticky in hand. "Here you go." She says. "It's funny the caller ID said Jake Lakewood, but I'm sure that was the number she called from." She hands me the sticky and looks at me as if she's waiting for more information. I don't like to feed the gossip chain. Especially in an office as small as ours.

"Thank you, Casey," I tell her "If she calls again, please come get me." I look at the number; it isn't a number I recognize. I have a meeting in five minutes. I should wait until after the meeting to call.

I make my way down the hall to the conference room, but my mind is on my last phone call from this mysterious *Gina* person.

I'm distracted throughout our meeting and don't even remember what we talked about as I make my way back to my office.

I take the sticky out of my pocket. Who knew the meeting would last two hours. My hands are shaking as I dial the number. I close my office door for more privacy. I want to know more about this 'Gina' and I want to know if she is telling the truth about Jake. Could it be true that he's been with her for the last week? Does he have another child?

I dial the number and hear the ringing on the other end. I am so nervous. My heart is pounding.

"Hello" the familiar voice answers on the other end.

Oh, shit.

"Hello?" the familiar voice asks again.

I hang up the phone right away. Tears fill my eyes. I stare at the phone, crying.

The door to my office suddenly opens and Eric comes into my office. "Laura, I need to get…" he stops mid-sentence when he sees me sitting there, my eyes filled with tears. "Oh my God, Laura, what's wrong?"

I look at him, the tears make it hard to see, "Jake." I tell him thru my sobs as I'm shaking my head "Jake answered the phone" I'm pointing at the phone.

Eric looks at me bewildered, not exactly knowing why Jake answering the phone was a bad thing.

I now have my head in my hands as I continue to cry. This can't be happening!

"Umm, hold on" he leaves my office and closes the door. I sit there trying to compose myself.

A few minutes later, Eric pops his head back in my office "C'mon, let's go get some lunch."

I need to get some air, so the invitation is welcome. I grab my purse and try to pull myself together. As we walk out, I see no one in their offices or the hallway. It seems strange to me, but I don't question it.

"I had Evan call everyone into a meeting in the back so, I could sneak you out," Eric tells me. "I don't need everyone seeing you like this." All of a sudden Eric seems so...protective. "Office gossip is like poison." He tells me. I feel so grateful for Eric right now. I would have hated for anyone to see me like this.

As we drive out onto the highway in his Black Chevy Tahoe, Eric looks over to me and hands me a box of tissues. "We can talk about it or we can just have lunch and forget about it," he tells me in a very calm, sincere voice. I don't think I've ever seen Eric in this light. "It's up to you. Either way, I want you to know, you're one of the strongest women I know, Laura, and whatever it is," he stops and glances over at me, "I'm sure it's nothing you can't handle." He seems so sure. I'm not.

I look at him and barely manage a smile. Thanks, I think? I'm not even sure if that was a compliment or what? Either way, I was glad Eric got me out of there. He's right. The office gossip would have been rampant with this one. Casey, especially, would have put two and two together.

"Eric, I think Jake and I are over" I manage to say after a long silence. I'm looking down at my ring. "I mean, I don't know, it's complicated, but" I stop and shake my head and stare out the window. Even with the unspoken words, I think Eric understands.

Eric looks over at me, a smile on his face. His grin throws me off. He seems cheerful over my last statements. He sees my confused look, "I'm sorry if I seem happy about that," he explains, "it's just that," he pauses and smiles again "the thought of you being available seems like a good thing to me." His smile is almost wicked. I can't help but laugh.

"Can you please be serious?" I tell him, trying to wipe the huge smile that is coming over my blushing face.

For a minute, I'd forgotten about Jake. Even if for just a minute. Eric's plan to take my mind away from the situation works. I pull myself together.

Lunch is filled with conversations about work and Eric's latest adventures with Evan. We manage to make it thru lunch without talking any more about Jake, and it's refreshing.

"Are you sure you want to go back?" he asks me, as we head back to the office. "I'm sure we can manage if you take the afternoon and handle what you need to at home." Eric has really been a gentleman this afternoon. I'm impressed.

"Thank you, Eric," I tell him. "I *would* like to take the afternoon. I feel I have a long night ahead of me." I take a long breath coming back to reality.

"You call if you need anything, ok?" he tells me as we pull into the Black Gold parking lot.

"Sure." I nod. "Thanks again for lunch, for sneaking me out, for… everything," I tell him. I lean over and give him a small hug.

As I get into my car, I can't imagine just how I'm going to *take care* of my problem with Jake. All I know is that Jake is not going to make a fool out of me!

I text Jake before leaving telling him I know he is back from the field, and we need to talk. He hasn't responded.

The entire ride home, my emotions are a roller coaster.

The 45-minute drive between work, picking up Matthew, and home, gives me time to cry, get mad, and cry again. I'm a mess. I still don't know what I'm going to say to Jake. As I pull into the driveway, I see his truck.

Here we go.

My heart is racing as I gather my purse and keys. I pull the visor down to look in the mirror and make sure the evidence of all my tears is not all over my face. As I'm doing this, I see a shadow in the corner of my eye. I look up and see Jake getting into his truck. What the hell? I quickly open the door to the car and get out.

"Jake!" I yell at him. His windows are up, and he is completely ignoring me. "Jake!" I yell again. I start to walk over to the truck when he pulls out of the driveway. Not once did he turn around to look at me. What the hell? I think to myself.

I take Matthew out of the backseat and head into the house. As I walk in, nothing seems different. Not right away, anyway. I place Matthew in the playpen and head down the hallway to the bedroom.

As I walk in, I see it. A note on my nightstand. Clothes missing from the closet and when I walk into the restroom, Jake's half of the restroom is now empty.

I'm shaking as I unfold the paper on my nightstand that just says 'Lori' on top.

>*Lori,*

There's nothing I can say that will make this any better or make you less mad. Maybe I wasn't ready for this. I'm sorry.

Jake

That's it. That's all he writes and with that, he is gone again. Out of our lives. He didn't even give me an explanation for what this Gina girl told me. He just left.

I look down at my left hand and see my ring and the tears are rushing down my face.

Why, God, why did he leave me? What did I do wrong?

I hear Matthew in the living room and start to make my way over when my doorbell rings.

Mami. Great. Now I have to tell her that my *almost perfect relationship with My Baby's Daddy* is no longer existent. I really don't need this right now.

I open the door. "Hi, Mom" she sees my face and looks at me with concern.

"Laurita, what's wrong?!" I leave the door open and walk over to the couch and she follows quickly behind me closing the door.

I guess now is as good as any to let her know.

Of course, Mami thinks I did something wrong to drive Jake away. I finally had to ask her to leave because she was upsetting me.

She and my Dad are going to visit my aunt in the Valley for the weekend. My aunt hasn't met Matthew yet, so, she asks me to come with her. I'm not up for any family visits. Not right now. Not like this. I don't want to see anyone. I can barely stand talking to my mother. So, she offers to take Matthew. I'm reluctant but think it might be good. He doesn't need to see me like this either. My mother, of course, has to throw in her two cents.

'it'll give you some time to think about what you did and what you need to do to make it right.'

Yes, Mom, *what I did!* I do love my mother, but she just doesn't get it sometimes.

Thank goodness tomorrow is Friday. I have all weekend to sulk.

Chapter 5

Falling Apart

I text Corey letting him know that I have a "family emergency" and will have to take tomorrow off. I mean, technically, I'm not lying. This, to me, is sort of an emergency. All I get back from him is 'K'. Good Ol' Corey, we can always count on him…for nothing. I think to myself.

Christine is out of town, so, I can't even go out for our regular Margaritas. I walk into my kitchen and open a bottle of wine. I settle into my couch and pop in my favorite chick flick, Titanic.

I can't imagine why I was so stupid for letting myself go thru this again with Jake. He's played me before even leaving me when I was pregnant and that is pretty bad.

And still, Laura, you let him back in so he can what? Hurt you again? Break the pieces that were left of your heart? Leave you without so much as an explanation. With so many unanswered questions.

If he does have another family, Jake is not the person I thought he was. Actually, if all this is true then I really *don't know* Jake at all!

Ugh. I have to get out of my own mind and try to find some peace. Please, Lord, just give me some peace. I pray to myself.

Four glasses of wine later, I cry myself to sleep.

****

I should have gone in to work. I have spent all of Friday morning in bed and I am still in my pajamas. I remember my favorite blanket from the couch, the one that still smells like Jake and I get up to get it from the living room. I take the blanket and find myself putting my whole face into it and taking in the smell.

Why? Why would he leave his family? It isn't supposed to be this way?

Suddenly, I find myself going thru my drawers looking for *anything* that will remind me of him, his smell, his touch, our time together. I am on a mission. I am obsessed.

I leave no drawer untouched, no shelf unturned. My house is a mess.

In the end, all I find is my engagement ring, a napkin from the Hard Rock Café that we both signed and dated the day Jake proposed, and my blanket.

I fall to the floor exhausted. I'm sick to my stomach. I can't cry anymore and frankly, I don't want to.

I lay there on the floor, wrapped in my blanket, with my engagement ring and what seems now to be a silly napkin signed by a foolish, foolish girl and the boy who took her for a ride.

I was so happy. But I see now, how happiness can blind you.

'Ay, Laurita, find a nice boy who will love and respect you'

I hear Mami in the back of my mind. But even in Mami's perfect world, that boy is Jake. If she only knew the whole story.

I can't help it and the tears start to fall again.

Another night where I cry myself to sleep once again.

****

It's Saturday and I've decided on a Chic Flick marathon.

I talked to Matthew this afternoon. Well, actually, my mom put the phone to his ear, and I said hi and he babbled and said 'Mami' a couple of times. He seems to be doing ok with Tia Lucy. I'm sure he's getting tons of attention. Mami had her usual words of wisdom.

'Put on a nice dress and invite Jake over so you all can talk.'

Ay, Mami, if only it were that simple. I think in my mind. I sometimes wonder if it *ever was that* simple. Were relationships so easy back in the day, that all you had to do was put on a pretty dress, smile pretty, and magically, everything was all better? I have to laugh to myself because I find that hard to believe.

I open a new bottle of wine because it seems the last one that was in my fridge has mysteriously disappeared. Ok, probably not so mysteriously, but this wine is going down extremely well. Besides, wine puts me in a better mood. Maybe, I can keep from crying today.

I look around my house and it's quite a mess. My obsessed mission to find memories of Jake is scattered everywhere.

"Geez, someone should really clean this place up," I say out loud to the loneliness in the room. I look around. "And I guess that someone has to be me." I pace up and down not having any idea where to start. "Maybe, I'll have another glass of wine first." Yes, I'm talking to myself. And why not? I'm usually talking to myself in my head, so why not just start talking out loud?

"Yea, Why not?" I say as I take my seat in front of my TV where another episode of *'Snapped'* has begun. I forget about cleaning.

I am restless. I walk to the kitchen to fix myself a small salad and grab a water bottle returning to the couch. I realize I haven't eaten since, well, since I had lunch with Eric. In a moment of clarity, I start believing that things are going to be ok. I'm going to be ok.

I can do this. I mean, I've done it before.

I had a baby without Jake. I don't need him! I'm kind of starting to feel better. I change the channel. I'm done watching the *Chick Flicks*.

I surf through the channels, and there it is, I catch the last part of 'Jerry McGuire'. You know, when he says to her *'You complete me'* I find myself getting emotional all over again. My eyes start to water once again. Why couldn't I complete Jake? This is just too hard. I hate this. I change the channel again.

Where's my wine?

And just when things seem to be at their worse, my doorbell rings.

"Who could be coming over now?" I am still talking out loud. I've got a good buzz going and I can't be responsible for what I might say. Even if it is Jake, I might tell him off! I almost hope it is. I'm ready to tell him exactly what I think about him!

I open the door without looking out the peephole.

"Holy Shit!" The words slip out before I can stop them. Standing in front of me is... Eric Johnson? I stand there thinking that maybe I shouldn't have just said that. "Umm, I'm sorry, Eric, I just didn't expect it to be you." I start laughing. Oh, no, I am a little tipsy. Ok, more than a little. And now, my boss is here.

"Laura, I just thought I would stop by and check on you," Eric says. "After talking with you on Thursday, I thought maybe you would need someone to talk to? A shoulder to cry on?" He lifts his hands and has a bottle of Jack Daniels in one hand and some Coke in the other.

I smile at him. Hell, I'm already on that road. "Wow, you read my mind!" I tell him. "come on in!" I over exaggerate my 'come on in' wave and Eric makes his way into my house.

"Please, Eric, excuse any mess you might see, but my fiancée just left me," I tell him. Pointing out the scattered remnants of my 'mission', sarcasm dripping in my voice.

"So, I guess talking with him didn't go very well?" he yells at me from the kitchen as he goes thru my cabinets looking for glasses to pour our drinks.

"The glasses are in the cabinets by the far wall," I tell him, and I take a seat at the bar. I bet I look so cute right now. "I look like a mess, don't I?" I ask him as I try to straighten out my hair. I'm still in my pajamas.

"You look beautiful." He tells me as he lifts my chin. "I don't think you could ever look any different." Why does he have to say that? Why can't Jake be like him? Jake doesn't like me the way Eric does. I might be able to 'complete' Eric.

"Jake and I didn't talk at all," I tell him, and I look down at the drink Eric just handed me. "He just left me a note." I accentuate the word 'note' and I take a drink of my newly poured Jack and Coke. It's yummy.

"What?!" Eric exclaims. "Are you serious?" He walks over and sits next to me at the bar. "That jerk didn't even have the balls to talk to you, he just wrote a note?"

I nod my head and I feel the tears coming on again. I thought I didn't have anymore, but here they are! It's amazing how many tears our bodies can produce.

Eric puts out his arms and I lean in for the hug. I start to cry right there in Eric's arms. I cry for what seems like forever, Eric holds me, running his hands thru my hair and occasionally saying "it's ok, let it all out." With his ever so calm and soothing voice.

Oh, Eric, My Protector. When I think I can't cry anymore, I pull my head up and look at him.

"I'm sorry, Eric," I tell him. "I think I'm done." I laugh. "and your shirt is soaked."

"Well," he says, and he starts to pull off his shirt, "we could just stick it in the dryer" He pulls it off and hands it to me.

Eric's chiseled abs throw me off. He really is Hot, with a capital 'H'. I'd always noticed that he was handsome, but Oh My God, not THIS *drop dead chiseled sixpack* handsome.

I giggle and Eric smiles. "What's so funny?" he says.

"I just never expected that you'd be so fit." I tell him, "I mean, you are always partying, when do you find the time to work out?" I take his shirt into the laundry room.

"Oh, see, this is where I can tell you that you don't know me at all, Miss Sanchez," Eric says as he takes a bite of an apple from my fruit bowl. He's so…sexy. Jake was sexy, too. I think to myself. I walk away headed into my room.

"I can check and see if I have another shirt you can borrow," I yell back at him. "Make yourself at home."

"That's fine," he tells me. "Another drink?" He yells at me as he gets up making his way into the kitchen.

"Sure!" I know I have to have something here that he can borrow. I open up one of my drawers and notice an old Longhorns T-Shirt. I bought this shirt after a road trip to Austin, thinking an old Star Football Player from high school would want anything to do with me. I was wrong.

I quickly check my face and throw my hair into a ponytail. I run into the restroom and quickly brush my teeth because God knows I must have horrendous breath. I look one more time in the mirror and see the evidence of the last two days of crying. My eyes are red and puffy and just plain sad looking. How could I let a *guy* do this to me? I think to myself. I stand there and want to cry again.

No, Laura! Get it together! Be Strong! You're better than this. I wipe my eyes and pour water on my face. There isn't much I can do to hide the redness in my eyes so, I just leave it alone.

I walk back into the living room and notice that Eric has since not only poured us some drinks but cut some fruit for us to eat. I throw the shirt at him.

"Well, Eric, you are always surprising me." I smile at him.

"Now, there." Eric says, "that's what I want to see," he comes up close to me and puts his hand on my chin and pulls my face up so that I'm looking up at him. "You have a beautiful smile, Laura." He says in the most charming voice. I can't help but smile again.

We spend the rest of the night drinking our Jack and Cokes and talking about work. I, of course, talk about Matthew, the milestones he has reached. Eric is a complete gentleman and does not once make a move on me even though he was always asking me out before. I wonder if he has lost interest because I'm a mother now? I look up at him, my head laying on his lap.

"Laura, you deserve someone who treats you right." Eric's expression is now one of adoration "Jake doesn't know just how special you are and if he can't see that, then he doesn't deserve you." He moves the hair out of my face and places it behind my ear. "One of these days, he'll figure it out, but it will be too late." As he says this, I wrinkle my nose and he puts his finger on it. "It's true." He tells me.

"He didn't make me feel very special on Thursday," I tell him. "I felt so small when he was driving away from me without so much as an explanation." A tear escapes and falls from my eye. Eric wipes the tear.

"Like I said, He is stupid if he doesn't see what he has right here in front of him." He's running one hand thru my hair, the other holding my hand over my stomach. I feel like we have been friends forever. I feel so at ease with him.

I look up at Eric. He is so handsome. I smile at him. "Thank you, Eric." I start to sit up. "Thank you for everything."

"I didn't want you to be alone." He says, "I can stay if you like,"

I turn to look at him and he must see the surprised look on my face. "In a strictly plutonic way, of course." He adds quickly with a smile. I smile back. It would be nice, I guess, to not be alone tonight.

"Really?" I look at him questioningly.

"Of course." He smiles his superstar smile. He has perfect teeth and the most beautiful face.

I turn on my usual movie and grab my blanket. I snuggle up next to Eric and I must have fallen asleep fairly quickly. I don't remember much of the movie.

I feel Eric taking me in his arms, carrying me. It's nice to feel so protected, so loved.

We're in my room now and he has already pulled back the covers on my bed. Such the Gentleman.

Why do we waste our time on the Jakes of the world? He places me ever so gently into the bed and covers me.

I hold his hand. "Don't go," I tell him. It might be all the alcohol in my system but right now, this feeling of adoration, love, protection, whatever it is, I like it and I don't want it to leave.

"Ok" Eric whispers. I hear him walk back into the living room to shut off the TV. He also has my blanket with him when he returns. He goes to the other side of my bed and proceeds to remove his shirt and pants, but he doesn't get under the covers. He stays on top of the covers and uses my blanket. He gets close to me and puts his arm around me, and I let out a long sigh. "Now sleep." He tells me and he kisses the back of my head. Eric knows exactly what I need right now.

Who would've known that Eric Johnson would be so thoughtful?

Chapter 6

Moving On

I haven't heard from Jake for about two months. I still sometimes take the ring out of my drawer and fantasize about what 'could have been'. It took me a little while to get back into my groove, but I finally accepted that Jake was gone and that it was over.

After that night with Eric, we had a long talk about our relationship and I had to draw the line between work and my personal life. Eric still asks me out, he wants more, but I have rules. I don't date anyone I work with. Much less someone I work *for*. I tell him, but he thinks it's a cop-out. And, I also told him that I wasn't ready to start dating after Jake. A little white lie, but I didn't want to take the conversation any further. Eric and I have a good friendship. Amazingly, it has grown into a very solid friendship. Something I would have never expected.

I am attracted to Eric but he's a party boy and that part of him has not changed. I need someone more stable, committed, who wants more than just a roll in the hay for a while. I've seen some of Eric's girlfriends and I don't want to be on that list. Besides, I feel like I am finally starting to move on and even have a date tonight.

Justin Porter.

Oh, Justin. Justin is an old friend from high school. He and I ran into one another last Friday on my girl's night out with Christine. He was one of the cutest guys in high school and hasn't lost his looks at all. He is still strikingly handsome and judging from his attire, he has made something of himself.

I am so excited about tonight. It's been a while since I've felt excited about something new.

I dropped Matthew off early at my parents' house so, I could spend more time getting ready. Justin will be here at seven. He's taking me out to dinner. It's about ten minutes to seven when my doorbell rings. I guess he's early, but I'm ready to go so, it's ok.

I answer the door trying to be calm and not show the obvious nerves creating knots in my stomach.

I go to open the door, only to be surprised once again. I see the face on the other side of the door staring back at me. My heart is racing.

I am angry, excited, and sad all at the same time.

The familiar hazel eyes are staring back at me.

Jake.

He looks good. But Jake always looks good.

Justin is handsome but Jake is ruggedly gorgeous. Maybe it is just my "love goggles" that make me see him this way. I look at him and my anger starts to show. I haven't spoken to Jake in a while. He left me a note when he left and didn't even have the decency to say goodbye to his son the last time I saw him.

"Hi, Lori, Wow," He looks at me. "You look gorgeous." I sneer at him. I hate that he thinks he can still call me Lori. Only my friends call me Lori. I think to myself. Why is he here? Justin will be here any minute and he shouldn't be here. Of all nights that he could show up, why did he pick tonight?

"What are you doing here?" I look at him and try to look as if I don't care that he is here. "It's not a good time. I'm getting ready to leave."

He starts walking in closer to me and puts his hands out as if he's asking for a hug. I am really not in the mood for his games.

"Hey, don't I get a hug. I haven't seen you in a while." He makes his move to touch me and pull me in, but I pull away. I can smell alcohol on his breath.

Great. He's been drinking.

Jake is not good when he drinks excessively. He can't hold his liquor and usually passes out or gets violent. It's a wonder he even made it to my house. He's been driving his truck, too!

His eyes are almost shut when he goes to hug me again and he practically falls to the floor. I catch him and hold him steady and lead him to the couch where I just throw him down onto the cushions.

I may not like the guy, but he is Matthew's father. I can't let him drive like this.

Ugh! I'm too nice. *I should leave him passed out on the lawn. He doesn't even deserve my couch!* I think to myself.

I walk into my kitchen and pace back and forth contemplating my next move. I could call the cops and have him removed? Or I could ask my neighbor to carry him out to his truck and leave him in there. No, I can't do that. What if he wakes up and starts driving like that.

God, what am I going to do? Justin will be here any minute.

I pour myself a glass of wine and think, there he is, passed out and probably out for the rest of the night. Jake really is bad when he's like this but once he passes out, he's out!

The idea starts to form in my head. I can always leave Jake here while I go out with Justin.

Why let him ruin my night? He probably won't get up anyway, he's out cold.

Justin texts me that he will be about five minutes late which gives me enough time to make sure Jake is out for the night. I manage to take off his boots and get him completely onto the couch. He is snoring and I throw a blanket over him. I am so upset with him, but I can't just throw him out. Not if it means him driving like this. I would hate for something to happen and have to live with that guilt. I stand over him and I can't believe that my mind jumps to how gorgeous he looks. Then, I think of the last time I saw him. Suddenly, the effect that Jake once had on me is gone. I'm happy that I have another date tonight. I gently slap his face. He may be passed out and probably doesn't feel it anyway, but it gives me a little satisfaction. I slap him again.

My doorbell rings. Justin is here. Just in time, I might have kept slapping Jake if he hadn't arrived.

****

My date with Justin is going really well. It's like something out of the movies. We're having dinner at a beautiful restaurant on the Riverwalk. This is definitely *not* the Hard Rock Café. Justin orders for me. I'm not used to these high-end restaurants so, I welcome him taking control. Dinner is amazing.

"Justin, tell me again what it is you do?" I'm trying to keep somewhat of a conversation going.

"Well, like a lot of people in South Texas right now, I'm working with a company that does business in the Eagle Ford Shale area. I'm currently in investments but we're looking at expanding." He is really good-looking. I do have to say, he has not changed much since high school. He just looks more… 'polished'.

I start to wonder if he knows of the company I work for. I, too, work in the Eagle Ford Shale. The company I work for, Black Gold, is growing quickly as well, but most companies in the oil-field are right now. I decide not to mention my work just yet. I want to know more about Justin before he knows everything about me.

I manage to fumble through dinner conversations without talking too much about myself. I don't know if I want to tell Justin about Matthew just yet either. Most guys run when they hear the word children, so, I'm trying to keep it under wraps for now.

I don't eat much but dinner was nice. I like Justin and his table manners are perfect. He is well-groomed and well-spoken. I love a man who can have a conversation and isn't looking at just getting in your pants. It also helps that his conversation is not limited to the latest movies or video games that are coming out.

"Would you like to walk for a bit?" Justin asks as we walk out into the beautiful San Antonio night. "We can walk down from here to the River Walk." He puts out his arm for me.

"Sure," I tell him as I put my arm thru his.

"You know, Laura, my home is actually in Austin. I am in San Antonio for business." I didn't know this. I thought he lived here. I just hope he doesn't have a wife and kids back home.

"Well, that explains why I hadn't run into you before," I remember he got a football scholarship to UT. It was a big deal in our school. He was a star Football Player. I tutored him his senior year to help him keep his grades high enough to keep playing. I had what you would call a school girl's crush on him, but Justin was too popular to notice me back then. I was just a silly, nerdy girl. "Your parents still live here, though?"

"Yes, they still do." He laughs. He has such a cute laugh. "We are closing a deal right now that could keep me here for a while but after that, I really don't know." He places his other hand gently over mine on his arm.

"Well, Justin, I believe there is a reason our paths crossed again." I want to ask which company he works for, but I don't want to pry. He can tell me when he wants to. "I really enjoyed dinner. The food was amazing, the dessert was awesome. I should have taken a picture of it. It was like a piece of art." I smile. I'm babbling. I think I'm nervous. I babble when I'm nervous.

He laughs and this time takes my hand in his. We walk for what seems like hours on the River Walk reminiscing about school and all our former schoolmates.

"I had the biggest crush on you in high school," I tell him. "I even went to your first game at Longhorn Stadium." Justin stops when I say this.

"You did?" He looks at me. I see the sadness in his eyes. "So, you were there the day I got hurt?" *Great! Good going, Laura! I completely forgot that was the day he got hurt!*

"Justin, I am so sorry. I forgot that was…" before I could finish I felt Justin lean over and kiss me. It's a quick kiss.

"Laura, it's ok. Football was my dream back then." He takes a big sigh. "My dreams have changed since then. "After my knee surgery, I had to re-evaluate my life's direction." We start to walk again. "I can't complain. I love what I do, and I live comfortably." He smiles and I notice we are back at his vehicle. I can't help but notice he drives the typical Black Chevy Tahoe of the Oilfield.

He opens the door for me and waits until I get in and sit down, closing the door behind me. He is such a gentleman. Is he for real? He is everything a guy should be. He opens the door for me, pulls out my chair, and even stands up every time I leave the table. Everything that Jake is not, plus the looks. I bet Justin would never leave me with just a note on my nightstand. Have I mentioned that I really like Justin?

He is a true gentleman which is something I am not used to. Jake is definitely rough around the edges. He occasionally opened doors for me, never pulled the chair out for me or held my coat out for me to put on and I really don't think Jake knows about designers, much less, designer suits.

Justin is handsome. The chiseled features of his face, his perfect dark hair, and blue eyes accented by his designer suit and his manicured hands. Yes, Justin Porter is definitely a catch. And tonight, he is out with me.

The drive home is quiet. I'm lost in my own mind, thinking about him. He fits the description of the perfect man. Who wouldn't want to be with him? I'm amazed he is still single.

Don't let this one get away, Laurita.

I hear Mami's voice in my head.

'A true gentleman doesn't try to sleep with you on the first night.'

Justin barely kissed me, I doubt he will try anything else.

I'm almost sad that the night has to end as Justin walks me to my door. Then I remember what is on the other side of *that* door.

Now, I'm worried.

Please, Lord, don't let Jake ruin my night. I'm silently praying that Jake is still passed out on the couch.

Oh, please, let Jake still be passed out.

"It was really nice seeing you again, Lori," Justin says as he reaches down to kiss my hand. He called me Lori. He used to call me Lori in high school. "I only hope that you give me the pleasure of your company again." He brushes my hair out of my face and kisses me again. Only this time, he kisses me on the cheek. Then he flashes the most beautiful smile. He likes me. I can tell.

"I had a very nice time, Justin," I was about to tell him I'd like to see him again when the front door to my house swings open.

Oh, no.

Jake is awake. And by the look of it, still drunk, maybe even more intoxicated.

This can't be happening? Not to me.

"Well, *Lori*, whoosh your newf frien?" Jake slurs the words so bad he almost doesn't make any sense. I want to die right where I'm standing. I'm so embarrassed. This night was going so well, and now here I am with my Ex-*something* and my new *something* and I'm standing here stunned, in shock…almost speechless.

"Jake, go back inside." I push him back in and try to close the door. "Justin, I can explain. It really isn't the way it looks." I must have the look of horror on my face because Justin is looking at me with both confusion and pity. "Jake is my ex and tonight he-he just showed up," Just as I'm saying this Jake comes back out stumbling and barely holding himself up.

"Dosh he knowd we are getting married?" He trips and stumbles in front of Jake and puts his finger on Justin's chest "If I were you, Fool, I would take a walk before I …" I grab and push Jake back and start to close the door again. Justin is just standing there. He's watching me try to deal with this intoxicated individual in front of my house, I can only imagine what he is thinking. He says nothing to Jake or me. I finally get Jake inside. I hold the door closed behind me.

"Justin, I am sorry. Thank you for a wonderful night. I promise, I will explain this all to you later, but, obviously, I need to take care of this now." As I'm saying this, you can hear Jake inside. He is yelling obscenities and … is he puking? Oh, I hope he's puking into the trash can.

"Please, Justin, I hope this doesn't make you think less of me. I really am not with him or engaged to him and to tell you the truth I haven't seen him in almost two months except for to-night." Jake is still yelling in the background and puking. "I really gotta go. I am so so so sorry." I apologize to Justin and my heart is sinking with frustration.

"Lori, don't worry about it. Take care of what you need to." He looks disappointed.

Why would someone like Justin want someone with Drama? He's doesn't know about Matthew. So, in his mind, I just have this crazy ex at my house. He's probably never going to call me again.

"I'll call you." This time he didn't kiss me. He's never going to call me again. He walks away without a smile, without looking back.

Thanks a lot, Jake.

Ugh. He's still in there yelling and puking everywhere. Thank goodness Matthew is with my parents. He doesn't need to see this.

Chapter 7

Going Backwards

Three weeks. That's how long Jake stays this time. After that night with Justin, Jake tells me he has no place to go. After getting kicked out of his friend's house, he doesn't have a place to stay. It was supposed to be for a few days. Right. That turned into three weeks.

Well, for Jake. For me, after a few days, Jake turns on his charm. He apologizes for leaving us and says he "feels right" when he is with us. He says he wants to stay. Reclaim his family with us. He feeds me a story about how he missed Matthew and me, and he couldn't sleep knowing that he had done us wrong. Yea right. Run, Laura, Run!! Why don't we ever listen to those little voices in our heads?

He comes clean about Gina and says that it is over. He also finally tells me about his daughter. She's three years old, almost four. He says he wants a paternity test because Gina likes to sleep around and has told other guys that Blake is their daughter. I feel sorry for that poor little girl if that's true.

Jake assures me that his relationship with Gina was never anything serious and nothing like what he has with me. A little voice in the back of my head reminds me, that even *we* have a broken relationship.

Laurita, a man will only treat you how you let him treat you.

Run, Laura, Run!! Again, I don't listen. I don't know why, but I can't tell him no.

I love him and he *is* Matthew's Daddy. My heart wins again while I hear everything else telling me to go!

Jake has lost his job with the company I sent him to a couple of months back. He and the supervisor had differences in opinion. At least that's what he tells me. That should have been my first red flag. Jake likes to show up when he's broke or out of a job. I start to make some calls and get him some interviews at other Oilfield companies.

I could have easily got him a job at my company, but I don't want Jake to work at Black Gold. That would be too weird. They would hire him, for sure, but I don't mix my work with that part of my life. I have rules.

After two weeks, he starts working at Premier Disposal, a Saltwater Disposal in Carrizo Springs. He is getting paid more than at his last job so, he ends up making out better.

After only one week at Premier, yup, you guessed it; Jake's stay at 'Chez Laura' is over. No explanation. No Call. And this time, not even a note.

Again.

This time, though, Jake stoops to a new low. He took my income tax refund with him. I had left it in my drawer. Stupid me. I should have taken it straight to the bank. I was finally going to get a new car and was going to use that as my down payment. Jake found it. So, not only was he leaving us again, he had escalated to theft.

I can't believe I blew off Justin because of Jake. Why was I always allowing him to do this to me? Am I so Stupid that I don't see when he's using me?

I keep the breakup to myself and don't tell my family right away. Christine has always been my shoulder to cry on. I sometimes expect her to be judgmental and say something like '*I told you so*' but she never does. She always has something good to say that will make me feel better. This time, though, I avoid telling even her. For a while, anyway.

It's been almost a month since Jake left and I decide to call Christine and cry about it. I've been avoiding the subject, fearing the *I told you so's* from my family and even though Christine has never done that to me, from her as well. I'm just afraid one of these days, she's going to snap and just lay it all out there and tell me one big 'I TOLD YOU SO!'.

I'll take my chances, though. She'll know how to make me feel better.

As I dial the number, I start to think how lucky I am to have Christine. I hear Christine on the other end of the phone. She sounds like she's been napping but it's the middle of the day. She sounds out of it, anyway.

"Hello?" I always try to start our conversations with something witty, but today I am not feeling it.

"Was I the only one who couldn't tell that Jake was just using me again until he got back on his feet?" I wait for her response, but I really want her to lie to me. At least, I don't want to know that I *WAS* the only one.

"Laura! Jake is the one with problems, not you. If he can't see what he's missing when he leaves you and little Matthew, he's got issues that neither you nor I could fix. You want to give Matthew a complete family, Sweetie, and it's perfectly normal to want his Daddy in the picture but you are just going to have to come to terms with the fact that Jake can't be fixed." She pauses for a little bit and a tear is coming down my face. "When you decide to let go, you won't let him do this to you anymore. I will always be here for you no matter what." She pauses again, I really love that she is there for me. I don't know what I'd do without her. "So, tell me, are Margaritas called for?" She knew what I needed. We always went out after a breakup.

"I have to ask my Mom to babysit, but, yes, Margaritas are definitely called for." I knew she wouldn't judge me. She never does. That's why Christine and I have been best friends forever.

<h1 style="text-align:center">Chapter 8</h1>

Moving On… Again

I dropped Matthew off at my Parent's house for my night out with Christine. My Mom is not happy about it and gives me the 'You'll never find a nice boy if you're a party girl' speech as I'm going out the door. Even though it doesn't stop me, it stays in the back of my mind. I love my mother and I do respect her. I have never picked up guys in bars.

Mom, of course, is not happy that Jake and I are no longer together. Again.

'You have to give him his space, Laurita, men don't like women who nag.'

I don't know where my mother got the idea that I am a nag.

Christine and I head to our favorite watering hole, Benny's. Benny's has the best Margaritas and their music isn't all Tejano like a lot of these local bars. They play classic and current Rock and R&B. There are a few pool tables and some dart machines. Just the way we like it. There's a small dance floor in case people want to dance.

We like to hang out at the tables by the bar. If you get here early enough, you can get a good table. This place can get pretty packed. It has become very popular recently.

Christine is her usual self. Bubbly, beautiful, and ready to party. I swear Christine could easily have a boyfriend if she wanted one. She's had a couple of short relationships here and there but nothing that she ever took seriously. She does have one guy who is ALWAYS coming around. Joseph has been around for about 5 years. He and Christine have a unique relationship. They don't go out or waste time trying to impress one another. They just kind of get together whenever they want to, you know, *get some*. I think he's married but Christine doesn't care enough to find out.

"La La, you need to take a sip of this Margarita and remember that you are the better one" She calls me LaLa when we're out so as not to give my real name to anyone we don't want to. I call her CC. It sounds dumb but at least we know that if a guy calls us by our nickname, it's probably because we didn't like him enough to give our real name. She pushes over the Texas Size Margarita, Benny's Special, and puts hers in the air waiting for me to toast.

"Here's to us. We are strong women. We say who, we say when" She stole this from Pretty Woman, "and we always keep our head up. Drink up, LaLa" She practically pushes my drink into my mouth.

"CC, have you talked to Joseph?" I hadn't really talked to her lately and didn't know what was going on with her. I never understood how she could just sleep with someone with no strings attached. She and I are very different when it comes to that. I'm not clingy but I'm also very "picky" about who I share my bed with. I can't just sleep with someone where feelings aren't involved. Christine on the other hand was all about Casual Sex.

"Oh, Joseph, Joseph, Joseph… LaLa, you were right. He *is* married. I saw him at the Grocery Store with his family" My jaw drops, and I move in closer to the table to hear more. I wonder if she is hurt or how she feels about it. I know I'd be furious.

"Oh my God, CC, what did you do? Did you confront him?" I take another sip of my Margarita, it is especially strong and I'm starting to think Christine ordered mine with a double shot.

"Confront him? What? Are you on Crack? I bought my milk and got the hell outta there!" She laughs and takes a drink. She starts nodding her head, "I don't want to get in the middle of that mess."

"What are you gonna do?" I ask as I take yet another drink and wonder again if my drink has a double shot. It's really strong.

"What do you mean what am I gonna do? He's not my boyfriend, LaLa. We never had *that kind* of relationship. I don't care what he does when he's not with me." I look at her amazed and she can tell the look on my face. "What!? You know I don't care. He's good for one thing. There's nothing else there. Punto. Finito." She always uses her Spanish 'Punto. Finito.' instead of just saying 'period'.

"You're so bad, CC. You need to be careful because the last thing you need is some Loca Esposa coming after you." I lift my Margarita and take a drink. I think I need another one.

"Girl, he better take care of business cuz I don't want any of those problems." She lifts her hand to wave the waitress over. "Do you need another drink, I got a double shot in that last one." She smiles. I knew it! "You needed to loosen up, Sweetie. You're such a Prude!" She breaks out laughing with her oh so contagious laughter. I start laughing and start to think that I might sometimes be a little uptight but I'm definitely NOT a prude!

"These drinks were already paid for by the gentleman at the bar." The waitress tells us as she places two more Margaritas on our table and points to the bar. A guy is standing there who lifts his beer at us. I lift my drink and mouth the words 'Thank You'. He's really cute.

"CC, he's really cute. Maybe he could be another one of your victims." This guy was cute, but I don't generally like meeting guys at bars. I know I kind of met Justin at a bar, but that was different. I already knew him. We just happened to run into each other at a bar. CC looks over at him and smiles.

"Maybe you should melt some of that ice and take him home with you." She smiles at me with her mischievous smile.

"I'm not an Ice Queen! I just got dumped by my Baby Daddy. I can't just go and pick up some other guy!" I was really starting to feel these Margaritas with their double shots.

"Nothing helps you get over one guy better than another guy on top of you!" She lifts her glass again this time chugging what is left. She starts laughing. "You know I'm right!"

"CC, you ARE definitely crazy, Girl. But I still Love you." I get up to go to the restroom. Oh, My, I am definitely feeling these Margaritas. "I'll be right back. I have to break the seal."

"LaLa, I'll have our friend over here for you when you get back." She still has that mischievous look in her eyes. She will go over there and get him. She always could attract people to her.

One night we ended up with about 10 people at our table just laughing and having a great time. She has such a great personality that she draws people to her. That's why I say she could have a boyfriend if she wanted to. She can get any guy she wants.

"CC, don't you dare." I point my finger at her in a motherly way, "Bring him over if you want but don't you dare tell him it's for me."

I start to walk away, and I hear her say, "We say who, we say when!" and she burst out laughing. She really is a great friend.

As I walk back, I see the guy from the bar is already in deep conversation with Christine. He looks really into her and she is going on about her job and some of the crazy things that go on in her workplace. I walk up and Christine stops and puts her arm around me.

"Rudy, this is my closest and bestest friend in the world LaLa." Ok so, we're still using our nicknames.

"Hi, Rudy." I reach over to shake his hand. "Thank you for the drink." Yes, thank you. I am really feeling these Margaritas. I think to myself.

"No problem. I saw you ladies sitting over here and thought I would break the ice with a couple of drinks." He looks at my glass, "Do you need another one?" I really shouldn't.

"Sure" What am I doing? I shouldn't drink anymore. "CC might need one, too" Where is she? Christine has left us alone and is at the bar talking to some other guy already. Why do I feel like she set me up? I turn back and look at Rudy "Never mind, I'm sure he'll take care of her."

"So, Rudy, tell me about yourself." I guess I have to make the best of it since Christine is now at the bar flirting.

Rudy turns out to be a great guy. He makes me laugh. I mean, it could be the four Margaritas I've had so far, but I really think Sober Laura would really like this guy.

Finally, at about midnight, Christine comes back to our table. It's a short visit coming to let me know she is going home with this random guy she's been flirting with for the past two hours.

"Ay, CC, please be careful. Call me when you get home. Text me his address in case he turns out to be some psycho, I know where to send the police." I smile at her. I don't really know what else I can do, she is an adult and can make her own choices.

"Yes, LaLa, I'm so sorry, I know I said I would take you home."

"Don't worry about it. I'll just call a taxi." I start thinking that I should call the taxi company now if they are going to get here soon.

"I'll text you, Sweetie, love ya!" She hugs and kisses me on the cheek.

"Take care of my girl." She winks at Rudy and walks away.

"Well, I'd better go out and wait for my taxi," I tell Rudy trying to make our departure as easy as possible. I really don't want to give him the wrong idea. I really *don't* pick up guys in bars.

"I can always drive you home, LaLa." Rudy offers. I really shouldn't. I don't know him.

"I don't want to make you go out of your way," I answer almost shyly. "besides, I already called a taxi."

"It really is no problem at all. It would be my honor." He stands up straight and offers me his arm.

How could I refuse?

"Well, ok, I guess."

Chapter 9

Bad Hangovers and Regrets

I hear my alarm ringing and I grab my cell phone to turn it off. I turn around in my bed and there he is. Rudy. I still can't believe I actually let him in last night and much less that I actually slept with him.

I'm going to hell. Mami voice is in the back of my head again.

'Men will not take you seriously if you're easy'

Mami would kill me if she knew what I was up to last night.

My first one-night stand. Wait. It's not a one-night stand yet. I mean, it's only considered a one-night stand if I never see him again, right?

Oh my God, I probably look crazy right now. I'd better go wash up and fix my hair a little bit. I don't want to scare him away.

"Hey, there, Where are you going?" Oh no, he's already awake. He puts his arm out to pull me in.

"I have to go to the restroom" I pull away and run into the restroom. I really can't believe that I did this. This is not me. I don't do this kind of thing. Plus, I have to go pick up Matthew and need to get Rudy out of here.

I take my time, brushing my teeth, washing my face, and just standing there looking at myself wondering what I've gotten myself into.

I hear him rustling around the room.

Good. Maybe he's getting ready to leave.

As I come out of the restroom, he's sitting at the edge of the bed, fully dressed. Thank God.

"Rudy, I –I just want you to know that what happened last night," I sound nervous and I'm rambling. "I don't or I have never brought anyone home with me." I'm gripping my hands trying to get the words out without sounding like a real idiot.

"LaLa, I had a good time. Grab your cell phone" he motions for my cell phone on my nightstand. I go to pick up my phone and notice I have four new text messages. I'll check them later. I look at him. "Dial 210-555-1016."

I dial the number and hear his cell phone's ring tone, AC/DC's Back in Black. Good song.

He takes his cell phone out of his pocket.

"That's me." He says. He shows me his cell phone with my number on his screen "and now I have you."

Is he really going to call? I mean, why should he? He's already seen it all and had it all. Men like the chase and I allowed him to get it all in one night. There is no way this will ever turn into a relationship.

I can hear Mami's voice again.

'why buy the whole cow, if he gets the milk for free.'

At this rate, I'm going to be alone forever. With Mami in my head all the time, I will always find faults.

"I'll make sure to save you to my contacts," I tell him wondering if I should even waste my time.

"So… am I programming you as LaLa or are you going to tell me your real name?" He's good. How did he know that's not the name I always go by?

"Laura" I'm looking at him and he really is cute. I guess he could've skipped all of this and just left. Maybe he isn't such a bad guy. Of course, I'm trying to justify this. He's still a guy. A very good-looking, great in bed, I wish we had more time to do what we did last night but this time sober, kind of guy. I'm a little disappointed in myself but what's done is done.

"Laura is a much better name for you." He gets up and walks over to me. He puts his arms around me, kissing my forehead. I smell last night on his body, but it doesn't, for some reason turn me off. "Don't worry, Laura, I don't think any less of you. I can tell you're a good girl." He's really holding me tight. I didn't realize how much I missed being held like this. I just wish…Oh, who am I kidding? I have to enjoy this moment. Right now. I may not see him again, right? I return his embrace. I take in his muscular chest and rest it on my cheek.

I'm a hopeless romantic and that is why, *LAURA!,* I scream at myself, we don't do one-night stands. We want more, remember? I do, I so, do want more. I start to take in the reality of the situation. Slowly, I let go just a little of my, *I never want to let you go bear hug.* He's still holding me.

"I know this might sound unbelievable to you, but I don't usually take random girls home either." He pulls back just enough so that we are face to face. "You are different," he says, "Someone I could talk to." That was a line. A commonly used one, too.

"Rudy, I'm sorry, I hate to push you out, but I really have to go." Matthew is still at my parents and they are probably wondering why I'm not there yet. I bet they would never guess it's because their daughter just discovered *one-night-stand sex with a hunk from the bar last night isn't as bad as she thought but now doesn't know how to get him out of her house* is the real problem here.

"Ok, I will call you. I really had a great time" He kisses my forehead again and makes his way to the door. He looks back before walking out and winks at me. Then he disappears behind the door.

*****

I'm on my way to pick up Matthew when I remember that I really should check my messages. I will check as soon as I get to my parents' house.

"Hola, Mami" I call out to my Mom as I walk in. She's making breakfast and Matthew is in his highchair.

"And Good Morning to you, My Love," I tell Matthew as I lean down to kiss him on his forehead.

"Mami!!" Matthew yells and lets out the cutest giggle. I smile. It's hard to believe that this little boy is really the only one that holds my heart.

"So, did you and Christine have a good time last night at that Sin Palace?" My mom can be so dramatic sometimes.

"Ay, Mami, it's a bar and I'm 28 years old. I'm allowed to go into them now" my mom hates my sarcasm. I really should check my text messages. I reach into my purse and pull out my phone.

"Oh, no!" Mami yells, "no phone, Laurita, you are going to eat breakfast without that thing on the table!" She's waving the spatula at me.

Geez, she might throw it at me if I don't listen. Yea, right. I laugh a little inside.

"Mom, I just have to check to make sure Christine made it home ok last night..." Oops. Did I just tell my mom I didn't go home with Christine?

"You mean to tell me she left you alone at the bar?" She doesn't sound happy. "Laura, that girl is going to get you into a bad situation one of these days. What if some loco would have taken you, being all alone like that?" Mami's drama.

I roll my eyes. "Mom, it wasn't like that." I surely can't tell her I went home with Rudy, either.

"We left at the same time. She didn't *leave me* there." Please, God, let this conversation be over.

My mom purses her lips "You are never going to meet a nice guy, Laurita" Oh, God, here we go again…

"Yes, Mom, I know!" I cut her off. Putting my hand in the air between us.

"Well, it's true," she snaps back. "You think your father married me because I drank and went to bars?" I look at her, one eyebrow up. Does she really want me to answer that?

"No, he married me because I was a good girl and I went to church." Of course, she had to throw in the Church thing.

"Mami, you and Dad got married ages ago. It's a different time." I roll my eyes.

Yea, like, didn't they have arranged marriages back then?

"Boys still don't want Party Girls!" She's raising her voice to make her point, but I'm bored of this conversation. She really should just record it and play it for me every time I go out. She loves to give me the guilt trip. "You have to think of Matthew now. You should be trying to get Jake back!" She really didn't just say that. My mom is delusional. I didn't *get rid* of Jake in the first place! He left me.

"Mom, when are you going to understand that Jake. Left. Me." I tell her slowly and sarcastically. "I don't want to talk about this anymore, Mom. So, just stop."

I go into the living room with my phone and start going thru my messages. Christine texted me at 2 am.

She made it home ok. She mentioned this guy was a douche, I really have to remember to call her.

"Ok, Mami, let's eat," I tell her. "I have to go soon. I promised Christine we would go shopping today." A lie but it will get me out of here sooner.

Mom is still not happy with me. I take my seat at the table when I see my Dad making his way down the stairs.

"Hi, Dad," I tell him with a smile on my face. "Hmm" he doesn't even mutter a hi. He leans down and kisses Matthew on the head.

"So, Dad, my car is making a funny noise," I tell him. "I was wondering if you could take a look at it." I wait for him to answer. He sits there as if he's mentally going thru a schedule. He still doesn't make eye contact with me.

"You really should get a new car, Laura," he finally says, "I thought you were going to get one when your income tax came in?" Oh, yea, that. I didn't tell my parents Jake left with my money. "Haven't you gotten that, yet? I could help you negotiate a good deal if you want." I think my Dad is coming out of his shell finally. He isn't looking at me directly but he's offering his help, that's a good sign.

"Well, I was, but…" my voice trails off and I take a bite of my bacon. How do I put this?

"But what?" My dad scolds. "Did you already throw away that money on *cochinadas*" (translation: crap) He doesn't sound happy. And now, he *is* looking at me.

"No!" I tell him right away. "It's just that, well," It's hard to tell my parents the truth about Matthew's Daddy. "Jake took it," I say flatly, ashamed and I look down at my plate.

"What?!" my Dad says in a tone I know only too well. "Why would you give Jake that money?"

"Dad," I look at him and I almost want to cry at the memory, "I didn't *give* it to him." I'm looking down. I'm ashamed. "He took it when he left me."

"Laura, why didn't you tell us this before?" my mom butts in, almost wanting to sound concerned.

"I just didn't think it was important," I tell her. "I was already going thru a lot and I didn't want you guys to worry." I look back at my mom, "besides, you were more interested in what *I did wrong!*" I jab at my mom.

"Laura, I don't need you to get smart." My mom quickly fights back. "I just think that sometimes, you are difficult and make it hard for people to love you." Oh, no, she didn't just say that.

"Mama! Jake has another family. Another woman. Another baby!" I yell back at her. "Is that because of me being so unlovable or just him being a jerk?"

My mom looks surprised. "I- I had no idea." She says, now looking at me with pity. My dad doesn't say anything at all. He looks back down and finishes his breakfast. I can only imagine what goes thru his head. Breakfast is not so surprisingly quiet after that. I eat as quickly as I can and get Matthew's things together.

I pick up Matthew and go into the kitchen where my mom is washing dishes. My Dad has since gone outside to work on one of the many do-it-yourself projects that he delves in since his retirement.

"I'm leaving, Mom" I lean over to kiss her on the cheek. "Thank you for watching Matthew."

"Bye, Laurita," I still hear the concern in her voice "you really need to start going to Church," she tells me. I can't help but roll my eyes. She kisses Matthew on the head. "Bye, Bye, Little Baby!" she says to Matthew in a high-pitched voice and Matthew's eyes widen and a huge smile comes across his face.

"Tell Dad I said Bye," I tell her as I walk out the door. I'm so glad that is over. I have to check on Christine.

****

I drive to Christine's house and see her car in the driveway. Good. She must be home.

I walk up to the door, Matthew in tow, and ring the doorbell.

Christine opens the door, and motions for me to come in.

"Chris, Oh my God, what happened last night?" She's still in her pajamas and slippers. She's obviously sulking.

I put Matthew down on the floor with his toys and baby blanket.

Christine sits across from me on her chair while I sit on the couch.

"Laura, I don't want you to *ever* tell anyone about this, ok?" Christine tells me as she starts talking.

"Christine, c'mon, you know I wouldn't ever gossip about anything you tell me." I'm almost insulted that she would even ask. Christine really should know better than that "Laura, this guy was an ass." She then starts to tell me about this guy. "When I got to his house, he broke out with some coke." I look at her puzzled. "Coke, Laura! Cocaine!"

"Oh, Shit! What did you do?" Christine and I don't like to be around people who do stuff like that. It makes us nervous.

"Well, I told him I didn't party like that and he didn't like that answer." She gets up to go to the kitchen. "Do you want something to drink?" she asks me.

"No, I'm fine," I tell her, and I follow her into the kitchen. "What happened, Chris? When you said no? Did he get mad? Violent?" I really want to know if he hurt her.

"No, No, No, nothing like that." She says. "He got mad. Yes. But I was able to calm him down." She looks at me as she takes a drink of her water. "I had to have sex with him." She looks away. "that's the only way I could get his mind off of it." She looks away like it's a bad memory. For the first time, I don't think Christine had sex by choice.

"Oh, Chris." Those were the only words I could mutter.

"Then he took like another three hits, and he was out of it," she says so nonchalantly "That's when I left. I snuck out."

"How do you feel?" I asked her.

"I was scared shitless last night, I'm not going to lie," she said, "I'm just glad I'm home and in one piece." She picks up Matthew and takes him in her arms. "Maybe your way of life is not so bad after all." She smiles at me.

"Well," I look at her smiling shyly, embarrassed. "I wasn't exactly the Ice Princess you know and love last night either." I'm all kinds of shades of red.

"What?! No Fucken Way!" She gets closer to me and puts her hands on my shoulders. "Are you telling me that you actually melted that ice and picked someone up at a bar?" She looks into my eyes as if she's proud of me.

"Yes," I giggle like a little girl. "Rudy offered me a ride home and well… he ended up staying," I say shyly.

"Oh, shit, My Laura is all grown up" She hugs me tight. "You had your first one-night-stand." I think she actually *is* proud.

"Well, it's only a one-night-stand if I never see him again, right?" I tell her quickly, correcting her.

"And there it is, you poor thing, you still have that ice creating illusions, telling you that you didn't have a one-night-stand." We both burst out laughing.

I love Christine. She really is the only one I can talk to.

Chapter 10

The Merger

I show up for work early, but it seems we all had the same idea. Corey is already here, and I see Eric and Evan's Tahoe's in the parking lot as well. Evan is Eric's twin, Their dad Patrick T. Johnson, is one of the richest men in Texas. He has many investments throughout the state and it was no wonder that he would invest in the shale. Now, he's selling off half of Black Gold to a phantom company, and leaving the other half to his sons, Eric and Evan.

It's almost 11 o'clock and the new partners have not shown up. I wonder if they are still downtown signing papers with Mr. Johnson. I thought the deal was already finalized but I don't know anything about the paperwork it takes for a merger.

Who knows. These guys have their own schedule. They show up when they want after doing their rounds at breakfast, then sitting around telling stories about all their business ventures. Really it isn't interesting. I bet they'll show up at 12, right when I want to take my lunch. It always happens that way.

I have four clerks that work for me. Casey, our receptionist, Janice and Michael, my accounting clerks, and Maria, our Human

Resources Clerk. They are all very good employees. I was blessed with such a good team. We are still understaffed for the size of our company. I take on a lot of the accounting duties to make up for the deficiency. We should at least have another two accounting clerks, but that's a whole other story.

"Casey, can you please let me know when they arrive?" I tell Casey as she sits at her desk filing her nails. I tell her mostly because I want to hint to her that maybe now is not a good time to be filing her nails.

"Oh, are they on their way? Corey told me he was meeting them for lunch and that they wouldn't be here until later." Really? Why didn't Corey tell *me* that?

"Oh, well, in that case, I guess we'll wait until Corey gets back." I walk back to my office.

I can't believe Corey didn't tell *me* he was going to meet them for lunch.

Oh, well, I guess this is just more time for me to get some work done.

At about a quarter to two, I get a text message from Corey. They are headed to the office and he wants to make sure the coffee and doughnuts are in the conference room.

Since when do I make coffee?

I get on the phone with Casey. "Casey, Corey, and the rest of the group are on their way back and would like some coffee. Can you set it up in the Conference Room, please?"

"Sure thing." She is always easy to talk to. She never gives you the *'that's not my job'* speech. I like that about her.

I'm sure the twins are going to be here, too. This means I will see Eric.

Eric always looks good. He continues to ask me out, but I have rules. I always remind myself of that. *'Rules are made to be broken'* he tells me each time, but even if I did I don't think that Eric could ever have a serious relationship with his partying lifestyle. And I'm not the type to have a Casual Relationship.

I'm a hopeless romantic who is waiting for her *Knight in Shining Armor* to come to sweep her off her feet and take her away into the big castle.

I have no idea why I thought Jake could be that Knight.

I think I'm supposed to gather the staff in the Conference Room to meet the new partners.

I'm not sure if I should do it now. I don't know how long it is going to be before they get here. Heck, I can always text Corey. We all know he is glued to that phone of his. I get a response almost immediately

All I get back is '10m Yes' Geez. Such a conversationalist.

"Casey, can you announce for everyone to please meet in the conference room for a meeting. Like, right now, five minutes." We don't have a big office, but I only have 10 minutes so, the intercom is the way to go.

"No Problem, Miss S," she hangs up the phone and she immediately goes over the loud speaker.

"ATTENTION IN THE BUILDING. WILL ALL EMPLOYEES PLEASE REPORT TO THE CONFERENCE ROOM? AGAIN, WILL ALL EMPLOYEES PLEASE REPORT TO THE CONFERENCE ROOM? WE WILL BE HAVING A STAFF MEETING IN 5 MINUTES. THANK YOU"

I walk into the Conference Room and it seems like everyone is there. This is good.

I really love my job and I take pride in what I have helped build here at Black Gold. I look around the room and still see some familiar faces. I feel better knowing that we haven't lost some of those people that I helped recruit from the start.

"Hello, Everyone, If you will all please find a seat." People are standing and moving around all over. There is also a lot of talking. "As you know Black Gold is undergoing a transition. We have new Management. Eric and Evan Johnson will still be Superintendents over Operations, but Mr. Johnson's portion of the company was sold to the PSM Corporation. Today, we are going to meet the new partners. I expect that you all may have some questions and we will try to get to all of them today. Corey should be here any minute with them. So, let's just keep the talking to a minimum and start thinking about some questions we might want to ask" I felt like a school teacher in front of her students telling them to be quiet in the library. My mom always said I was bossy.

I look out the window and see Corey's Black Chevy Tahoe pulling into the parking lot. They're here.

I'm nervous. My palms are sweaty. That is so gross. I'm going to have to shake their hands and my hands are sweating. I quickly go into the Women's restroom and wipe my hands and run back to wait for them at the door.

Corey is the first one in followed by Eric and Evan. Both Eric and Evan hug me. Eric's hug is especially tight, as always, he smells good, too. What is it with me and smells? Evan is followed by two young gentlemen. They are wearing designer jeans, designer blazers, cowboy hats, and cowboy boots. Yup, the typical Texan Suit.

"Trace, Brent this is Laura Sanchez, our Office Manager." Corey introduces us. "Laura this is Trace Smith and Brent Martin." I hear the door open again as I am shaking their hand.

"Nice to meet you," I tell them. They flash their oh-so-white smiles back at me.

"Oh, and here he is" Corey yells as another person enters the building. My back is towards the door so, I'm unable to see who it is.

"We thought you got lost," Corey tells him.

I turn around and…

Ay, Dios! This can't be happening.

"Justin Porter this is our Office Manager Laura Sanchez." Justin flashes his beautiful smile, and he puts out his hand.

Are you serious?!

No way!

Justin?!

Holy Shit. I feel what seems like all the blood in my body rush to my face.

"Miss Laura, it sure is a pleasure to meet you," Justin says in his slight twang.

This can't be happening. I shake his hand and smile but can't get any words out. I'm absolutely speechless.

"These three guys are what makes up PSM Corporation. They are the *head honchos,* you might say…" Corey says in his wonderful Texas accent.

Sure, it makes sense. Porter Smith Martin. PSM.

Oh my God. This *is* really happening? My head is spinning.

Snap out of it, Laura! Get it together. This is your job!

Finally, I find my voice, and words start to come out.

"Well, I have everyone ready to meet you all in the Conference Room" my voice is shaky and almost cracks. I really need to pull it together! "They are anxious to meet their new Bosses." I smile and start leading them down the hall. I think I'm going to faint, I feel sick to my stomach. Nervous doesn't even begin to describe this feeling. I think my knees are going to buckle.

Is it hot in here? I need some air. Oh, Dear, what's wrong with me!?

Justin has not taken his eyes off of me. I feel his stare going thru me, not to mention that I think Eric has noticed Justin's interest. Eric makes his way next to me and even puts his arm around my shoulders as if he's claiming his property.

"Laura is the backbone of this office," Eric says, "We'd be lost without her." He takes his arm off.

Thank God, that was making me very uncomfortable. I also noticed Corey's dislike of Eric's statements. I don't want anyone to think that anything is going on with Eric and me. For some reason, I think Eric wants just the opposite.

I stand by the door and show them into the Conference Room. As Justin walks in, he winks at me and I smile. I guess he has no hard feelings for me not returning his calls before. I know I am going to have to explain myself eventually. This is going to be interesting. I don't like mixing business with pleasure, and I think this definitely is a trying situation.

For once it's not Mami in the back of my head, instead, it's Christine. *'Fuck all that other shit, if you want him and he wants you, just do it! It's that simple!'* Of course, she was talking about Eric back then and now it's Justin! Oh my God, why is life throwing me all these curve balls?

Eric stays behind in the hallway and stands next to me by the door. What's his game? Is he trying to make it seem like we are an item?

"So, My Dad isn't your boss anymore." Uh oh. I know where this is going. "Maybe now you'll go out with me." He bites his lower lip and nods his head. He is so sexy, and he can make me laugh with his sense of humor. Right now, though, more important things are on my mind. "Or… are you still not dating?" He whispers in my ear and looks at me as if he knows that I was lying when I told him that before.

"Eric, I don't think right now is the time to be talking about this." I signal with my head at the meeting going on. "There are more important things going on, don't you think?"

Eric smiles. A very sincere smile that doesn't fit his 'Party Boy' persona. Still, he's the type to love you and leave you. I don't need that kind of guy and I think that I've mentioned this before, but Eric can charm the pants off of you. I don't need the party boy.

And *now*, Oh dear, now… Justin is here, too.

What am I going to do?

Stick to your rules, Laurita!

My pocket is vibrating. Is that my phone? Almost everyone who would be calling me at this time is in this meeting.

I pull out my phone.

Are you serious? Rudy? I can't believe he's calling me right now. I wonder what *he* wants. He hasn't called me since that night.

I hit 'deny call' and take my seat in the conference room. We went out about 4 times after that "one night", but It always seemed like he only came looking for me when he wanted some. You know, like he was my Joseph and I was his Christine.

I mean, come on, we only went out four times in three months. I liked him but I think he just liked what I did for him.

I really should be paying more attention to the meeting. For all, I know there could be some major changes that are going to affect us.

Brent is talking right now. These guys are all very young. They are nothing like the people I expected. But you can tell they all come from money. I knew Justin had money, but I never knew he *had* money.

"So, please, everyone, rest assured that we are not here to bring in our friends or to disband the company." Brent was talking, reassuring our employees that their jobs were safe. "We like the way the company is running, and we might make some changes here and there, but we promise that we will make every effort to keep all of the existing personnel." He seems to be putting everyone at ease. Even Corey looks like he's more at ease. "Does anyone have any questions?"

Mr. Martinez in the back raises his hand. He was one of my recruits from the beginning.

He speaks with a very thick Mexican accent, as do most of our drivers. His question is about benefits.

Justin stands up and addresses Mr. Martinez.

I feel my phone vibrate once again. This time it's a text message. From Eric.

I turn to look at him. He is sitting right behind me. He smiles.

Have dinner with me.

I smile. Oh, Eric. Always so persistent. But I have my rules. I quickly text back.

Pay attention ☺

Justin is saying something about benefits. Maybe I should have been listening instead of texting with Eric. I look over at Justin. He is amazingly dreamy. And looking around, I see all my clerks think so, too. They are all drooling over him. Including Michael.

I am in quite a pickle. I really need to talk to Christine about this. This is some good drama. She'll love to hear about it. It really amazes her that I am so careful with my love life and yet, I can get myself into the most interesting situations.

The meeting ends and everyone seems ok with the transition. Most of the employees who were nervous or afraid of the changes now seem much more at ease.

I walk back to my office. As I walk back, I wish I could just close the door and lock it to avoid any weird run-ins, but I know this will be impossible.

It was inevitable. Corey and the *'Head Honchos'* had some coffee and pastries while they sit around and talk a little more in the conference room. I usually don't stay for their shop talk. The meeting keeps Eric busy and out of my office and for now Justin, too!

Suddenly, out of nowhere, Justin pops his head into my office. I guess I thought wrong.

"Hey, Lori, are you busy?" Oh, dear. He called me Lori. People are surely going to know that I know this man on a personal level! The walls in this building are very thin. I don't need everyone at work to hear me explain to Justin why I didn't call him back. I don't need them to know that he and I went out at all! Please don't bring up our date. Please.

"Justin" I sound shaky again. Like a schoolgirl. "No, of course not, come on in." I stand up and motion for him to have a seat in one of the chairs in front of my desk.

"I hear that you are THE original employee for Black Gold." Oh good, he's not bringing up our date or the horrible events that happened after our date.

"Yes, I was the second person to be hired for this location. Karl, my ex-boss, interviewed me and hired me as Office Manager. He was the first to be hired but he was let go." I wanted to say he was let go to allow a college friend with no experience to get a six-figure salary and almost drive this company to the ground. But I think I will leave that part out.

"That's great. I also hear that you are the go-to person and that you pretty much run this place." He's looking at me with his beautiful smile, perfect lips, perfect hair, and perfect tan. Why did I ever blow *him* off for Jake? I really am off my rocker sometimes.

I hear Mami in the back of my head,

You always go for the bad boys and never listen to me!'

Yes, Mami, not now.

"Is that right? Who is saying this?" I ask quizzingly. "I'm the Office Manager and Corey is District Manager. Corey runs the daily operations. I run the administrative operations." I didn't want to take credit and step on anyone's toes. Even though it was true, I have been doing Corey's job for about the last three months. If not, Black Gold would have really sunk.

"Evan told me." He's leaning into my desk. He's talking real low now. Almost like he's interrogating me. "He said that Black Gold was going down, then suddenly, it started doing better again and they didn't know why. They started doing a little investigating and they found out it was you. Only you were letting Corey take the credit." As he's telling me this, I'm just looking on thinking to myself, there really wasn't anything else I could do. I had to save the company. This is my job and my livelihood. I have to protect it because it supports and provides for my son and me.

"Justin, it sounds crazy as your telling it, but…" I pause and look around the office " I only helped Corey out." He's looking at me now with concern. "There are a lot of people who rely on Black Gold for their income, including me" I wasn't lying. Our economy is not the best right now and I did hire a lot of people who were receiving unemployment before. "I couldn't let the company fail."

"I just helped out where I could," I told him. "Corey and I both worked together." This was somewhat true. I did the work and then turned it over to Corey to take credit for it.

Justin is looking at me with his gorgeous smile. He leans back in his seat and looks around my office. I have so much stuff in here it isn't even funny.

Has he seen the pictures of Matthew? He could think he's a nephew or something.

"I really am looking forward to working with you all," he says. "Black Gold has nowhere to go but up and I think you can help us get there."

"Would you like a tour of our office?" I really want to get him out of here before it gave him a chance to ask about that horrible night.

"I would like that." He says as he gets up off his chair.

We walk out into the hallway as Casey approaches me. "Miss S, you have a message." She hands me a pink message slip. "He called while you were in the meeting." Casey stands in front of me. Clearly enamored by Justin. Smiling widely from ear to ear.

"Justin Porter, this is our receptionist Casey Wilder." I introduce them. Justin quickly smiles his superstar smile and puts out his hand. "Casey this is Justin Porter, One-Third of PSM Corporation."

"Nice to meet you, Ms. Wilder," Justin says. "I look forward to working and speaking with all of you here at Black Gold." He tells her.

Casey is obviously giddy, Justin's good looks are by far, very distracting and her red cheeks make her look like a flirty school girl. "Please, call me Casey." She says nervously, "no one here is so formal. We all go by first name." The smile is locked on her face. "I really am looking forward to working with you, too." Casey is single and obviously in need. I could swear she is staring into his eyes like he's some kind of movie star.

"Ok, well, I am going to give Justin a tour of the office" I break the uncomfortable silence and Casey's stare! What is wrong with her, really?! She needs to get a grip!

"Miss S, I would be happy to show him around with you being so busy and all." Casey butts in. Unbelievable! Did she really just say that? I never knew she was such a flirt.

"Well, I" I start to say uncomfortably, but before I can finish, Justin stops me.

"Actually, Miss Sanchez and I have some business to discuss but thank you for the offer, Casey" So, I guess he isn't oblivious to her game or maybe he really does have business to discuss with me.

Oh, Laura, stop it! Why does it bother me so much that Casey is falling all over herself for Justin? It's not like he is mine. I mean, we went out once on a date I can only describe as perfect, up until the end at least. And then I avoided him. Who knows if Justin is even still interested in me. Besides, I don't mix business with pleasure, remember? I have rules, for God's sake! Oh, God, what am I going to do?

Christine's voice is in the back of my head again. *'You're going to find a dark room in the back and take him and make him yours!'* Shut up, Christine. I could never. After the way I avoided him, he can't still be interested. Can he?

I continue my tour of the office with Justin, introducing him to the rest of the staff, reliving the ogling eyes and flirtatious smiles. Even Michael was visibly drawn to him. I feel like I have to apologize to Justin, obviously everyone in my office is sheltered and has never been exposed to handsome before.

I proceed to show Justin his choice of the four empty offices on the opposite end of the building. I ask him what he would like for himself so that I could get the phone and computer lines up and working.

"Well, they all seem to be the same distance from your office so, I guess it really doesn't matter." He smiles and winks at me. He's flirting with me? Oh, geez, the butterflies in my stomach tell me that I like it but everything else tells me that I am in unfamiliar territory. Remember your rules, Laura! Justin is now *your boss.* I look at Justin up and down, briefly reliving that moment on the River walk as we walked hand in hand.

Ay, Laurita, you've really gotten into a pickle this time, haven't you? Justin turns to look at me and I smile nervously knowing he's caught me in my gaze.

He puts his hand on my shoulder "as long as I have a window, I'm good. So, I guess, the second one will do. Plus, I noticed you are not married." He points towards the second door in the hallway. What was that about me not being married?

"Ok, I'll make sure to get everything ready for you in there. I can order your computer, but it will take time to get here." I tell him and I walk into the second office, and he follows behind. I'm trying to keep to business and not sway away from the subject. "No, Justin, I'm not married." I decide to answer him but quickly get back to the subject. "We need to get a list together of office supplies so I can put in one big order," I tell him trying to stay on point.

"How about this, Lori," he tells me as he moves in closer to me. Oh, Gosh, will you please not call me Lori. It really does things to me. Wow, he's really close.

"I know these guys are not going to want to wait for computers and office equipment to come in," he looks serious but has a smile on his face. I can smell the subtle smell of aftershave, "so, why don't you and I make a trip to the store and buy what we need?" He and I alone on a supply run? Seriously? Oh, dear. That can be trouble. I hesitate as he waits for my answer.

I can't help but smile and I look down. "Um, when did you want to go?" I ask him, trying not to sound nervous, "it's kind of late to go today, we can go first thing in the morning?" I tell him before he can answer. Trying again to stay on the matter of business. My heart is racing, and I wonder if he can hear it. I know I can and it's distracting.

"Ok," he says, "Let's do that. In the meantime, I will make sure to get a list of supplies from these guys as to what, specifically, they want." He says, very matter-of-factly. I smile at him and look into his eyes. His beautiful blue eyes.

"There you all are!" Eric's loud voice interrupts the sound of my heart and the moment between Justin and me. He makes his way into the office

"I was just showing Justin around. He has picked this as his new office." I tell Eric nervously moving away from Justin.

Eric quickly notices the tension between Justin and me and looks back and forth at the two of us a couple of times before saying a word.

"Well, Justin, Laura here is one of our most loyal, dedicated employees." He gets close and puts his arm around me just as he did earlier. "There is no one like her and we are truly lucky to have her." Geez, I'm thinking that statement was overkill. I really wish he wouldn't put his arm around me. It makes me feel like he's trying to claim his property or something.

"Thank you, Eric," I tell him, smiling shyly, trying to pull away. Eric pulls me in closer. "I just do my job, really." I smile half-heartedly.

"Justin, I hate to steal Laura from you, but I need to speak to her regarding one of our accounts if you don't mind?" Eric looks over at Justin as he starts to walk out of the office finally releasing me from his tight hold.

"No, of course not," Justin says to him, and Eric flashes a not so sincere smile at him.

"Laura, can we talk in your office?" Eric tells me from the doorway. I'm still standing in the middle of the office staring at Justin. Why does Eric want to talk to me about an account? We've never talked about accounts before, why now?

"Um, Eric, go ahead to my office," I tell him. "I will be there in two minutes. Justin and I are just finishing up on some plans." I hold up two fingers verifying the fact that I said two minutes, in case he didn't catch it. I'm really nervous but Eric shakes his head in agreement and leaves the office.

As Eric walks away, I turn to look at Justin. "So, tomorrow morning then." I smile at him.

"Yes." He tells me and starts walking towards the door. He turns suddenly and is standing right in front of me, a smile on his face. "You'd better hurry. Eric needs to *talk* with you." He sounds… *jealous?* I'm not sure. He's closer than before and I can almost *feel* him next to me. He has caught me off guard and I'm definitely at a loss for words.

"Eric is just.." I tell him, almost in a whisper. Eric is just what, Laura? I can't even think! He is so close to me my mind is spinning!

"Eric is just trying to keep me away from you," I say finally, and I break the spell. I step away from Justin and I smile at him. I pull myself together.

Justin smiles a mischievous smile and looks over at me, one eyebrow up "is that so?"

I take a deep breath, smile, and walk out of the office. Oh, Perfect Justin.

Walking back to my office, I see Eric standing in my doorway. He is also movie-star handsome; a beautiful man and he's staring at me with his longing eyes as if he's hurt or begging.

'*Ay, Laurita, what have you gotten yourself into?*'

I hear Mami in the back of my head.

"We need to talk," Eric tells me as I walk into my office, and he closes the door behind me.

"Okay," I say as I walk in.

Chapter 11

Shades of Green

I can't imagine what has Eric so upset. I walk into my office still flustered from the events with Justin. I'm still holding the message Casey had given me when I look down to read it. Rudy? Rudy called the office? What? Why is he calling me at the office? He has never called me at the office! Oh, now I am mad.

"Laura," Eric startles me out of my own mind. "Um, can you tell me about Gulf Coast?" he says in a sort of unconcerned way. Only thing is, he's pacing in my office and he closed the door.

"Gulf Coast?" I tell him. "Eric, did you really call me in here to talk about Gulf Coast?" I look at him doubtingly. "We haven't had any problems with the Gulf Coast account since we started doing business with them 4 years ago," I say sarcastically.

Eric stops pacing and turns to look at me. "It's just that…" he stops mid-sentence and decides to sit down. I'm still standing so he points to my chair and signals for me to take a seat. Oh, Dear, is it that bad that I need to be sitting? I pull out my chair and sit down.

"Laura, I don't know, I am getting this vibe, you know?" Eric is quite nervous and very fidgety.

I have no idea what he is talking about and I'm sure the look on my face isn't making it any easier for him.

"You see, as soon as Justin Porter walked in, I sensed his interest in you and…." I sit back, I feel my face turn red. Eric tilts his head to the side "and well," he tilts his head to the other side "well, I don't like it! There I said it!"

He sits back in his chair putting his hands in the air like a big weight has been lifted off his shoulders. "I probably saved you from what could have become a sexual harassment issue." He says next in a more sarcastic tone.

I'm looking at Eric in astonishment. Clearly, this is why I do not mix business with pleasure. I really don't have time to deal with this drama at work. I start to laugh and sit upright in my chair again, leaning in towards him on my desk. Is it nerves because I've been caught or am I upset? I really am not sure but right now I want Eric to believe that I am upset.

"You find this funny?" Eric tells me with a glimmer of a smile on his face. "Really? I can't believe you're laughing at me!" He is tone is serious.

"I'm not laughing at you, Eric" I'm trying to stop laughing, but my smile is still there. "It's just that, this is exactly the reason why I could never go out with you." I lean back on my chair again and tap my pen on my desk. I'm flustered.

He suddenly sits back and his eyebrows furrow as if he's confused. "What? What are you talking about?"

"I can't have you questioning everyone who talks to me or looks at me wondering if they are interested in me," I start to tell him, my hands are nervously waving everywhere, "and then have you go off and get all upset because you think they are hitting on me or about to *sexually harass* me!" I start nodding my head, "this is the kind of drama I just don't need at work." I tell him. "You con tinually trying to get in my pants or wondering who else in this office might be trying to."

That was low. Maybe I went too far with that last statement. I look over at Eric wondering if it's too late to take back what I just said.

"Laura, please," Eric is again sitting at the edge of his seat, "don't get me wrong, I just want you to be careful. I – I care about you," he says. His tone now gets deeper angrier. "I care about you and I thought I had already made that clear to you. It's not just about getting in your pants, you know?" He's visibly upset and looks away. He looks at me again. "It's never been about that with you." He looks at me like I'm an idiot for not knowing this and starts to get up.

"Eric, sit down," I tell him. I feel bad. I didn't mean to hurt his feelings or *upset* him. He has always been the perfect gentleman with me. He didn't deserve that. I owe him an explanation. He stops and takes a deep breath. "Please," I say. He turns back and sits down.

"Look, I owe you an explanation." I start to tell him. I don't know how much I want to tell him, but I do know he needs to know there is a history there.

"Justin and I know each other. From before." Eric's eyes light up, and he sits up a little straighter in his seat. He is now intently listening to me.

"Justin and I went to high school together," I smile at him and he lets out his breath as if he'd been sitting there holding it. "that's probably why you saw us carrying on in familiar terms," I tell him trying to put him at ease. It seems to be working. He is now sitting in front of me with his head in his hands as if he's embarrassed.

"Laura, I never would have guessed," he says placing his hand over his mouth now in disbelief, "I mean, I still think he is interested in you. Did you date in high school?" he asks me quickly.

"No – No, we never dated in high school." I begin to tell him. I leave out the part where we did go out on a date not too long ago, "I was the nerdy girl, you know" I say rolling my eyes, "I never got much attention from the jocks." I laugh but inside I feel a little sad because this is all true. I *was* a late bloomer.

"I did help him with his homework, though," I go on, "so you see, Eric," I try to sound justified, "what looks like interest is just two old friends who are past the formalities and can have a normal conversation," I tell him. "I didn't want anyone to know that we knew each other because I would hate anyone to think that I am getting any kind of special treatment, you know what I mean?" I am sitting there hoping that Eric is satisfied with my story and hoping he doesn't ask any more questions. Because I really do hate to lie.

Eric nods as if he agrees, but he still seems a little doubtful. "I would still be careful, Laura." He says pointing his finger at me as he walks towards the door. "You are definitely not the nerdy girl anymore," he smiles and looks at me with those adoring eyes, "and I know Justin Porter noticed." He opens the door.

Before walking out, he looks over at me and smiles. I do love Eric's smile. For some reason, his smile is always a sincere one. No matter how much of a party boy he is. "How about we go out for a few after work to celebrate this transition?" he tells me. "I promise, no funny business," he puts his hands in the air, "all of us are going. My brother, Corey, and our new partners will be there, too!" he says. Oh. That means Justin will be there. That can stand for some uncomfortable situations.

"I promised a friend that I would meet her for dinner, sorry," I tell him. I'm lying, of course, but I'm not ready to be in that situation yet.

"Well, the invitation is open if you change your mind." He smiles again and winks as he leaves my office.

It's almost time to go home and I text Christine.

Long Day. You will not believe what is going on at work!

I almost instantly get a text back from Christine.

I could use a drink. How bout you? Bennys?

Christine read my mind. I get on the phone with my mom and ask if she could pick up Matthew at daycare. I tell her I'm going with the new partners to dinner and she reluctantly agrees.

I text Christine back.

Ok. We're on. Meet you there after work. ☺

Christine texts back a smiley face and suddenly I feel better knowing that I can talk to someone about today's events.

I start getting ready to go when Justin comes into my office.

"So, we are all going out to celebrate," he says looking at me with his gorgeous eyes. Something about his dark hair and his blue eyes just makes me swoon. "would you like to join us?" he asks me.

"I'm sorry, Justin," I tell him as I look inside my purse for my keys. "Eric asked me as well, but I already had plans with a friend of mine." I look at him apologetically. "Maybe some other time, I tell him" he looks at me questioningly. I flash a smile at him. He smiles right back.

"Ok, then. I guess I'll see you tomorrow morning then." He walks out of my office.

Just then, Corey, Eric, and Evan are leaving and pass my office and all three at once yell out, "Good night, Laura!"

"Good night!" I yell back. Justin is standing in the hallway.

"Well, Good Night then." He tells me.

"Good Night, Justin," I say as I walk out closing the door to my office.

He joins Brent and Trace, who are waiting for him at the entrance, and they leave the office together.

I let out a long sigh. Thank Goodness this day is over.

As I get in my car, my cell phone rings.

Rudy. Great. I'd better get this over with.

"Hello?" I really didn't want to answer but I want to know what is so important that he had to call my work.

"Laura, it's Rudy." He says like I don't know it's him.

"Yes, Rudy, I know it's you," I tell him. Still annoyed and upset over him calling my office.

"Well, I was just wondering if you were busy tonight?" he starts to say.

"Um, yes, I am busy. I haven't heard from you in like two weeks, Rudy. Why now?" I ask him.

"Laura, I like you. I'm sorry I haven't called you." he starts to say but I interrupt him.

"No, Rudy, you don't *like* me. You like what I do for you." I jab at him. My car swerves. I really shouldn't talk and drive.

"Yea, well, I've been busy, and it's not like that. I do like you." he fights back.

"I'm sure you have," I sit there rolling my eyes, thinking about how many other women he must do this to, "maybe we should both just lose each other's number, ok?" I tell him in a very cold voice. I don't think I've ever been this cold before.

"Laura, I thought we could talk about this over some drinks." Are you kidding me? Is he trying to negotiate? Over drinks, no less! Oh sure! Get her drunk again and she's all yours!

I hear Mami's voice again.

'Who knows what can happen when you are out drinking? You could be taken by some loco?'

Who knew that Rudy was 'the loco' (translation: crazy guy).

"I'm sorry, Rudy. Please, don't call me anymore." I end the call and feel almost relieved that I finally did that. Rudy never made me feel special. He made me feel like I was just a piece of meat, good for one thing. It's a very empty situation. My feelings are mixed. I almost understand all of Mami's crazy sayings.

Besides, I have enough Male drama at work to keep me busy.

I smile thinking about Eric and Justin. It's almost a wicked smile, one I am not familiar with coming from me.

Why is this so intriguing to me? I have always separated my work and my personal life. I have seen work relationships and the drama they can cause. That's why I have rules. Drama is *not* for me.

It's been difficult. Knowing that I am attracted to Eric, I have had to tell myself over and over again that he is no good for me. A party boy. *'He will just love you and leave you, Laura.'* This is how I mentally prepare myself to deal with Eric. He's a player and I can keep clear of him for this reason. And now, Perfect Justin? What mental game am I going to have to play to keep me away from Justin? And with Eric in the same building? Why does it bother me that it might hurt Eric if I go out with Justin? I am so screwed up in the head right now. I really need to talk to Christine about this.

I pull up to the parking lot at Benny's and see Christine's car. Good. She's already here.

I pull down my visor to check my face and put on a fresh coat of lip gloss and a little retouch on my eyes. Bennys has a small kitchen so Christine and I should be able to get something to eat. This is good since I skipped lunch.

I make my way into the club and quickly spot Christine at our usual table. She's already got a Margarita waiting for me.

"Hey, CC," I walk up and grab the Margarita. I take a much-needed drink. As if all of today's events can magically be washed away. I notice Christine is not her usual bubbly self. "What's wrong, Pumpkin?" I tell her playfully.

"Oh, La La, I saw Joseph today." She's pouting. Christine actually sounds depressed. I don't think I've ever seen her this way. "He came over like he usually does, and" she takes a huge drink putting her whole face into her glass, "and we started to, you know…" she shakes her head at me for acknowledgment. I nod my head letting her know that I know what she means. "Well, stupid me, I go and tell him that I saw him, you know, at the store," she takes another gulp. Suddenly a Texas-size Margarita seems too small for Christine. It almost seems like she wants to cry. "and I tell him I saw him… with his family." She's waving her arms. She stops, looking down at her empty Margarita glass. "I don't know why I brought that up, La La." She puts her hand over her forehead. Leaning her torso on the table. Chris is a mess. I never knew she had these kinds of emotions. Chris has always been the tough one. Made of steel.

"What did he tell you?" I place my hand over her head and run it thru her hair. Obviously, it wasn't good if she is acting like this.

Christine laughs nervously as she pulls herself back up on her seat. She looks over at me, "He just looks at me and says 'So'," she mimics his face making an idiotic expression. "Can you believe that?!" she yells at me. "That's all he could say was, 'so'" Her rendition of his idiotic expression back on her face. Her eyes are watering. She grabs my napkin to wipe trying hard to contain them. She picks up her empty glass again pouting her lips, I quickly slide my Margarita over to her and call the waitress over.

I'm watching Christine and I'm in shock. I've known this woman almost all my life and have never, and that is Never with a capital N, seen her get like this over some guy.

She puts the Margarita down long enough to continue her story, "So, I ask him why he never told me he had a family, and you know what that asshole tells me?" her eyes are small, she's upset, angry, and hurt.

I try to contain my emotion, *my* anger, and sarcasm, "Do I really want to know?" She sits back pursing her lips.

"Why should I tell you anything about that part of my life," She is visibly upset. "You and I fuck, Chris, that's it." She looks at me with a look of horror and upset in her eyes. But now, I really see the anger building up. Her tears are drying up and I see her aggravation.

"Oh, CC, you *did* have feelings for him, didn't you?" As I say this, she starts to cry.

"I don't know, La La, I think after that one night, I was feeling, I don't know, I guess a little vulnerable, and I wanted, something, someone," she says and takes a drink of the new Margarita the waitress just brought over. "I wanted to feel like someone thought I was special, I guess." She says this and her voice cracks. "I can have a boyfriend!" she exclaims loudly, hitting the table in the process. "I've wasted 5 years with this man, just…fucking, apparently." She waves her hand in the air, rolling her eyes. She looks over and sees that I haven't been drinking. How could I? I've been listening to her and got caught up in her story.

"Hey, are you going to drink or what?!" I'm staring at her in amazement and I snap out of it. I grab my Margarita and take a long drink. We sit there quiet for a couple of minutes, both of us lost in our own minds. I finish my drink and look over at her.

"CC, it's only natural to have had feelings for him," My expression is serious, concerned for my friend. "I knew you did. I would have thought you were weird if you didn't." She looks at me with her pouty face and she leans into the table putting her finger on my chest.

"Well, I wish you would've fucken told me!" she yells at me. I can't help but laugh. Oh, Chris, don't hold back now. Just say what you feel.

We sit there waiting for our next round of drinks. I guess I can tell her about my day and get her mind away from Joseph.

"Well, I guess we both had equally interesting days," I tell her leaning over so she can hear me. Our third Margarita has finally made it to our table. "You are not going to believe what happened at work today!" I look over at her and she seems preoccupied like she isn't listening.

She looks over at me and pulls out a mirror from her purse. She starts to check her face and retouches her makeup. "WELL!" she yells at me from behind the mirror, "are you going to tell me or what?!" she waves her lipstick at me.

"Well, you know today was the transition thing at my work, we were supposed to meet the new partners," I move in closer. I wonder if she is really listening.

"Oh, yea," she puts her mirror down, "Don't tell me they fired your ass?" she asks demandingly.

"No, No, I still have my job," I explain to her, "we met the new partners today and of course, the twins were there, too," I tell her. "Eric was there." I smile just thinking about him.

"Don't tell me," she interrupts, "you finally broke all your rules and made that Fine Piece of Ass yours!" she smiles wickedly, and her eyes open widely.

"CC, can I tell the story, Please?" I tell her trying to keep from laughing along with her, but before I could go on, my cell phone notification goes off. I look at my phone and see I have a text message from Eric.

"Oh, Shit, CC, Eric just texted me!" I tell her. "It's like he knows we're talking about him," I start laughing. As I read the text message, my eyes get wider.

I thought you were going out to dinner?

What? How did *he* know? Christine sees the look on my face.

"What did he say?" she asks me. "Is he asking you out again?"

I hold up my phone, showing her the text message and I shrug my shoulders. All of a sudden another text message comes thru.

Margaritas don't count as dinner ☺

I start looking around the club. This could only mean one thing.

"Oh, Shit, CC, I think Eric is here," I tell her as I show her the second text message.

Just then the waitress comes over with two new Margaritas.

"These were paid for by the gentlemen sitting at the table in the back corner." She points at a table in the far corner of the bar. I can barely see but I make out at least five figures.

"Oh, Shit, CC, they're here!" I tell Christine. Suddenly, I see all six of them, Brent, Trace, Evan, Eric, Corey, and Justin all making their way to our table. "AND they're coming over to our table!" CC sits up in her chair and she starts to frantically fix her hair. I see Eric, then Justin. Oh, Shit! This can't be happening!

"Fancy seeing you here," Eric says as he comes up to me and hugs me, especially tight as always. I introduce everyone to Christine using her real name and we drop our nicknames immediately.

I see the look on Christine's face when she sees Justin. She is in complete shock, I almost want to laugh. She turns to look at me and mouths the words 'Oh My God' as if finally acknowledging why my day was an interesting one.

She lifts her glass taking a long drink. She is needing one just thinking about the kind of drama that could have gone down today.

We all talk for about twenty minutes, a little shop talk, glances from both Eric and Justin are making me extremely nervous. Eric is sitting beside me, while Justin is sitting directly across from me. Both are trying to keep my attention but all I want is to talk to Christine alone.

"Umm, will you all excuse us," I smile politely, "we are going to powder our noses," I hold out my hand for Christine and she quickly takes it.

"You know, I'll never understand why women have to go to the restroom in groups," Corey says, "it's like they're afraid to pee alone." Oh, Corey, sarcastic as always. Both Eric and Justin get up from their seats as we get up from ours and pull out our chairs. Such gentlemen.

We walk into the restroom and I let out a long breath.

Breathe, Laura, Breathe. I tell myself. Christine looks over at me, her eyes wider than usual.

"Holy Shit, Lori! No wonder you're all flustered!" Christine tells me as we both sit in the loungers and she begins to laugh, "Justin is one of the new partners? How the hell did that happen?" she asks me in between gaggles of laughter.

"Chris, I don't know." I'm nervously laughing but mostly I'm just nervous. I feel sick to my stomach and I'm shaking just a little. "I was surprised myself. You should have seen me when he walked into the office!" My face is pouting. How do I get myself into these situations? I'm still trying to catch my breath. "I wanted to crawl in a hole and never come out." I look at her and she is still laughing. "Don't laugh at me, Chris, this is a serious situation!" I want to laugh, too, because it is kind of funny.

"And then with Eric there, I bet you are all tied up in knots." She rolls her eyes in an exaggerated fashion mimicking I don't know what. What did she mean by that?

"Eric isn't a problem, Chris," I tell her matter-of-factly. Looking down at my hands.

"Oh, really?" she looks at me, finally trying to put on a straight face except for the huge smile. "Girl, that boy has it bad for you!" She gently pushes my leg with hers. I know Eric likes me, but that isn't the problem here. It's Justin.

"That doesn't mean anything," I tell her, laughing. "I've never said yes. I told you I'll never go out with him." I slap her on the arm.

"What you say and what you feel are two different things, My Dear!" she says mockingly, pointing her finger and waving it around in front of my face.

I think to myself for a moment trying to figure out what she means by that. I'm confused. Chris isn't making any sense. She's talking in code.

"What are you talking about?" I make a face as if she just said the most idiotic comment ever.

"Look, Lori, you didn't tell *me* about Joseph but I'm going to tell *you* about Eric," she's pointing into my chest, "you got it bad for that boy, but you have convinced yourself that you don't." I really don't know what she's talking about.

Do I?

"I think you've had too much to drink, Chris, really." I snap back at her. There's a huge smile on my face. I can't wipe this smile off my face. What's wrong with me? Maybe, I'm the one who's had too much to drink.

"And *NOW*, Perfect Justin is back, and you are in quite a pickle, aren't you?" she teases, still smiling and giggling. "Cuz I know you like him, too!" she says this as if she knows me so well. Who does she think she is? Some kind of mind reader? My best friend, who knows all my deepest, darkest secrets? Who apparently can read between the lines?

I look at her, pouting because as much as I hate to admit it, it's true and Christine does know me. She knows me better than anyone.

"You're drunk, Chris," I tell her smiling, still not wanting to admit it. "These situations don't happen to good girls like me, remember?" she starts laughing hysterically.

"That's what makes this even more comical!" she yells out, "the fact that you are SOOOO careful and you are still in this situation!" she keeps laughing at my expense. I really wish she would stop laughing at me and help me figure this out.

"C'mon, they're going to wonder what happened to us," I tell her as I get up from the lounger. I offer my hand to help her.

"Ay, Laurita, what are you going to do, Mamita?" she's mocking me again, staring at me, batting her eyes.

"I can't be with either of them, Chris," I say with the most serious voice I can find at the moment. "I work with both of them." I put on my best pouty face and then break out laughing. "C'mon, let's go back, I don't want to talk about this anymore!" She finally gets up and we head out the door.

As we walk out of the restroom, we see Eric in the hallway. Oh, gosh, he is handsome, and I've had way too much to drink to be around him.

I hear Mami's voice in the back of my head.

'Alcohol makes a girl do things she wouldn't normally do.'

You got that right, Mami.

"Hey, You, is everything ok?" he walks over to me. Tall, sexy, and smells wonderful as always. "You all were in there for a while." He smiles his award-winning smile. And then there it is again locked on my face, that stupid grin! Really, what is wrong with me?!

"I'll leave you two to talk," Christine says as she heads back to the table. Smiling her wicked smile as she trots off.

"Fine," I smile back at Eric, shyly looking down. He puts his hand on my chin and raises my head so that I'm looking at him.

"How much have you had to drink, Laura?" he asks me, his other hand now on my waist.

"Ummm, I think we were on our third when you all sent over another one," I say to him. A huge smile *still* locked on my face. "How much have *you* had?" I ask him playfully pointing at his chest.

"I can hold my liquor." He answers smiling a mischievous but still, beautiful smile.

"So can I," I fight back, "I'm doing ok, Eric. I don't need you to be taking care of me." Always my Protector.

"Ok, Ok, I just want to make sure." He flashes another great smile. This one more playful.

"Why do you do that?" I ask him.

"Do what?" He looks at me with his sparkling green eyes.

"Flash that smile like it's going to fix everything," I tell him. He smiles and he runs his hand across my cheek. I'm entranced.

In the corner of my eye, I see Justin headed towards us or at least headed towards the restrooms. I quickly snap out of my little fantasy land.

I tip-toe so that I can reach to whisper in Eric's ear. "Justin is headed this way. Maybe we should head back to the table?" Eric looks back. He takes my hand and starts to lead me back to the table. He nods his head at Justin as we pass him. Instinctively, I pull my hand away from Eric and smile at Justin as he passes us. I see Justin staring at us, at me. Justin smiles looking at me the whole time.

Oh my God, What am I doing? I'm playing with fire.

I hear Mami's voice in my head.

'You're playing with fire, Laurita'

I know, Mami. I just said that.

I am so confused. I feel the knots in my stomach.

I feel Eric take my hand again only this time I don't pull away.

Christine is right. I do like Eric, but I know Eric. Eric *is* a party boy. He lives a fast life with fast girls. I don't fit into his lifestyle and not to mention, he's my boss, one of the partners.

Then, there's Justin. I like Justin, too, but now Justin is my boss, too, another one of the partners. Perfect Justin.

How could this be happening to me?

I'm quickly interrupted from my internal struggle by what I can only describe as a 'Bar Rat', aka Skank.

She comes up to Eric, getting in between him and me, forcing him to let go of my hand. Um, did she not see me?

"Hi, Eric." She presses her body against him and hugs him and kisses his cheek. I almost want to get in between them, so she acknowledges my presence, but I decide against it. He isn't my boyfriend and if he wanted to, he would introduce me.

"Oh, hey, Mona" he doesn't sound interested but she doesn't get the hint.

"Your party on Saturday was great." She tells him. "will there be a repeat this weekend?" she asks him. Ah, yes, the famous parties that the twins like to throw at their bachelor pad. Suddenly, I'm reminded why I can't date Eric.

I decide I've heard enough and leave him with *Mona* and I start to walk back to the table by myself. Before I get there, though, I cut to the bar. I turn back once, and Eric is still talking to her.

Why do you care, Laura?! He isn't your boyfriend and you don't want him to be your boyfriend, remember?!

I'm standing at the bar when I feel someone come up behind me. I wonder if Eric is done talking to '*Mona*' I think to myself, but I refuse to turn around.

I'm pouting? Really, Laura.

"What can I get you?" the bartender asks me.

"Shot of Patron, salt, and lime," I tell him.

"Make that two!" the person behind me yells out. That's not Eric. I turn around. Perfect Justin.

"Hi." He tells me with the cutest smile on his face.

"Hi back," I answer. "You like Tequila?" I ask him, a sly smile on my face.

Who is this person? I am really not myself today!

"Are you kidding? I *am* from Texas. It's like drinking water." He laughs. The bartender sets up the shots in front of us.

I smile as I look up at him, he's at least six feet tall and he smells delicious. I take the shot in my hand and I gently tap his. "to Black Gold" I tell him. He smiles and we both take our shots.

I don't even know if I'm ready for this. All I hear is Mami in the back of my head.

'Laurita, you're never going to meet a nice guy if you're a Party Girl.'

I'm not much of a Party Girl, the shot goes down rather harshly. I lick the salt and suck on my lime hoping to help ease some of the pain in my esophagus. Justin looks at me and laughs.

"Are you ok?" He's making fun of me. I put my shot glass back on the bar and let him pay. I start to walk back to the table.

My internal struggle starts all over again. I am really getting myself into a lot of trouble with these two, and I shouldn't be here. It's bad enough that I'm confused but adding alcohol to the situation was not going to make *anything* better.

I make my way back to the table, Justin right behind me. I see Eric's face when he notices Justin's hand on my waist.

I sit there for about 2 minutes when it dawns on me.

'What are you doing here, Laura?' I shoot Christine a look. She reads my face instantly.

"Hey, Lori, walk with me. I think I see some of our friends over there." She says as she gets up, pointing randomly into the crowd. She turns and looks at our guests, Eric is back at the table and Mona has followed, but she's talking to Evan now. "Please excuse us." She says politely. Justin gets up from his chair as we do. Ever the gentleman. I am not feeling so polite, I just get up and follow her.

We walk back to a far corner but it's much too noisy to talk so, we walk back to the restrooms.

"Laura, I see it all over your face. What's wrong?" she tells me as we walk in. The lounger is free, and I quickly take a seat. I know I've probably had too much to drink and that tequila shot is playing tricks inside my stomach.

"Christine, I shouldn't be here." I start to tell her. "It's a bad idea being here with both of them." I point out the door as if both Eric and Justin are standing right outside.

Christine purses her lips, "Oh, but you were handling everything so well, Sweetie, what happened?" she tells me in a very sweet, therapist, '*I really want to help you*' kind of voice.

"Alcohol happened, Chris!" I pout my face. I hate when you realize you've done something wrong only it's too late to change it. "this is the reason I didn't want to go out with them tonight in the first place!" I tell her.

I proceed to stick my head into the lounger and Christine starts running her hands thru my hair. "I'm sorry, I didn't know it was this bad." She's playing the role of supportive friend to her crazy, lunatic friend.

"That's just it!" I yell at her as I pull my head back up. "It isn't that bad, it isn't something I can't handle, but when you add alcohol, it turns to shit and…" my voice gets all pouty "it turns to this!" I tell her.

"I want to go home." I tell her finally. "Can you go back and tell them that I wasn't feeling well or something and…and that I had to leave?" I'm begging her to do this for me.

She leans back on the lounger and thinks about it for a moment. "Girl, you want *me* to go back there and tell them that *you* left?"

she says doubtingly, "Ay, por Dios, Laurita, why can't you just tell them that you need to go and excuse yourself?" she asks me.

"No, you don't understand, If I tell them I want to leave, either Eric or Justin are going to want to take me home." I start to tell her. "I don't want to have to choose tonight. Please?" I ask her again putting my hand on her arm.

"Ok, but you owe me, BIG TIME!" she says in her Mexican Accent that only comes out when she's been drinking.

"Let me go out to my car, give me some time to leave so, they can't catch up to me in the parking lot, ok?" I take the keys out of my purse.

"Girl, you are all kinds of paranoid." She tells me. "Let me walk you out then. So, I know you're gone." She gets up and starts to walk to the door.

As we come out of the restroom, I'm almost afraid we might run into Eric or even Justin again, but they aren't there. We head for the front door and Christine gets her hand stamped so she can return.

"Thank you so much, Chris," I tell her as I give her a huge hug, "I love you."

"You know you owe me for this?" she tells me pointing at me, she then points back at Benny's, "Cuz in there, that's your Drama, Mama, and you better figure that shit out."

"I know, I know" I feel like I'm getting scolded. I look down as I get into my car.

"Hey," she yells back at me "it's easy, pick the one that loves *you*." She smiles a sarcastic, mocking smile at me.

What is that supposed to mean? I really don't understand Christine's wisdom at times, but I really do love her.

I pull out of Benny's parking lot relieved that I don't have to put up with *that drama* anymore.

At least not until work tomorrow and sober Laura can handle it.

Chapter 12

Girl, What are you gonna do?

If there was ever a morning where I needed coffee, today is it. After last night's activities, I am not feeling so hot. I ended up staying at my parents' house because I didn't want to risk driving home with Matthew in the car.
Of course, that means I got an earful from my mother.

'Laura, what are your new bosses going to think of you now?' she said. *'They're going to think you are an alcoholic'* she continued *'irresponsible and crazy'* she added in there. *'Heaven only knows all the bad things they could be thinking right now.'*

Ay, Mami, if you only knew what my bosses thought of me and the things I go thru at work. I tell myself.

I'm sitting in my office when Justin walks in.

"Good Morning, Sunshine," he tells me smiling slyly. "You ducked out on us last night." I manage a smile and take a drink of my coffee.

"I'm sorry, Justin," I begin to tell him, but just then Eric pops his head in my office completely disregarding Justin.

"Good Morning, you feeling okay?" he asks me, one hand out with his thumb up.

"Yes, I'm fine," I tell him and smile. "I guess I shouldn't have taken that tequila shot." I laugh.

"I could've taken you home, you know?" Eric tells me this, completely   disregarding Justin's presence in my office. "Next time make sure you tell me before leaving like that." He points at me, scolding me. Oh, Eric, always my protector. He turns to look at Justin, then looks back at me, "Next time, I mean it!" he tells me.

"Yes, Eric, Ok!" I tell him, smiling and he leaves my office never acknowledging Justin's presence.

"So, are you ready to go?" Justin asks me. I almost forgot we are going on our supply run today.

"Yes, of course," I tell him. "Give me about ten minutes? I just need to send out a couple of emails." I ask him and he nods his head.

"Sure, I'll be in Corey's office whenever you're ready." He tells me.

Geez, my head is throbbing. I take out some Motrin and take two pills. "I swear I am never going to drink again" I whisper to myself and I even laugh a little. If I had a dollar for every time I've said that.

I finish up my emails and wonder if I'm up for this supply run. Being alone with Justin, I smile to myself. It can't be all that bad.

I call Casey and let her know that I'll be out of the office. I grab my purse and make my way to Corey's office.

Corey is, as usual, texting away on his phone. I knock gently and he looks up.

"Hey!" Corey yells, "well if it isn't the Life of the Party!" I can always count on Corey to be his sarcastic self. He smiles coyly, "I guess we should all be glad you didn't puke all over our table, huh?" Oh, Corey, sometimes I just wish I could tell you to shut up. I smile a half-ass smile and look over at Justin.

"Are you ready?" He looks at me and looks over at Corey. He seems bothered by Corey's statements.

Justin gets up from his seat and adjusts his coat. I start to walk out of the office when I hear Justin speak. "You know, Corey, being an asshole is not in your job description." Corey looks surprised. "Maybe, you should leave that at home next time." I can't believe Justin just said that. I look over at Corey with a stunned look on my face.

"Well, I," Corey tries to explain, "I was just messing around with her. She knows that!" Corey points at me.

"Miss Sanchez, after you," Justin says standing at the door. He looks at Corey and if looks could kill, I think Corey would be six feet under.

Corey looks nervous as we leave, but he doesn't say another word. I wonder what the repercussions of this will be between Corey and me.

Justin and I are walking down the hall and I want to laugh. I look at him, "Thanks," I tell him.

"I don't have patience for men with no respect," Justin tells me flatly.

I smile at Justin. "You have no idea," I say to him thinking of the many times Corey has been an asshole. Justin opens the door for me and we make our way into the parking lot.

"Well, I'm sorry you've had to put up with that," Justin says, and I stop walking.

"Justin, I don't want anything to happen to Corey because of me," I nervously tell him. I'm starting to realize that I have an impact on Justin and his decisions. "He has a family and they don't deserve…" my voice trails off.

"Laura, trust me, anything that happens to Corey, will be Corey's fault," Justin assures me.

He opens the passenger door to the Tahoe and I get in. He gets into the driver's seat, and we leave the Black Gold parking lot. I look at my phone and there is a text message from Eric.

Be Careful. Remember, you're not the nerdy girl anymore. ☺

I smile to myself. Oh, Eric, always the protector. I put my phone on silent and into my purse.

Justin looks over at me. "You have a beautiful smile, Lori," he tells me and flashes his perfect smile over at me.

"Thank you," I answer back.

It's amazingly quiet and I'm not sure I want to be the one to start the conversation. I'm looking out the window thinking of last night's happenings. I still can't believe I'm in this situation.

Suddenly, Justin looks over at me "You didn't tell me you had a son," he says. I'm not sure if that was a question or just stating facts. I look over and smile at him

I'm clearly starting to get nervous. He probably found out about Matthew last night. I wonder who told him?

"Yes, Matthew. He's fourteen months old." I say to him.

"His dad?" he looks over at me, I see the questioning in his eyes. I wonder what he's heard about that? I think to myself. I can only imagine.

"The guy you kinda met that night at my place." I say, "that was him." I stare out the window. I'm not sure if I want to tell him the whole story but I guess he deserves to know that Jake wasn't just some crazy ex-boyfriend at my house that night.

"You know, that night we went out; Jake, my son's father is Jake, he showed up on my doorstep. Drunk. Right before you picked me up." I begin to tell him. "He ended up passing out on my couch and well, I couldn't let him drive like that, so I left him there while we went out." I look over at him, trying to read his face.

He looks over at me as if he is absorbing all the information. He furrows his brow and looks over at me. Should I keep going? Should I mention that Jake and I stayed together for three weeks after that? Maybe, I'll leave that part out.

I look over at him and he is clearly in wonder over all of this.

"So, during our date, your son's father was passed out on your couch?" He says with a look of disbelief.

"Yes, but I promise you that before that day, I hadn't seen or heard from him in over two months," I explain. I must really sound stupid. I mean, this sounds like a real story. A made-up story.

Justin looks over at me again. He is holding his hand over his mouth and his expression is blank, I really cannot get a read on his face. He pulls into the store's parking lot and places the vehicle in Park.

We sit there in silence for a moment with the motor still running. Finally, Justin turns my way again. "And you're not with him anymore?" he asks me, and I shake my head no. "Why didn't you return any of my calls?" He asks me. I knew this question was coming and it is the one question I wish I didn't have to answer.

"Justin, I'm sorry." I start to say, "I don't have a reason for not calling you back except that I was embarrassed at what happened that night." I look down and I'm clenching my hands together; something I do when I'm nervous. "You don't deserve someone with drama," I tell him. "I'm sure you are beyond that," I say so sure of myself.

Justin quickly turns in his seat and takes one of my hands. "Laura, let me decide what I want in my life, ok?" he says in the most charming voice.

I take my hand away and I start shaking my head saying no. Justin is looking at me confused.

"It's too late, Justin," I say, my voice low, sad.

"What do you mean?" he quickly responds more confused than before.

"I work for you now," I start, "you are my boss." I place my hand on my forehead, leaning my elbow on the door. "I have a rule about dating someone I work with," I tell him. "And even more, someone I work *for*," I say.

Justin starts to laugh, "Now, Lori, don't make me go and fire you," he says sarcastically, and I turn around to look at him. I can't help but laugh.

"What?" I tell him. He's playing with me; his smile says it all.

"Things don't have to be complicated, Lori," he tells me, "I don't like drama, either, so, believe me if you and I are dating, no one else has to know." He looks at me with a serious face. "Discretion is my middle name." he winks at me.

I can't believe what is transpiring. I'm in the middle of the Office Depot parking lot, negotiating with my boss on whether or not we should…*date?* Is this for real? There are so many thoughts going thru my head right now. The main one, of course, is Eric.

Why is Eric even a factor, Laura?! I think to myself. Remember… two words. Party. Boy.

"Justin, I don't know," I tell him, "what if things don't work out?" I look at him with concern.

"And what? I go psycho on you, fire you?" He leans back in his seat. "I guess I can see why you would be reluctant." He smiles at me. "I assure you, that's not me. I've never gone '*Psycho*' on anyone," he turns off the vehicle. "C'mon, we can talk about it more over dinner on Friday. Right now, let's buy these supplies!" He opens the door and gets out of the Tahoe.

Wait a minute. Did he just schedule a date?

I come around the side of the Tahoe and look at Justin. "Dinner Friday?" I ask him.

"Good. I'll pick you up at 7," he says smiling, and starts walking towards the store.

Well, isn't he the sly one? I can't help but smile. What have you got to lose, Laura? I ask myself and then Eric comes to mind. Why is Eric doing this to me? Of course, all it takes is the thought of *Mona. Fast Life, Fast Girls.* Yes, Laura, remember, this is why we stay away from Eric Johnson.

Still, I can't ignore that I do have feelings for Eric, and I do feel as if I am betraying him by saying yes to Justin. Even though Justin and I have been on a date before he was my boss.

I don't know what to do. I should have never blown off Justin for Jake. I guess this is my chance to make things right.

Chapter 13

Perfect Justin

This week has gone by so slow. The transition has gone pretty smoothly, and work is going well. I see some new accounts coming in, which is a good thing. Of course, with the good comes the bad.

With the increase in activity, my clerks have been stretched thin. I have worked until 8 pm every day this week and have spent hardly any time with my little guy. I feel guilty. Tonight, I have my date with Justin and I'm tempted to cancel. Maybe I can just change the time and make it a late dinner. Matthew deserves some of my attention.

I'm sure Justin will understand. Even though he is just across the building, I text him instead of going to his office.

Can we make it 8:30 instead of 7 pm tonight? Need to spend quality time with my little guy.

I can take Matthew to the indoor park for a little while. And Christine already volunteered to babysit at my place so, the change of time should not be a problem.

I don't get a response. I guess he's busy. I place my cell phone on my desk, waiting for his reply.

Just then my intra-company instant messenger goes off. It's Corey.

Can I speak to you in my office, please?

I can't imagine why Corey wants to speak to me. He hasn't really spoken to me since the incident in his office with Justin.

Sure.

I reply.

I get up from my desk and walk over to Corey's office. He's deep into his phone. Nothing new. I knock gently.

Corey looks up, "Laura, come in," he waves me in. "close the door, please." He says as he points to the door.

Oh, no, whenever the boss asks you to close the door it's not a good thing.

I do as I'm told and take a seat in front of Corey. It seems like Corey is in a good mood. Something I haven't seen in Corey for a while. Of course, it could be just an act to cover up what he's about to tell me.

Corey sits at his desk smiling for a bit while texting on his phone. I swear that man would die if his cell phone went out. He finally shuts it off and puts it into his drawer. He's sitting leaning on his desk looking at me, curiously. Searching for words, maybe?

"Laura, I think I owe you an apology," he begins to tell me. He isn't making eye contact with me, so, I don't know where this is coming from. I can't imagine that Corey truly thinks he owes me an apology for *anything*. He is having a hard time with this, I can tell.

I sit up in my chair and cross my legs. I'm feeling a little uncomfortable thinking that this is the consequence of Justin's statements earlier in the week.

"I don't understand," I nervously smile at him. I'm feeling quite uncomfortable.

"Well, it seems there are people here who value your opinion," the words are not coming out so easily and it is evident by his pursed lips. "Anyway, I may have underestimated your worth to this company." He lets out a breath. Almost as if he's reading from a script.

"Corey, what's this about?" I ask him.

"I'm trying to be nice, Laura," he snaps back at me, gritting his teeth. He lets out a long sigh again and looks at me. "Look, you wanna know the truth?" he finally blurts out.

Looking at him, I just put up my hands like 'duh.'

"I know you have helped me a lot around here," he has trouble looking at me when he speaks, "and I know that you let me take credit for a lot of your work." Wow. Did that really just come out of his mouth. I am now officially intrigued. He continues, "and I know that I sometimes give you a hard time." After saying this, Corey looks up at me. "I've always been one of those people that has a sarcastic sense of humor, you know?" He puts his hands together in front of him as if he's praying. "I'm sorry if I took it too far with you." He says finally.

I sit there pondering what he just said, and I'm still in awe that he actually said it. I am looking for the right words to say and I turn around to look at him. I figure I have two choices; I can tell him it's ok, I understand. Even though it isn't ok and actually, I hate his sarcasm. Or I can accept his apology gracefully and leave it at that.

I hear Mami's voice.

'A man will only respect you if you respect yourself.'

I'm sure Mami was talking about a different situation but it fits. I have to put a stop to this now.

I really feel bad when people's feelings are hurt on my account.

My good-natured side wants to tell him it *is* ok, not to worry about it. Still, my professional side says I need to draw the line. If I don't, he will continue to make his unprofessional comments and think it's ok.

I look over at Corey who is waiting for me to respond.

"Okay, apology accepted," I tell him. "Was that all you needed?" I ask him as I get ready to get up.

Corey is puzzled by my response. "Uh, yea, that was it. Uh," Clearly, Corey, was expecting this to go differently. I want to laugh because he really doesn't know what to say, "Thanks." He tells me as I get up.

But before I open the door, good ol' Corey finds his words "You know, you didn't have to get your boyfriend to defend you. You could have told me yourself if you were so *offended*." Ah, yes, there he is. The Sarcastic Corey I know.

Obviously, taking the "nice person" approach was not the way to go with Corey. Keeping my mouth shut this time is just not going to work.

"My boyfriend?" I ask him, hostility clear in my tone. I turn back and look at Corey, my eyes wide with anger.

"I don't know who you think you are?" I start walking towards his desk. "Justin heard what you said to me, Corey, he reacted in the heat of the moment. I didn't *ask* him to do anything!" I'm in front of his desk now staring down at him. I'm breathing hard and I feel the blood rushing to my face.

"Justin?" Corey looks at me confused, "Who said anything about Justin? I'm talking about Eric." I lean back and now I'm the one with the perplexed look. Corey goes on, "Eric come up in here and tells me that he heard what I'd told you and wants me to apologize." I cross my arms, "I mean, you were the one that told him about it, right?" He looks at me thinking he's figured every-thing out. "Who else could it be?" I step back, irritated by this whole meeting, and start to make my way out of the office. "You went crying to him about what I said to you."

I turn to look at Corey. "You really don't know anything." I say opening the door, "and he isn't my boyfriend." I make my way out.

"You could've fooled me!" he yells out as I walk down the hall and back to my office. I can't believe what just went down.

I walk into my office only to be surprised again to see Eric sitting in my chair.

I'm clearly upset. My face says it all.

I'm not sure if I'm upset with Eric yet, because I don't know how he found out about all this. I mean, really, the only way he could know, if I didn't tell him, and Corey didn't tell him, is from Justin. This is what I don't understand. Why would Justin tell Eric?

"Hey, there." Eric looks at me, only he doesn't flash his smile as usual.

"Hi" I mutter and take a seat on one of the chairs across my desk. We are both quiet as if we are lost in our own minds. We are just sitting there across from each other for a minute when Eric finally speaks.

"So, um, Justin said 8:30 is fine for dinner, he will pick you up at your place." I quickly shoot a look over at Eric. He is holding my phone in his hand.

Oh, no! I forgot that I left my phone on my desk!

Stupid, Laura, Stupid, Stupid, Stupid!

I take the phone from Eric. "So, you read my messages now?" I am trying to sound unbothered by this, but inside, my stomach is in knots. I didn't want Eric to know about my date with Justin

 "No," he sighs. Eric doesn't look like his cheery self, "I came in here looking for you, to warn you," his voice is different, "about the meeting with Corey. Obviously, I was too late because you were already in there." He points to the wall between mine and Corey's office.

"Right, so, get to the part where you read my messages," I tell him flatly.

"Well, I decided to wait for you and was making some calls from your desk phone when your notification goes off." He points to my desk where my phone had been.

Of course! These darn smartphones. It shows the message on the screen. I understand now and roll my eyes.

I look down. I don't even know what to say to him.

"Eric, who told you about the incident in Corey's office?" I ask him. Trying to get away from the subject.

He looks over at me. He seems distracted, distant. "Michael." He looks down at his hands.

"His cubicle is right across Corey's office. He heard everything." He starts gathering his portfolio.

Wow. Michael coming to my rescue, too. Who would've thought?

"He was really upset by the whole thing, and it upset me, too, when I heard about it." He zips up his portfolio and looks over at me. His voice is sarcastic now, "I guess you're lucky Justin was there to protect you, huh?" He smiles at me, only this is a smile I don't recognize from Eric.

"Eric," I start to say when he gets up and heads for the door.

"You don't date anyone you work with, huh?" He tries to hide the hurt in his eyes with sarcasm, but I can see it.

I sit there speechless as he walks away.

'Ay, Laurita, you've really done it this time.'

My stomach is starting to hurt.

I feel absolutely terrible, and I want to talk to Eric. Only I have no idea what I want to say. I'm still sitting in the chair across my desk with my head leaning back looking at the ceiling.

I *have* to talk to him. Eric's office is five offices down from mine. Come to think of it, his office is directly across from Justin's, except that the cubicles cover the view in between. I see Corey leaving the office for lunch.

It's lunchtime and there aren't very many people in the building. I walk slowly to Eric's office. Mostly because I still don't know what I'm going to say. I'm glad no one is around because I hate when people see me going into Eric's office or him going into mine. I know they are mentally making up their own scenarios. I am well aware of the office gossip. That is why Corey called him my boyfriend.

I knock gently on the door and wait. I don't hear anything. Maybe he went to lunch, too. I think to myself. I open the door ever so slightly.

"Eric?" I call out to him.

"Ya, come in." He's in there.

Ok, here we go. I'd better figure out fast what I'm going to say.

I walk slowly into his office, closing the door behind me. Eric is sitting in the dark. He hasn't turned on the light to his office.

"Eric, I feel I owe you an explanation." My stomach is really in knots.

"Laura, it's fine. You don't *owe* me anything." He smiles at me. "Everything is great. You and Justin make a great couple and Black Gold is going to be great." Wow. He said great three times. One more time and he might believe it.

I walk over next to him on his desk. He is nervously typing away on his computer. Walking over to the edge of his desk, I sit on the edge. I'm trying to get him to look at me, but he won't.

"I'm sorry, Eric." I start to apologize.

"Sorry for what? Hey, don't worry about it. We're good." He flashes a smile at me but again this is a smile that I am not familiar with. One that seems very insincere.

"Eric?" I put my hand on his shoulder. I really am having a hard time finding the right words for this.

"I know I said I wouldn't go out with you because we worked together," the words start to come out before I can stop them, "but the truth is, I was afraid to date you because you're such a…" I stop. I hesitate long enough for him to turn around and look at me. His eyes have changed. There's a longing in them and he is waiting for me to finish. "such a party boy." I finally admit.

"*Party Boy*" He repeats those two words and looks at me with a new look. A wicked, devious look. I feel his green eyes on me and I'm intrigued. I've never seen Eric like this.

Oh, please, Eric. Nothing has changed. I am still afraid of you. Afraid of what you will do to me, to my heart. Don't make me tell you anymore. Please, just forgive me and let's go back to being friends. I look down, lost in my own head hoping that this is enough for Eric. I don't even realize that he is now standing right in front of me.

I feel his hand on my chin and he gently lifts my face so that I'm looking up at him. He takes my hair out of my face and places it behind my ear. My hands are at my side clenching to the edge of the desk, but I suddenly feel like I want to hold him. I let go of the desk and I put my arms around him, resting my head on his chest. I can smell him. He puts his arms around me and holds me tight. I feel his lips kiss the top of my head. I feel better. My stomach is no longer in knots and the lump in my throat is gone. Does this mean he forgives me?

"Are we good?" I ask him, still holding him, my face on his chest.

"We're good." I feel him squeeze me a little tighter.

"I'd better get back to work." I whisper, letting go.

Before I can turn, Eric grabs me, takes me off the desk and pushes my back against the wall. Suddenly, his hands are holding my face and I feel his lips on mine. He kisses me and I feel his body pressing against mine. We kiss and I feel his arms around me. It's a long, sensuous kiss and I'm lost in the moment. There is a tingling sensation coursing thru my body. Eric stops and looks at me, he kisses me again.

Oh, I want this. It feels so good. Again, I am lost in the moment.

Wait. I can't! No, I can't! Laura, you have to stop!

I pull away from him.

"Eric, no!" I hold out my hand. My heart is racing, and I can only imagine what my hair looks like. Not to mention that I'm probably flustered.

"We can't," I tell him.

"Why not?" he laughs slightly, "because I'm a 'Party Boy'?" He says mocking me. I can't believe he's making fun of me.

This makes it easier for me to compose myself. My knees are shaking, they're weak. Wow, I always wondered if someone could actually make you feel 'weak at the knees'. I guess they can.

Get it together, Laura!!

"C'mon, you know you like it!" Eric's smile is crass, smug. I don't like it.

"Don't treat me like one of your skanks!" I scold him.

With that, I pull myself together and walk out of his office.

It seems people are just now getting back from lunch so, I got out just in time. I walk back into my office and close the door. I need some alone time. I've had an eventful morning. I pull out my mirror, checking my face. My red cheeks are testimony to my escapades. I can't breathe. I need to get some air.

I grab my purse and phone. I notice I have a new text.

It's from Eric.

I would never treat you like a skank.

Whatever, Eric. I think to myself. I don't even respond, I'm so upset with him. Maybe. Well, not that upset. I don't know, I guess it wasn't that bad. Another text message comes in.

You don't know how long I've waited to kiss you like that.

I quickly reply to that.

Never going to happen again.
I have rules remember?
And no one else needs to know.

His response is again immediate.

never say never
our secret

Whatever, Eric. I tell you why I can't date you and you make fun of me?! Even use it against me. Unbelievable!

I really should get back to work.

****

Matthew enjoys his time at the park. My little guy really holds my heart, everything he does makes me smile. It's amazing how kids have that effect on you.

Driving back from the park, my mind wanders to the day's happenings. I still can't believe what went down between Eric and me. I'm not sure I want to tell Christine about it. At least not yet. I've never been in this situation. I feel weird, kissing a guy this morning, now I'm going on a date with another this evening? Surely, that is a sin or something. There *has* to be a rule about that somewhere, right?

I get home and Matthew is so tired and fussy. I give him a bath and put on his pajamas. It should be an easy night for Aunt Christine. He's so ready for bedtime. It's 7 pm and I jump in the shower.

Christine is already at my place when I get out. She has let herself in and is playing with Matthew in the living room. She picks him up and walks over to my room.

"How dare you try to put him to bed before I got here." She threatens me playfully.

"He was fussy, Chris," I tell her. "After his bath, he was dozing off."

"Well, we are going to play tonight. It's not every day that Mommy lets me watch you!" Christine tells Matthew.

"Thanks for doing this." I look over at her. "I didn't want to tell my mom I had a date and get her hopes up, you know?" I roll my eyes.

Christine starts laughing, "Oh, I know!" she sits on my bed, "If they still could arrange marriages your Mama would have married you off a long time ago!"

"You ain't lying," I tell her. I pick out my dress and begin the production of getting ready.

Christine pours us a glass of wine but she's too busy with Matthew to really talk to me.

My doorbell rings at 8:30 pm, on the dot. I walk over to the front door, kissing Matthew on the way out.

"Thank you again, Chris. I'll see you later tonight." I whisper as if someone might be listening.

I open the door slowly. Justin looks handsome as always. In a faraway place in my mind, I was afraid there was someone else on the other side of that door.

"Good Evening, Lori." Oh, Justin. Ever the Gentleman.

"Good Evening, Justin." I take his hand and we're off.

I drift off to Eric's office during our ride to dinner. Earlier today.

His lips on mine. His body pressing against mine. His intoxicating scent. It's our secret, I think to myself.

Secret.

I have never been one for secrets. I'm not even sure I can keep a secret.

I've tried all night to stop thinking about Eric. Dinner is quiet. Justin seems preoccupied, too, constantly checking his phone. Something must be up at work.

"A penny for your thoughts." Justin tries to start a conversation. Oh, no, Justin, you don't want to pay for *these* thoughts, I think to myself. I smile.

"Justin, it seems Black Gold still needs a lot of work to get where we need to be." I finally break the silence. I rehearsed a speech in front of the mirror on why Justin and I should *not* date. It still does not sit right with me, since we work together.

"Yes, but I know we can get there." He says confidently.

"Well, this is what I think," I start "Why don't we concentrate on getting Black Gold where it needs to be. In the meantime, we don't have to complicate things with a new relationship." This sounded a lot better when I was talking to myself in the mirror. "What I mean is, you're busy with a new company and all that comes with it. Why add the stress of a new relationship as well?" I look at him for a reaction. "Do I make any sense at all?" I look over at Justin who is studying me.

"I understand what you're trying to say, Lori," Justin reaches over and places his hand over mine, "does this have something to do with your rule about dating co-workers?" I look down, shaking my head in agreement. Damn, he saw right thru that, "Life can't be just work, work, work, Lori." He pauses for a little bit. "I want to take time to smell the roses" He smiles at me and pulls a piece of my hair out of my face, I can't help but notice that he doesn't put it behind my ear the way Eric does, "and you are a beautiful rose, Lori." I smile.

"It was just a thought," I say knowing that I've been defeated.

"I've been meaning to ask you," Justin pauses and looks at me with a serious look on his face, "I don't usually give merit to office gossip but it seems that there are those who believe," he looks at me as if he doesn't want to continue, but he does anyway, "that believe that you and Eric have" he pauses again. I'm almost afraid to hear where this is going. "have or had an affair at one time." He glances over at me as if to assess my reaction.

I'm a little offended by the question, my expression has changed and Justin notices.

"What do you think, Justin?" I answer defensively. I look at him square in the eyes. He smiles as if that will pacify me.

"Well, I know that Eric cares about you a great deal." He starts to say. This throws me off and I tilt my head back. What does he know about Eric's feelings? "I saw it that night we went out. He's very protective of you." He looks at me inquisitively. Searching for answers in my eyes possibly. I don't give him anything. At least, I don't think I do.

"Well, I would go with your first instinct to discredit office gossip." I can't even look at him and start to fidget with my silverware.

"The funny thing is that people don't believe that you have slept with Eric, but they also can't believe that he would love you so much if you hadn't." He adds making this even more comical.

What? This gossip tree is out of control.

I laugh. "Justin, please. What people?" I keep laughing, "This is too funny. Eric is not in love with me. That's preposterous!" I mean, really. *People* should mind their own business.

"So, there's no secret love affair going on there? Your baby isn't really his?" I almost spit out my food when I hear this.

"Justin!" My voice is higher than before. "Are people really saying these things?" Now, that is just ridiculous!

He laughs. "You'd be amazed at the information you can get from Michael." Oh, yea, Michael. The one who snitched to Eric about Corey's comments. Now it makes sense why he would go to Eric! I mean, Eric is my *lover*, after all.

"Misinformation, apparently," I say to him, still upset over this whole conversation.

I can't believe Justin would ask me about office gossip. He really should know me better than that. I know he probably just wanted to make sure but there were other ways, better ways to find out.

Overall, I've had a good time tonight. We steer clear of office gossip, once Justin sees that I was clearly offended by our last conversation. We find a nice Jazz bar by the River and the night goes smoothly.

"Lori, please, let's do this again." Justin kisses my hand and looks over at my front door, "and I can only hope there are no drunk ex-boyfriends on the other side of that door." His Texas accent is really coming out. I wonder if that is the result of the wine we had at dinner. I like Justin.

Justin walks me to the door. "Thank you, Justin," he is still holding my hand; "I had a good time, too." He slowly pulls my hand in towards him and I feel the rush go thru me. Not like before, when I was in Eric's office, this is more like…fear? I find myself scared again at the thought that I might be doing something wrong. Kissing Eric this morning and now Justin this evening?

I feel his lips kiss me ever so gently. I feel his arms around me and I turn away and place my head into his chest. It doesn't feel right. Earlier today I'm with Eric and now I'm here with Justin. This internal struggle has me tied up in knots! I hug him and he hugs me back.

"Good night, Justin" I let go and put my hand on the door.

"Good night, Lori," his beautiful blue eyes look right thru me. Questioning, wondering why I won't kiss him.

I'm sorry, Justin, I can't explain. I think to myself.

I open the door and go inside. Closing the door quickly behind me, I stand there behind the door. I am so glad that is over! I can't breathe. I'm frozen.

Chapter 14

The After Date…Date?

Christine walks over looking at me with a crazy look. "Hey, you ok?" she starts to snap her fingers in my face. "snap out of it." She tells me. Suddenly all I want to do is tell her everything. *Everything!* With Eric. With Justin. With Corey. The Office Gossip. I just need to spill.

She's standing in front of me. "It was just a date. Yes, he's Mr. Perfect, but there's no need to get weak at the knees." She's holding me there against the wall making a serious face.

"No, no, Chris, it's not that." I start laughing. "Eric and I made out this morning." I begin to tell her. Her eyes suddenly grow, and she tightens her lips, "I mean we really…Made….Out." I'm especially expressive with those two words. "Anyway, and I had to tell Corey off and then Eric found out about Justin but that was before we made out and then we did make out and it was good, Chris, Oh My God, it was good." I'm really talking fast, and I see Christine trying to tell me something with her eyes, but I keep going.

"and then I tell Justin that maybe we shouldn't see each other cuz you know, he should concentrate on the company and he says no but then he asks me if I'm having an affair with Eric? Can you Believe that? He says he heard it from Michael. Michael is one of my clerks." I'm talking faster and trying to take off my shoes now. "So, Michael says he doesn't think I'm the type to do Office romances, but they can't imagine that Eric would love me so much If I wasn't putting out…." I stop talking. Christine is sitting at the bar drinking her wine, but I see someone else in my peripheral vision.

If my eyes don't deceive, I believe that it might be… Eric?

I tightly shut my eyes, when I realize what I've done, and I turn around.

"Oh…My…God" I say as I see Eric sitting there smiling, his green eyes sparkling.

Christine lets out a burst of hysterical laughter.

"You two are priceless, you know that?" She points back and forth at the two of us, still laughing holding her wine.

"Laura, Eric stopped by to check on *me*'" Christine puts her hand to her chest, "*and* to make sure Matthew was doing ok." She says this in a very suspicious, I really don't believe his story kind of way. "Of course, I told Eric that I think the real reason he is here is that he knew you were going out with Justin tonight, and he wants to cock block." My mouth drops open. Leave it to Christine to just come out and say it.

"Chris!" I yell, throwing my shoe at her.

"What?! You know I have no filter." She says ever so bluntly again, "Especially, when I drink." I look over at Eric and he is laughing. He gets up and walks over towards us.

"And I told Christine that I wasn't here to cock block because you would never sleep with Justin on the first date." Eric is looking at Christine so sure of himself. "And I was right." He points to Christine, who proceeds to roll her eyes.

I look over at Eric. How do you know what I would or wouldn't do? I think to myself.

The three of us stand there for a moment and it's Christine who finally breaks the silence.

"Well, Pumpkin, I can't drive home, so I'm sleeping in your bed tonight." Christine puts her hand on my shoulder. She is quite tipsy. She bows her head to Eric. "Good night, Fine Sir, thank you for taking care of Matthew and me in our time of need." She's so sarcastic. I laugh and almost push her over. She cracks me up.

"You know where the PJs are if you need to borrow," I tell her as she walks into the room. She waves her hand over her head.

I look over at Eric, who is now standing by the bar pouring two glasses of wine. He hands me a glass and signals me over to the couch.

"Um, you were talking really fast, but I thought I heard you say that making out with me was really good." He says, teasingly.

I take a drink of wine, "I said a lot of things that you weren't supposed to hear and that's all you're coming at me with?" I tell him, embarrassed that he did hear everything I just said.

"How was *your date?*" he sounds sarcastic.

"It was fine." I really don't want to go into the details of my date with Eric. I want to ask him why he is here but then I really don't care. Of course, it doesn't matter. Weirdly, I'm kind of glad he's here.

"I know this wasn't your first date with Justin, you know." He takes a drink of his wine and looks over at me with a serious expression. "He told me that night at Benny's after you left." He turns over to look at me. Apparently, there was a plethora of information exchanged about me that night, AND at work.

"Oh, what, he just turned around and said, 'Hey, I went out with Laura.'" I make a goofy face at him and he laughs slightly. I'm sure there's more to this story.

"No, we just got to talking and I told him that you had told me that you knew each other from before." He stops as if he's remembering. "He's the one that mentioned your date. You know, where your ex was here, drunk and threatening him and was just all over the place." He stops again and takes another drink. The mood has suddenly changed.

"Oh, yea," I say. How could I forget? I put the glass to my mouth finishing my wine. I really *don't* want to get into that story.

The expression on Eric's face conveys his intolerance as he says, "I wouldn't have just stood there.".

"Anyway, I think we talked about you the rest of the night." He smiles, taking a deep breath. "He and I have one thing in common, I guess." He gets up and heads for the kitchen, taking our empty wine glasses with him. "Jack and Coke?" he asks me.

"Sure," I tell him. That explains why Justin believes that Eric cares for me. If the conversation that night was entirely about me, there would only be one conclusion.

Eric hands me my drink and places his on the coffee table. He walks over to the TV and hits play on the DVD player. Amazingly enough, Titanic starts to play.

I look at Eric and I think to myself, why is he making this so hard?

"What?" Eric looks at me bewildered. "That's your movie, right?" I nod my head yes and he disappears into the hallway. I can't help but wonder what he is up to.

When he appears back into the living area, he is carrying two pillows and my favorite blanket. Is he for real?

"Eric, really?" I say in complete disbelief.

He smiles, the smile that I am so used to. The smile that I love.

"I don't forget anything you say or do, and I make note of the things that you like." He tells me as he covers me with my blanket. He's so kind, thoughtful.

He sits next to me and I snuggle up next to him. His arm around me. Tightly embracing me, protecting me. And although I had a date tonight with Perfect Justin, there is nowhere else in the world that I'd rather be than right here. Right Now. I feel his lips kiss the top of my head. This is what I like. It isn't complicated being here holding this man. Perhaps, Eric is in love with me.

 "I actually came here to apologize for today." Eric breaks the silence and I'm baffled. Is he apologizing for the incident in his office? I do not get up to look at him. I stay frozen, with my head on his shoulder.

"I should *not* have read your message and I should *not* have reacted the way I did."

Oh, he's apologizing for that. Well, I cannot help but think that I probably would have done the same thing. And being in his position, I may have reacted the same way! I still don't move or say a word.

"Laura?"

Darn, he wants me to respond. I slowly sit up. For some reason, I cannot make eye contact with him.

"It happens." I shrug my shoulders at him. "We all have our moments, I guess." Those are the only words I can think of at the moment. I am sure he is not satisfied with that answer. He puts his hand on my chin and lifts my face.

"Laura, I also don't want to make you uncomfortable," sincerity in his voice, "so, what happened in the office today…" he stops and looks away from me, "If I overstepped my boundaries, I apologize for that, too." He looks back in my direction, but he is looking down.

"Eric…" Geez, I feel like he thinks I am fragile or something. "It wasn't like I was asking you to stop." I say shyly, "well, not until the end, anyway." I place my hand on his forearm and grasp it tightly. "You didn't do anything I didn't want you to, ok?" he looks over at me and smiles. I feel as if I need to explain myself a little more. "It's just that…" my voice trails off. I don't know how to explain to him that I'm confused. It's him. It's Justin. It's work. My rules and all the drama.

"Because I'm a '*Party Boy*'?" Eric replies mockingly. He has turned his whole body on the couch, so he is facing me now.

"Well, you are," I say in my most audacious voice. I look up at him and smile. I think back to all the times I've been around Eric, just the two of us. He has always been the perfect gentleman. He has always surprised me, never acting like the 'Party Boy' I claim him to be.

"You've got it all wrong, Lori." He brushes his hand on my cheek. He just called me Lori. "My brother Evan is the '*Party Boy',* I just tag along to take care of *him*." He smiles. I really do love his smile. I always have. "I mean, I'm not a stick in the mud. I like to have a good time as much as anyone, but I know my limits." He tilts his head, "Evan, no. Evan likes to get out of hand. He likes to *test* my limits." He laughs.

So, I was wrong about him. He still has a reputation, though, a long list of girlfriends.

"Your long list of girlfriends?" I tell him in a low voice. "You have a reputation. The 'love 'em and leave 'em' type." I say almost in a whisper like I can't believe I'm confronting him with this.

"Laura, when you have money, you attract…" he stops and is at a loss for words, or at least it seems that way. "You attract women with ulterior motives." He finally says. Maybe he was looking for a good way to say *that*. I think to myself. "I don't have time for women who want me for my money." He really sounds honest, I see it in his eyes. And his explanation doesn't really sound too far-fetched.

It still does not change the fact that we work together. Of course, I can't even use that excuse now that he knows I went out with

Justin.

"I'm sorry, Eric." Is all I can say. "I thought. I mean, I assumed and that was wrong of me." I tell him clenching my hands together nervously.

Eric starts laughing and I look at him curiously. I don't understand why he is laughing.

"Laura, you don't need to be nervous?" he finally says pulling at my clenched hands, "It's not like I'm going to make you choose between him and me." He takes the drinks from the coffee table and hands me one. He read my mind. "I know you need time to sort this out. I'm in no hurry." He tells me in a very understanding voice. I look at him skeptically. He smiles at me and takes a drink. I can't believe what is happening.

I am now completely in unfamiliar territory. I have never had to 'choose' between two men before. Much less had two men pursuing me at the same time!

Mami has never given me advice on this before. I wonder what she would say if I told her.

'Ay, Laurita, did you lead them both on and now have them fighting against each other?'

'How could you let this happen, Laura, you should have stopped it before it went too far.'

She would somehow turn this on me. I just know it.

I grab my blanket and pull it over me. Eric takes the glass from my hand and places it back on the table. I place my head on Eric's lap, thinking about today. I'm back in Eric's office. His smell, his lips, his arms around me. It felt so good.

I fast-forward to dinner with Justin. Perfect Justin. Holding his hand, great conversation, the kiss at my door before he left.

Oh, Dear God, what am I going to do? I think in my head as I feel Eric's hands running thru my hair.

Chapter 15

Do you even know what you want?

"Rise and Shine, Sleepyhead," Christine whispers, her hand shaking me. I smell bacon and eggs. Oh, yes! I love it when Christine cooks! I hear Matthew on his highchair. My head hurts. I lift my head from the pillow and see Christine. She is standing behind the couch. "I guess you all had a pretty good talk last night." She says pointing over me to the ground." My eyes are still sleepy and barely open, but I turn to look. Eric is lying on the ground asleep.
I put my hand on his shoulder, "Eric." I shake him. "Eric, it's morning. Are you ok?" I tell him. Poor thing. The floor cannot be comfortable. I could have pulled out the sofa bed if he would have asked.

"Yea, I'm fine." He mumbles and takes a deep breath. "Restroom?" He asks me.

"Sure. You know where it is." I tell him. He took off his shirt and he looks sexy wearing only jeans. He quickly gets up and heads for the restroom.

Christine smiles her wicked smile and I get up headed for the master restroom.

"You all could have asked *me* to sleep on the couch," she yells back, "I would have moved." Oh, Christine, she knows better than that, I think to myself as I start to walk a little faster because I realize I really have to go.

I take my time brushing my teeth, washing my face, and making myself somewhat presentable.

I change into some comfortable sweat pants and a t-shirt and head for the living area.

I hear Christine and Eric talking. I stop in the hallway to listen.

"So, did you tell her?" Christine asks Eric.

Tell me what? I guess Christine and Eric had quite a talk before I got home last night.

"It's not that easy, Chris." Oh, so now Eric can call her Chris, too. I guess they're best friends, too? "Laura needs time, you know?"

"If you just freaken tell her. She'll snap out of it." Geez, Christine can be so blunt sometimes.

I decide I've heard enough. I walk into the living area.

"So, what are we talking about?" I tell them and they both look at each other like they've been caught. Eric looking at Christine like a hawk.

"Nothing," Christine says exaggeratingly. "Eric and I are fighting over who is going to take you out tonight." She looks over at Eric and smiles at him deviously.

"Of course, whoever doesn't take you out, gets to stay here and watch Matthew." She says as she attacks her scrambled eggs in the pan.

"I-I don't know if I want to go out tonight." I look at Christine wondering what she is up to. "Besides, I'm sure Eric has other plans," I say uneasily. I really don't like Christine's little game.

"Actually, I do," Eric says and quickly, Christine's plan is shattered. "I'm sorry, it's a family thing." He looks at Christine, then me.

"No, that is fine," I tell him, and I look at Christine glaringly, upset that she put him on the spot.

"Well, let's eat!" and just like that, we change the subject.

Christine always makes a great breakfast, pancakes, eggs, and bacon. Matthew loves it and it shows all over his face.

Eric is sitting directly across from me on the table, and he is sitting next to Matthew as well. He interacts with him while we are eating and Matthew smiles and giggles at his silly faces. I like that Matthew is comfortable with him.

We finish eating and I start to pick up our plates. Christine gets up to help me.

"You come with me, Little Guy, let's get you cleaned up." Eric stands and takes Matthew out of his high chair. He carries him over to the restroom in the hallway.

Christine pushes me gently with her elbow. "Did you see that?" She whispers excitedly, she is smiling in astonishment. "He's so cute! He's helping you with the baby!" I think Christine is more surprised than I am.

I am, however, truly in awe. Eric Johnson is not making this easy for me. Everything I thought he was, he has proven to be the complete opposite. He is so protective, thoughtful, loving...tell me again, why you do not want this man, Laura? I ask myself in this daydream.

Christine and I as a team can wash the dishes fairly quickly. I make my way back to the table where I start to clean Matthew's high chair. The evidence of our breakfast is stuck in places I would never have thought.

"Look" Christine whispers. I feel her tugging on my arm as I'm wiping the table. I look up, Eric is walking back into the living room. Matthew is in his arms holding his favorite stuffed animal, his monkey. He's in a completely new outfit, his face clean as a whistle. My smile is almost instant. Eric gently places him in his playpen and looks over at me.

"What?" He smiles, "I have a nephew. My sister's son. He's two now." Oh, Eric. You are the complete package, aren't you? "I'm sorry, Laura, I really have to go." He walks over to me. He gives me his usual tight hug and kisses me on the cheek. I'm a bit sorry he has to leave. "Thank you for everything." He makes a turn to look at Christine.

"Chris, as always, a pleasure. Great breakfast," He hugs her, "until next time."

Chris looks at him as if she is displeased, "Yes, next time." She hits his shoulder and speaks through her teeth. Something is going on between these two and I really need to get to the bottom of it.

He smiles and winks at me as he walks out the door.

I stand there for a couple of seconds mesmerized. I realize that Chris is staring at me. She has an *I told you so* smile on her face.

"Uh-huh." She beads her eyes at me, "I suppose you're going to keep telling me that you have no feelings for that man?" She's staring at me, and I feel like she can see way down into my soul.

"Chri-i-i-s" I sing her name, stretching it out, like that might help to avoid the question. "Why did you put him on the spot like that?!" I get mad at her. Changing the subject.

"Ay, Por Dios!" Christine throws her arms in the air and walks back to the living room. "The two of you have me like a loca!" (translation: crazy person) She yells at me. "Ever since that night at Benny's, Laura," she points at me. "It's like I'm dealing with *your* drama more than my own!" She throws her hands in the air, rolling her eyes.

"Christine, what are you talking about?" I ask her. After that night? She and I haven't really talked since that night.

"After you left that night, I had Eric upset with me cuz I let you leave." She says. She's breathing hard like she's been holding all this back. "And then Perfect Justin is grilling me asking about you, saying that he didn't understand why you had all these walls up." She uses her hands to show makeshift walls in the air. "Then Justin and Eric are being all sarcastic with each other, like 'Oh, yea, I saw the way you were looking at her' and 'well, what about you, hanging on her like you were trying to claim her?'" She's using different voices and is talking really fast. It's crazy but I understand everything she is saying. "Ay, Laurita, both these men have it bad for you. I sat there the whole night just listening to them. They went back and forth, back and forth. Believe me, Girl, I was tempted to leave, but I wanted to hear what they were saying cuz it was about you, you know?" she's waving her hands and I'm listening intently. We are now sitting on the couch.

"Anyway, I don't know if you know this, but that man that was just here," she points at the door, "he is all about you." She crosses her arms and sits back. "And when I say all, I mean *all about you.*" She emphasizes.

"What do you mean?" I ask her.

"Girl, he knows what you like to eat, your favorite color, your perfume, how you like to wear your hair, you know what I mean? *Everything!*" She uses her hands waving them in a circular motion when she says 'everything'.

"Like in a stalker kind of way?" I ask her uneasily.

"No, No. In a cute, I have a crush, kind of way." She smiles. "Only he's got way more than a crush." She purses her lips. "He's very protective of you. Eric is all about giving you space, Lori, and letting you come to him when you're ready or at least letting you figure things out. He's not going to push you. He's afraid to mess it up." She says.

"What did you all talk about last night, Chris?" I'm super curious what their conversation could have been about.

"Oh, well, that, I will let him tell you all about that." I can't believe it! Chris has never held out on me.

"What? Are you serious?" I'm amazed. "Chris, you are supposed to tell me everything, you're *my* best friend, remember?" I look at her in a way that can only mean, 'duh'.

"Yes, Sweetie, but as much as I want to," she sighs, "this is something that has to come from him." She gets up from the couch.

"I'd better go." She grabs her purse. "Before you try to beat it out of me." She smiles.

I'm not happy. Chris has never left me hanging like this.

"Don't worry, Lori, it's nothing bad." She tells me as she walks out.

More secrets. I hate secrets.

Chapter 16

La Familia Sanchez

I t's a tradition in my family, Sunday is family day. We all get together at my parents' house, have a huge dinner usually grilled outside and spend quality time together. This Sunday is no different. Mami calls to make sure I will be there. Matthew and I are headed out the door when my phone notification goes off. I look at my phone and see it is a message from Justin.

Hi. How are you?

I smile. Perfect Justin is writing to me.

Good. On my way out. Family day.

I write back to him. I strap Matthew into the backseat and settle into the driver's seat. I get a response from him

Nice. Just checking in to let you know I was thinking about you.

That was nice of him. I think to myself. I don't know how to respond. I text back the only thing that makes sense to me.

Have a nice day. See you at work tomorrow. ☺

I'm glad we're going to spend time at my parents' house. I want to talk with my mom and maybe get some advice from her. I will have to do it without giving away too much information, though. I'm not ready to let her know about Justin and Eric.

****

Walking up to the front door of my old house, I already hear the loud talking coming from inside.

My brothers must already be here. I have two older brothers, Alejandro and Manuel, or Alex and Manny for short.

I'm walking with Matthew carrying his diaper bag when the front door swings open.

"Hey, Little Sis!" It's Alex. His big smile tells me he has already started drinking. Family day would not be Family day without beer. That would just be unheard of.

He opens the screen door and walks over and takes Matthew from my arms.

"Wow, Matthew is getting big!" My parents were gone last weekend so, it's been a whole two weeks since he's seen him. I guess he could have grown, I think to myself.

"How are you, Alex?" I give him a big hug, I'm happy to see him. "Is Gracie inside?" Gracie is Alex's wife. They have a very tumultuous relationship. We never know if they are going to be together or on a break again when Sunday comes around. Thank goodness they don't have kids.

"Yea, she's inside." He answers right away. "Oh, and don't tell her anything about her weight." I look at him befuddled. I don't think I would ever mention anything about another woman's weight but why would he mention that?

"Alex, what? Why would I?" I ask him curiously.

"She's pregnant." He whispers loudly. "We haven't told Mom and Dad yet so, don't say anything." He doesn't look happy about it.

He makes a face.

"Alex, didn't you learn anything from me?" I pinch his arm, jokingly.

"Hey!" He starts laughing loudly. "I know, huh?"

I walk into the house and immediately I am swarmed with hugs from everyone. My brother Manny is the only one I do not see. His wife Janet is here, as well as their two boys.

"Janet where is my brother?" I ask her as she chases one of my nephews down the hall.

"Oh, he's around here somewhere." Janet, by far, is my favorite sister-in-law. She's so down to earth. She isn't a drama queen, and she simply adores my brother. That's a big one for me. I may be the 'little' sister but I'm very protective of my brothers. "It's good seeing you, Lori. We need to talk!" She yells as she grabs my nephew and drags him to the backyard. My dad doesn't like kids running in the house.

"Hey, Sis!" I hear Manny yelling from the kitchen.

I walk a little faster and hug him. "Wow, Brother, life is good, huh?" I tell him as I feel his tummy.

He laughs slightly and holds his tummy. "I'm watching my weight," he says, "that's why I keep it right here where I can see it!" He laughs out loud. I guess he's been drinking, too.

"Where's my drink?" I tell him. I see Mami behind him make a face.

"C'mon!" he waves me to the back door. "I have a cooler in the back."

We step out to the yard. Alex is already grilling some chicken and it smells great.

"Hey, Lori, you'll never guess who came to work for me." Manny looks over at me as he hands me a beer. Manny has been working for Republic Disposal Services, a saltwater disposal located in

Karnes county.

"Are you still at Republic?" My contacts helped him find the job, but Manny is more than qualified. He landed the job on his own merit.

"Yea," he raises his arm and shakes his head, "I'm a supervisor now."

"That's great, Manny" I open my beer and take a drink.

"But let me tell you who is working for me." He says excitedly. I look at him, my eyes wide. "Jake!"

I start to cough. I think I almost choke on my beer. Did he say Jake?

"Jake?" I confirm. "Jake Lakewood? Matthew's father?" I tell him, my voice is laced with just a bit of anger.

"Yea. That Fucker started working with us on Monday." He sits down next to me. "At first, he didn't recognize me, you know? Cuz I only saw him like what, two, three times, maybe?" he tells me. "and even when I did see him, that guy was shady, like he didn't talk to us much. I never liked that guy."

I look over at Manny. "Hey, that's Matthew's Dad, you're talking about?" I say defensively.

"Yea, Lori, but after what he did to you?" he questions me, his voice upset.

"That doesn't matter, Manny!" I tell him. "I never want Matthew to hear you say a single negative thing about his father, you understand?" I'm pointing at him. He doesn't understand, I can tell by the expression on his face.

"Look, let's say you and Janet got divorced. God forbid." I tell him, knocking on the wooden picnic table, "You wouldn't want her talking bad about you in front of *your* kids, would you?" He makes a face, shrugging his shoulders.

"I guess, Sis." He comes over and sits down. "I just hate that guy for what he did to you, you know?" he looks at me and puts his hand on my shoulder.

"Why don't you tell him about the money he stole from you?" I turn around and My dad is standing behind me. I don't know how long he's been there or how long he's been listening to us talk.

"Dad, I didn't see you standing there." I walk over and hug him. He does not hug me back.

"What money?" Alex is the one yelling now. "Lori, he stole money from you?!" Telling my brothers, while they are drinking, that my ex-boyfriend stole my money is not a good idea. What is my dad trying to do?

"That's just history." I look over at my dad scornfully. "Don't worry about it. Matthew and I are fine." My brothers are both looking at me, Manny has his hands clenched in fists. "Really, we are fine." I grab Manny by the arm and move him back to the table to sit down.

I can't believe my Dad just did that. If he was standing there long enough to hear that Jake works with Manny, why would he instigate? He could cause major problems. My brothers are very protective of me. I don't need Manny going to work and making a scene because of me.

To my surprise, my Dad walks over to the picnic table to join us. My dad is staring at me and I feel a little uncomfortable.

"Manny, can you make sure that Jake pays your sister child support?" My dad says out of nowhere. My brother looks at me surprised, concerned even, then looks over at my dad.

"Well, that depends." He answers my Dad and looks over at me.

"Do you have a child support order?" He asks me. I shake my head yes. I can't believe we are having this conversation.

"I can talk to HR and make sure that the order gets put thru." He says to my dad.

"He needs to be a man and take care of his responsibilities," my Dad starts to say, "So, far, he has been anything but."

"I'll talk to HR, Dad." Manny looks at me. "Laura, he'll be making more money with us, you might want to try to get more child support." I don't want more child support. I don't even want to get the child support that is ordered. I don't want anything from Jake.

"I think I'm gonna go inside and talk to Mom." I excuse myself from the table. I am very uncomfortable with this conversation.

I walk into the house and see Janet and Gracie talking in the living room. I don't understand how Alex and Gracie can think that my parents don't know she is pregnant. It is very evident. I quickly make my way past them and walk into the kitchen.

I see Mami making her famous rice. I see her getting ready to make a salad.

"Can I help you with anything?" I ask her as I come in and take a seat on one of the bar chairs.

"I'm just about done, but you can help me with the salad if you like." She points to the lettuce and tomatoes on the counter. I take the lettuce and start to help her.

My mom is quiet, humming to herself.

"Mami, did you ever date anyone other than Dad?" I look over at her. Her humming stops and her expression is confused.

"I mean, was Daddy your *only* boyfriend *ever*?" She starts cutting the tomatoes for the salad. She seems to be having a memory because I see a slight smile come across her face.

"There was one boy, Michael, that liked me." She says, the smile on her face clearly saying that my mom liked him, too. "But it was a different time, Laurita, women didn't *date* casually like they do today." Her smile is gone.

"This was about five years before I met your Dad. Michael lived in the next street from mine." Her smile is back. "He used to walk me home from school," I remember my mom telling me that she and my Dad went to different high schools. They met at a dance years after high school. My Mom was twenty-four when they got married.

"Your grandfather was very strict, Laura, he didn't want me to talk to *any* boys." She closes her eyes as if she is remembering. "But, I was seventeen and I thought I knew better." She looks over at me. Wow. My mom was a bad girl? Way to go, Mom!

"Mom!" I say in astonishment, and she smiles.

"Ay, Laurita, I let him walk me home from school that is all." She says and she throws a piece of lettuce at me. "Your grandfather didn't like him. He used to tell me he came from a bad family." She is closing her eyes again. "I should have listened to my father." She looks sad now, a different look on her face.

"So, you all never went out on a date?" I ask her inquisitively.

"It was a different time, Laura. If we wanted to go out on a date, he would have to talk to my Dad. I already knew your Grandfather would not approve." She says. "We met every day at the corner and exchanged letters, love letters." She smiles at the memory. "We didn't have cell phones or Facebook back then." She laughs.

She pauses for a minute as if she is reliving the moment.

"One day, he wasn't at our regular meeting spot. I waited with my letter, but he never came." She is shaking her head. "I went home, and I thought maybe my father had found out about us and told him to stay away. I didn't understand what other reason would keep him from showing up." Her eyes are getting watery now. My Mom is getting a little emotional. "You see, Laurita, sometimes you think you know someone." She puts her hand over mine. "The next day I went to the corner again and he never came. I was so hurt. I went home and read his letters over and over." She is looking down shaking her head again. "I never saw him again. A friend of mine said he got another girl pregnant and married her. I never knew because I didn't see him again." She looks on as she gets the salad together.

"Ay, Mami." What a story. "Does Dad know about him?" I ask her.

"I told him once about the letters, but it was years before I met your father." She smiles. "When I met your father, my heart belonged to him from day one." She has a huge smile now.

I wish things were still that simple. My mom knew the day she met my Dad that he was the one. Thirty-eight years later, she still loves him. I see it in her eyes.

"Are you seeing someone new, Laurita?" she asks me inquiring. I do not want to tell her about Justin just yet. It's too soon. I'll tell her if it gets more serious.

"No, Mami," I smile, "There is someone interested in me, but I don't know if I'm ready yet." I look at her and her face is concerned. "You know, after Jake." I look at her sadly.

"Laurita, you're young. Not every person you go out with is going to be a potential husband." I can't believe what I just heard. Did my mom just say that? "You have to date to figure that out, Mija." She walks over to me and moves the hair out of my face. I love my mom. I smile.

"Don't let Jake ruin you for someone else." She's smiling down at me. "You're a beautiful, young woman with a good heart." My mom does not compliment me very often and it feels good hearing it. I kiss her on the cheek.

"Thanks, Mami." I help her carry the food outside to the picnic table.

Chapter 17

Decisions, Decisions!

Friday night has become a regular date night for Justin and me. Tonight, we are going to Benny's with Christine and her new Beau. She has been quite secretive the past couple of weeks as to who she is dating so, I am very curious.

It's been about three months since my first date with Justin when Eric showed up at my house. Justin has been the perfect gentleman. Perfect boyfriend.

Still, Perfect Justin.

Coincidentally, last week was the first time Justin stayed over. I held off sleeping with him because of Eric. I wanted to make sure, there was nothing there between Eric and me. But for some reason, Eric has been avoiding me. His conversation is always about business. Since that night at my house he seems…distant. I'm not sure if it's because of Justin or maybe the fact he is distracted. At today's staff meeting, Evan mentioned that Eric was in a new relationship. I wanted to ask him about it, but I guess I have no right to question him about it. I *am* with Justin, after all.

It's about a quarter to five when Eric pops his head in my office.

"Hey, You, I haven't talked to you in a while." He makes his way into my office and sits across from me.

"Maybe you've been busy," I tell him, a hint of jealousy in my voice.

He smiles the smile I love so much. "Busy here at work, yes." He tells me reassuringly. "Outside of work, Not so much." He looks at me waiting for my response.

"But your brother said…" I catch myself.

Stop, Laura, you have no right to say anything to him. You're with Justin, remember? I put my head down. "Never mind, it really is none of my business."

"That's why I came in here, Lori, to clarify to you what my brother mentioned in the meeting." I'm writing into my log and my heart skips a beat when I hear him call me Lori. I look back up at him. I am shaking. I feel it. My heart is pounding but I don't know why.

Why am I feeling this way? I'm with Justin. I think I am in love with Justin. I *slept* with Justin! Why is Eric making me feel this way?

All of the sudden, I am startled by Justin's voice. "Umm, excuse me, Lori?" He walks into my office and sees Eric sitting there but doesn't say a thing to him, his glare saying it all. Eric doesn't make a move to leave, though.

"I'm going to have to cancel tonight." He whispers. "Something came up." He looks preoccupied, nervous.

"Oh, Ok, then," I tell him, a little disappointed. "It's ok. Take care of what you need to." I put my hand on his arm, "Call me later." I tell him.

He makes his way to the door and turns back.

"I will." He pauses, looking down at Eric "call you later, I mean." And he walks out the door. He really is acting weird. I hope everything is ok.

"So, I was saying." Eric continues his conversation.

I look over at him. He sees my expression, the disappointment on my face.

"So, you all go out a lot?" Eric asks me, pointing out the door where Justin was standing before, changing the subject.

"Every Friday night." I smile. Eric smiles his beautiful smile and I am taken back to that day in his office. I recall the heat between us, the emotion, his lips, and his smell. Oh, Dear. I should not be thinking about this.

I quickly sit up in my seat. *Is it hot in here?*

I turn to look at Eric who seems to have been studying me for the last few moments. I smile again nervously.

"Yea, every Friday and tonight we were supposed to go to Benny's with Christine," I tell him. "She has a new love interest and I'm supposed to meet him tonight." I look at my phone at the time. It's after five. I need to get going.

"I can take you if you like." Eric quickly offers. I quickly look up at him, raising one eyebrow.

It isn't a *bad* idea, I think to myself. I mean, I would hate to be the third wheel when I meet Christine tonight.

"You don't mind?" I ask him, "I mean, we would go as friends, of course."

"Of course." He says, making a face as if I offended him.

"Okay." I get up and gather my purse. "Can you pick me up at eight?"

"I'll be there." He flashes his smile. Please, don't do that. I think to myself. That smile is like an aphrodisiac for me.

"Ok, thanks. I really appreciate this." I get up and give him a quick hug. "I'll see you at eight, my place." I run out of the office and head home.

****

It's almost eight o'clock and Mami has not come by for Matthew.

I grab my cell phone to call her for the fourth time when I hear the front door.

"Laurita, I'm here." It's my mom. I wonder what kept her.

"I'm sorry I'm late, Mija, but Janet asked me to babysit, too." She looks tired. "I had to pick up the boys and take them home, then come all the way over here." I smile at my mom. She's forgiven.

"Mami, you should have told me you were doing that. I could have brought Matthew to you." I tell her. She makes her way to the kitchen for a glass of water.

I notice the time. It is almost eight. Mami is going to be here when Eric arrives. I haven't told her about Justin *or* Eric yet so, she's oblivious. She might think Eric is my 'Mystery Boyfriend'.

I'm startled by the doorbell.

And there he is.

"Is someone picking you up?" Mami turns to look at me.

"Um, yea, sort of." I smile back at her.

Her curiosity builds. I haven't finished getting ready and she looks at me.

"Well, you go finish getting ready. I'll let him in." She shooshes me away to my room.

I am reluctant but I go ahead.

This is going to be interesting. Mami is going to meet Eric. I can only imagine how that is going to go.

I have never gotten ready so fast in my life. I go into Matthew's room and grab his diaper bag, making sure he has his night-clothes and plenty of formula.

I walk out into the living area. Mami and Eric are sitting on the couch.

Eric stands up. He looks gorgeous. His smile just sent a tingling sensation to my stomach. I am nervous. I don't know why.

This isn't even a date.

It's Eric.

"You look beautiful, Lori." He looks over at my mom, "And now I know where she gets her good looks." He says smiling at Mami.

My mom smiles big, from ear to ear. She is completely won over.

"Eric, It was a pleasure meeting you." She puts her hand out to shake his. Eric gives her his hand.

"And you Mrs. Sanchez." He says. Mami walks over to the playpen for Matthew and Eric quickly walks over.

"Mrs. Sanchez, Please, let me." He says and he bends over and picks up Matthew out of the playpen.

Mami's face says it all. She is in complete awe. He proceeds to carry Matthew out to her car and places him in his car seat for her.

I hug her before she leaves. "Thank you, Mom," I tell her.

"I really like him, Laurita" she whispers in my ear. Ay, Mami, if you only knew, he is *not* my boyfriend. I think to myself.

I keep that bit of information to myself, I don't want to break her heart. I smile as she drives away.

I look back at Eric suspiciously.

He smiles playfully. "Mothers like me. What can I say?"

Yea, right, Eric. That was you trying to win my mother over and you know it. I say in my own mind.

"Let me grab my things and I'm ready to go," I tell him as I make my way back in.

****

Benny's is in full swing when we arrive. I find Christine at our usual table.

"What the?" Christine says when she sees that I arrive with Eric.

"Long story," I tell her, and she smiles wickedly. "Not *that* kind of story, Chris, we're here as friends," I assure her.

"Uh-huh." She nods her head at me in disbelief. "Hi, Eric. It's so nice to see you again." She looks over at Eric and puts out her hand.

"Chris, always a pleasure." Eric shakes her hand.

"So, where's your mystery man?" I say to her looking around.

"Oh, he got a call and went outside cuz he couldn't hear." She uses her hands to mimic a telephone in her ear.

"Oh, ok." I'm looking around and Benny's is pretty packed tonight.

"I'm going to the bar to get us some drinks," Eric whispers in my ear. I shake my head in agreement.

Chris looks over at me. "So, where's Mr. Perfect?" she says sarcastically.

"Something came up. He had to cancel." I yell over the music and voices.

"I still think something is up with him, you know?" she yells back at me. "The fact that he doesn't want anyone to know you all are dating. Having you give *me* specific instructions that I am not to give out his name to anyone," she wrinkles her nose, "What the hell is that about?"

"Chris, we have to be discreet, you know?" I tell her trying to explain. "He's my boss and you never know who knows who. That kind of information can reach the wrong person and we can be in a lot of trouble, you know?" I look at her and she's making a face like she's not convinced.

Eric comes back with a Margarita and Jack and Coke. He pulls out the chair for me to sit down and I take my seat. He takes a seat right next to me.

"Oh, there he is!" Chris sits up straight and has an excited look on her face. "Baby, come, I want you to meet my best friend."

She grabs his arm. Suddenly, I feel Eric grasp my thigh…tightly. I'm distracted. I turn quickly to look at Eric. Eric's eyes are looking straight ahead, and he motions for me to look. I turn and standing in front of me is, none other than… Brent Martin?!

"Brent!" I am surprised. More than surprised. I am in complete shock. I look over at Christine as I shake his hand.

"Laura," he shakes my hand. He obviously expected me. "Eric?" But he obviously did *not* expect Eric.

He has a smile on his face, and he kisses Christine. I can't help but notice how happy Christine looks.

"How long have *you two* been dating?" I ask, the shock evident on my face.

"Well, since about a week after that night. Right, Babe?" Brent looks over at Christine.

"Yea," she looks over at me. "Lori, I completely forgot that I had given him my number, so, when he called me I was like 'Who the hell is this?'" She breaks out laughing. She really looks happy. Christine is glowing.

"I thought the office gossip about the two of you wasn't true." Brent interrupts pointing at Eric and me.

I feel my face turn beet red. I also feel Eric's hand on my thigh tighten once again.

"It is," I tell him, I see the big cheesy smile on Brent's face, and I quickly correct myself. "Untrue, I mean. The gossip isn't true. Eric and I are just friends." I turn to look at Eric, looking for him to verify my story.

Eric smiles at Brent. He doesn't say a word.

"My boyfriend couldn't make it tonight and Eric stepped in so, I wouldn't be the third wheel." I bet I sound crazy right now. I think to myself. I sound like someone making up some crazy story.

Christine is sitting back with a huge smile on her face. What is she smiling at? I glare at her. You're not helping!

"No, Brent, it's true." Christine finally butts in. "Lori and Eric aren't an item. I was surprised when he showed up here tonight, too." She smiles and winks at me, taking a drink.

I wonder if Justin found out that Brent was Christine's mystery man and that is why he canceled on me? I know he doesn't want people to know about us, especially at work. For some reason, he doesn't care that Eric knows. I wonder why? I roll my eyes.

Eric notices when I roll my eyes and he pushes my leg with his. I turn to look at him.

"What are you thinking about?" He asks smiling.

"I just think it's funny that Brent is Christine's mystery man," I look down. Eric places his hand on my chin and pulls my face up. "I wonder if Justin found out before we came here and that is why he canceled," I say dismally.

Eric pulls the hair from my face and places it behind my ear. "Probably." He says with a cynical tone to his voice. "He doesn't care that I know but he hides you from everyone else. Not even his *partners* know." He looks at me with a look of pity. I can only imagine what Eric thinks of me now that I'm dating Justin.

"It's complicated." I am making excuses and Eric knows it.

"It shouldn't be, Lori. I don't trust that man." I look away. Eric does not understand. He is biased because he likes me. Of course, he's not going to trust him.

"Snap out of it!" Eric yells at me. "We're here to have fun."

Brent comes back to our table with tequila shots and I look at Eric.

"Uh Oh. We know what those do to me." I tease him.

"Maybe, it's just what you need." He smiles and hands me a shot.

We all take our shots. I notice Eric's arm is around my waist. Christine notices, too.

"C'mon I need to go to the restroom." She practically drags me out of my chair.

"I'll be right back," I say to Eric as I'm being dragged away. He smiles at me as I leave.

We walk into the restroom and Christine quickly starts to yell.

"Have you and Eric talked?" She asks me. Holding my arm rather harshly.

"Talked? About what?" I ask her confused.

"Remember, that night at your place? I told you he had something to tell you." She is looking at me like I'm stupid. "Have you all talked since then? Cuz it doesn't look like it since, you say you're just friends and he's still looking at you with his googly eyes" Chris puts her hands to her eyes accentuating them, "and you're still going out with Mr. Perfect!" Chris can be so dramatic sometimes.

"Chris, calm down," I tell her. Smoothing my hand against her shoulder. "It's ok. Eric is seeing someone else, too." I tell her.

"Oh, really?!" I caught Christine off guard. She is in complete disbelief. "He's seeing someone else?" She is still looking at me, dumbfounded.

"Yes, so, everything is ok. Don't worry." I tell her. I really do have to go to the restroom, so I make my way to one of the stalls. "Let me pee, then we'll go back."

Chris is still standing there like she's in shock. I wonder why she finds it so unbelievable that Eric is seeing someone else.

"Hey, Lori, I'm gonna go back to the table, alright?" Christine yells at me while I'm in the stall.

"Ok," I yell back at her. I wonder why she isn't waiting for me. She always waits for me.

I make my way back to the table. I see that Christine is in a heated discussion with Eric. I look around for Brent and find him at the bar getting drinks. I wonder what is up with these two. Christine and Eric have something between them that they haven't told me. I really need to get to the bottom of it.

"Hey, what's going on?" I say to both of them when I get to the table.

Christine looks at Eric. "Nothing, Laura, everything is *just* fine!" sarcasm is dripping from her voice. She smiles at Eric.

"Eric, what's going on?" I ask him directly. I already know that Christine isn't going to tell me. I want an answer from him.

"Here we are!" Brent arrives at the table with our drinks.

I smile and take my seat next to Eric. He looks bothered. Possibly by whatever Christine told him. I turn to look at him. I slide my hand and place it on his knee, tightening it a little.

"Smile," I tell him. He looks over at me and smiles "We're here to have fun aren't we?!" I repeat his earlier statement right back at him.

He puts his hand on my chin, "Yes we are, Miss Sanchez, yes we are."

The rest of the night is uneventful. Christine and Brent look good together and I am truly happy for Christine. We say our goodbyes in the parking lot as if we are never going to see each other again.

"I love you, Chris. I'm so happy for you." I whisper in her ear.

"Thank you." She whispers back. She holds me tighter. "Don't be stupid, Lori, open your eyes." She whispers.

"What?" I ask her still whispering.

She lets go of me and looks over at Eric. "Goodbye, Eric." She hugs Eric.

I'm looking at her confused, but she never answers my question.

What do I need to open my eyes about? I think to myself. What is she talking about?

Eric opens the door to the Tahoe for me to get in.

"Thank you," I say as I climb in. He doesn't close the door. Instead, he stands there inside the open door next to me. He's looking down, fidgeting with his keys.

"Eric, what's wrong?" I ask him and this time it's me placing my hand on his chin and lifting his head.

"Lori, I tried to tell you this earlier." He looks nervous. I look at him intently. "What my brother said today in the meeting about me being in a relationship," He looks at me, waiting for a reaction. I feel my heart start to race. I really have no right to question Eric about his new relationship.

"Eric, you really don't owe me any explanation," I tell him sincerely, holding back my true emotions. Inside I feel just a bit jealous, but it isn't my place. I'm dating Justin and can't or shouldn't say anything.

"I just want you to know that this whole time..." his voice trails off. He looks out to the parking lot thru the windshield. "I mean, I've waited..." he stops again.

"Waited for what, Eric?" I ask him, getting his attention. "I don't understand."

"For You." He says finally. He looks down at his keys. He starts to fidget with them again. I don't know what to say. I care about Eric but I'm with Justin. I can't expect him to just sit around and *not* go on with his life. He can date if he wants to.

"Eric?" I look at him, question in my eyes.

"Lori, you always said you wouldn't go out with me because we work together." He stops and closes his eyes. "I figured one day you might come around. It wasn't until I saw that you were with Justin, that I realized that maybe it just wasn't meant to be." Eric stares into the sky, "I met her one of the nights I was out with Evan" Of course, I bet she's one of his typical skanks or gold-diggers. "She's an attorney," he smiles, "actually, she's an Assistant District Attorney." He looks at me again. "We've only been out a couple of times." He's staring at me, trying to read my face, but I'm trying to hold it in. I am truly bothered by everything Eric just said. I don't know if I would have felt better if she was just another skank, but the fact that she's a professional? That definitely changes everything. I feel my heart sink.

He looks at me as if looking for a reaction or even forgiveness. "Eric, I'm dating Justin. I – I really have no right to say anything about who you date." I look away. My heart hurts, my stomach is in knots and I feel pain in my chest.

"I just couldn't wait forever, you know?" Eric looks at me, taking my hand. Our eyes meet. I do know Eric. I know you've been waiting for me. I expect too much from you.

"Is this the reason you have been avoiding me?" I finally ask him; my voice is low. I can barely get the words out. "Since that night at my house, you have avoided me."

"The following Monday, Justin told me you all were going out again." Eric looks at me with his beautiful eyes. It feels like he can see right thru me. "I figured you had made up your mind." He shrugs his shoulders. "I met her about a week later" He smiles looking at me again. Why isn't he with her tonight, I wonder? "She's out of town this weekend," Eric answers as if he read my mind.

"Justin told you we were going out again that Monday?" I ask him. I am truly surprised. Justin wants *no one* to know about us, but apparently, he makes it a point to tell Eric personally that we are going out.

"Yea, he came over to my office, sat down, and said I needed to back off because you had decided to pursue a relationship with him. He had the most condescending smile on his face. Arrogant Prick" Eric is bothered by the memory I can tell. "I really don't trust him, Lori." The fact that Eric just called Justin an 'Arrogant Prick' does not sit right with me. But I also don't understand why Justin always insists that nobody knows about us, yet he is so quick to tell Eric to back off.

Eric is still standing next to me. I look over at him.

"Laura," He is looking at me, his eyes almost begging. "You really need to be careful with him. I mean, what do you really know about him? Other than the fact that he owns part of Black Gold and went to the same high school?" Eric looks worried now. "I can look into his background, you know, what he's been doing from high school to now if you want. I have some connections."

I smile. "Eric, I don't need protection from Justin. And I surely don't need you running background checks on the guy." I put my hand to his face. "I think maybe you are letting your feelings about me cloud your judgment," I tell him. I know Eric likes me, I have always known that, and I know he cares about me. "Well, the way you used to feel about me, anyway. I'm ok. Don't worry." I say as I turn back in my seat. Eric takes his cue and closes the door.

The ride home is quiet. In the back of my mind, I know Justin must have known that Brent was going to be there tonight. It makes sense why he would cancel. I know I was the one with the rules about not dating someone I work with, but Justin has taken it to a new level. When he said, 'Discretion is my middle name', he meant it. Justin absolutely wants no one, and I mean, not even my mother to know that we are dating. It upset him to know that I had told Christine, but he got over it. I guess he's right when he says that information like that, in the wrong hands, can cause more drama than either of us wants in our life.

Thinking about Eric with someone else is physically causing me pain. Pain in my heart, in my stomach. I'm jealous and I have no right to be. I really need to stop thinking about it.

As Eric pulls into my street, I notice the identical Black Chevy Tahoe already parked in my driveway. Is that Justin?

Eric looks over at me, "Was he supposed to be here?"

My expression says it all. I am just as surprised as he is.

"No. I – I had no idea." My stomach is starting to hurt even more.

What's wrong with you, Laura? Why are you nervous? You're not cheating on him! Eric is just a friend and you went out as friends.

"Well, this should be interesting." Eric's tone is sarcastic, with a hint of depravity. I sense he might even be looking forward to this.

"Eric. Maybe you should just drop me off and go." I tell him, fearing the worst scenario that can happen between two men, one woman.

"Laura, I can't just drop you off and drive away." He looks over, almost upset that I would even suggest it. "I mean, really, what can he say? It's not like we did anything. We went as friends." He shrugs his shoulders; his tone is now very matter-of-fact and calm. I sense that Eric is looking forward to this confrontation. "I have to make sure that you are ok before I leave." He tells me.

Ok? Why wouldn't I be ok? It's Justin. Justin wouldn't do anything to hurt me. Eric is just being over-protective.

As we pull up to the front of my house, I notice Justin is sitting in his vehicle. I turn to look at Eric again.

"Please, just drop me off. I'll text you and let you know I'm ok." I'm begging him now. I really don't want any problems to erupt here in front of my house.

Eric raises his hand and caresses my cheek. He's looking at me with his beautiful green eyes.

"Ok. Fine. But promise me, you will text me to let me know you are ok." He looks at me, his eyes still burning into me, "promise me!"

"Yes, Yes, ok," I put my head down. Eric lifts my chin so that I am looking at him.

"You're a good girl, Laura, you haven't done anything wrong." I know I haven't done anything wrong, but for some reason, I feel like I have. My stomach is hurting, and I am nervous. I don't understand why Justin is here, waiting for me.

"Good night, Eric, I had a good time tonight." I lean in and hug him, and he kisses the side of my head, on my hair.

"I love you, Lori." He whispers in my ear.

What? I pull back and I look at him. Did I just hear that correctly? Did Eric just tell me that he loves me? Isn't he dating little Miss Assistant DA?

I pretend I didn't hear his words, even though they linger in my mind.

"I will text you." I hurriedly open the door and make my way out of the Tahoe. As I make my way up the walk, I see Justin getting out of his vehicle. Eric is still watching from the front of the house. Why doesn't he leave already? I'm thinking in my head. Justin waves over at him, only with the dark tint on the windows, it's hard to tell if Eric waved back.

"Hey," I tell Justin, my voice high and nervy.

"Well, I trust you had a good time." Justin's expression is stern. "Eric, as always, stepping in to accompany you." He points at the Black Tahoe still parked in the front of my house.

I nervously turn and wave goodbye to Eric hoping he gets the hint that he needs to go.

"I just didn't want to be the third wheel, you know?" I tell Justin firmly. "I mean, we knew Christine was bringing her new boyfriend, it *was* supposed to be you and I, remember?" my voice is a little sarcastic now. I can't help but feel upset that he canceled but suddenly, is now here at my house.

"I don't like you going out with Eric, Lori," Justin tells me. I put my head down. I have never let a man dictate what I can and cannot do. I start walking towards the front door.

"You make it sound like a date, Justin," I tell him as I walk into the house, leaving the door open so he can follow me in. "We went as friends, that's all." I throw my purse on the couch.

I'm walking towards the kitchen when I hear Justin's voice. "I know Eric wants to be more than friends, Laura, and I don't like you going anywhere with him. You lead him on when you do that." Justin's face is different, I see the anger and he is talking thru his teeth.

I stop dead in my tracks and I turn around to face him. I'm surprised to hear him speak to me this way and I'm even more surprised that he is trying to tell me what to do. He is my boyfriend, but he doesn't own me!

I feel myself starting to become upset. I do not like fighting, but I can't allow Justin to talk to me this way, "Justin, Eric is a good friend. I drew that line a long time ago, way before you came into the picture! You don't have to worry about him!" I'm yelling now, upset, breathing hard, and still in shock.

I look up and see Justin standing there. He's pacing and looking over at me. It's almost as if he, too, is surprised by his emotion.

He finally stops pacing, he's looking down. "Look, Lori, I just," he starts but can't get the words out. He takes a deep breath. "I don't want to lose you, I don't know what comes over me when I see you with Eric." He says looking at me, his eyes asking for forgiveness, "And then Brent called me tonight, telling me that the two of you had shown up at Benny's together. He kept going on and on about the rumors and how you still denied they were true." He stops again and looks down. "I'm sorry, I don't know what got into me. I'm stupid. I saw red, Lori." He walks over to me and pulls me in for a hug only I'm not that easy to appease. I look at him, still upset.

When you think of gossipmongers and blabbermouths, people think of women, but working at Black Gold has taught me that men are just as bad. Why would Brent call Justin?

"Brent called you?" I asked him suspiciously, "He actually took time from his date with Christine to call you and tell you about Eric and me. Why?" I look at him with question in my eyes.

Justin hugs me but I don't reciprocate. "He knows about us, Lori. He knows that you and I have been dating and he thought you were stepping out on me." Now I am confused. If Brent knows about us, then why did he cancel tonight?

"Who else knows about us, Justin?" I ask him angrily pulling away from him, "Do *all* the partners know? Evan? Trace? Does *Corey* know?" I glare at him waiting for an answer. "And why did you cancel on me then?" I ask him, I really do want answers.

Justin tilts his head. "Well, the partners know. I don't *think* Corey knows." He says in a not so reassuring tone.

I cross my arms. "What happened to 'Discretion is my middle name'?" I can't believe that I've been the only one keeping this secret.

"Lori, c'mon." He gets closer, hugging me. "I've only told people that I know I can trust." He kisses my forehead. My stomach is still hurting but my nerves have settled. "C'mon," he says again, his lips gently touching mine. "Let's go to bed and forget all of this." He pulls me in tight, kissing my neck.

"Why did you cancel on me tonight, Justin?" I ask him again. He never answered my question. If Brent knew the whole time, where was he tonight?

"I'm trying to close a major deal for Black Gold and I had to take them out to wine and dine tonight. I hated doing it to you, Lori?" He looks at me sincerity in his voice now. I feel his body up against mine, hear his breathing in my ear. He kisses me lightly on the neck. Why am I letting him do this to me? Just minutes ago, he was trying to dictate my life, telling me who I can and cannot talk to, and now, he's doing this? He looks up at me and I see the changed expression in his eyes. "Let's go," he takes my hand and we start walking towards the bedroom. In a small part in the back of my mind, I hear a little voice telling me, 'a jealous man spells trouble' but the rest of me, allows him to lead me and we make our way to the bedroom.

****

I lie here with Justin next to me, weak from our lovemaking. Is that what they call makeup sex?

I suddenly remember I promised Eric I would text him. I gently make my way out of bed and walk over to the living room. I search for my phone in my purse and pull it out. I have three text messages. All from Eric, probably. I think to myself.

I touch the messages icon on my phone. Surprisingly, only two messages are from Eric. There is one message from Christine.

Eric's Messages:

12:15 am: Hello. Are you ok?

12:30 am: Hello?

I glance up at the time on my cell phone. It's almost three am. I text him back anyway.

I'm fine. Sorry I didn't text sooner

Almost immediately, he answers me. I can't believe he has been waiting for me to text him.

Good. See you Monday.

Christine's Message:

11:58 pm: Call me. I need to talk to you.

Well, it's too late to call Christine now. I will call her in the morning. I make my way back to the room, placing my cell phone on my nightstand.

I go to the restroom before laying back down.

I try to quietly make my way back into bed, so as to not wake Justin. I feel him move and get in closer, his body up against mine, he wraps his arms around me. I guess I am not as quiet as I think I am. Justin is obviously awake.

"So, do you check in with all your friends to tell them you're ok or is that just Eric?" Justin whispers in my ear, holding me tighter now. I look over at my cell phone on my nightstand. Did he go thru my messages?

"What are you talking about?" I say to him, not turning to look at him. Still puzzled.

"You texted Eric to let him know you're ok." He is still holding me tight.

I can't believe he went thru my phone. I lie there frozen, confused. I've never been in this situation.

I didn't do anything wrong. Eric is just a friend. He was just worried about me, that's all. I have nothing I need to answer for. Tell him, Laura!

"Justin, why are you going thru my phone?" I finally manage to say, almost afraid of the answer that awaits me.

"I was just curious, that's all." He says in a cynical voice, "who you could be texting at this hour." He finally let's go and turns around facing the other way. "Go to sleep. You must be tired after all of tonight's escapades."

I lie there for a while lost in my own mind. Justin wasn't himself tonight. I almost wonder if he's been drinking. Alcohol does things to people, it makes them act differently. It would explain Justin's weird mood.

That has to be it. Justin must be intoxicated. We all know these salesmen get together and they have more than their fair share when they get together to *'wine and dine'.* I think to myself.

****

I'm really moving slowly this morning. Justin woke up around six, saying he had to leave. His excuse had to do with work. The oilfield never sleeps, and nobody knows that better than me, so, I didn't question it. Besides, I think I want some me-time this morning, after last night.

I have to pick up Matthew, and it's already nine o'clock. I grab my cell phone to call Mami.

"Hello, Laurita, Good Morning!" Mami has always been a morning person. But this morning, she has an especially chipper tone in her voice.

"Hi, Mami, I just got up, I will be there for Matthew in about an hour, ok?" I'm still in bed and haven't even showered.

"Ok, Laurita, did you and Eric have fun last night?" Oh, that explains it. Mami is happy because she thinks I'm dating Eric. No wonder she isn't giving me a hard time.

 "Yes, Mami, I did. I'll see you in an hour, Ok?"

"Ok." I hang up the phone. I get up and see my clothes from last night strewn around the room and I want to laugh. Justin's eagerness last night shows in the way he undressed me and threw my clothes everywhere. It's like our fight beforehand brought out this animal intensity. It was actually kind of hot, my legs still shaking from our *activities.*

I quickly take my shower. Justin is probably just feeling a little insecure because of all the rumors about Eric and me, then seeing us together just made it worse. I throw on some jeans and a tee-shirt and head out to Mami's house.

****

As I walk into Mami's house, I smell the familiar scent of roses in the air. My mom always has rose candles and potpourri in the house. It always reminds me of home.

"Hola, Mami," I say as I walk into the kitchen where my mother is cooking.

"Hi, Laurita" she looks over at me.

"Where's Matthew?" I ask her as I look around, the house is really quiet. I can tell there are no kids here.

"Oh, he went with your father to drop off the boys." She tells me. I take a seat at the table.

"Laurita, how long have you been seeing Eric?" she asks me. I should have known she was going to ask me. My mom really liked him. I really should tell her we are *not* dating.

"Well, that's a matter of opinion," I say to her dancing around the question. I smile at her. "We're just friends, Mami." I break it to her. I look down, smiling shyly

"What do you mean opinion? And the two of you are fooling no one saying you're just friends" You, too, Mami?! I think to myself. She stops what she is doing and comes over next to me. "You like him, I see it on your face now just as I saw it on *his* last night, you can't lie to me. I'm your mother" Her tone is serious, scolding but she tenderly touches my face with her hand.

"I've known Eric for four years, Mami," I say to her, looking down again trying to get this smile off my face.

"Four years? Como?" Mami asks a little confused.

"He works with me." I look at her. She is looking at me, I'm sure she is doing the math in her head. Going thru my time with Jake, when Matthew was born. She is listening to every word. "I have a rule about going out with someone I work with. I …" I look down again. "I won't do it. " I look her way again. I shrug my shoulders.

"It's complicated."

"Love finds a way, Laurita." Mami looks at me earnestly. "It doesn't know anything about your rules." She makes an angry face but then smiles at me. "He really cares about you." Her smile is wider now, one she cannot contain. "I can tell. His eyes lit up when you walked in the room." I know I can trust Mami to tell me the truth. Believe me, Mami, will tell me even if it hurts my feelings.

I smile. She goes back to the stove now, leaving me sitting on the stool.

"He is the one that sent you the roses when Matthew was born." I look over at Mami, How did she know that? She smiles at me as if she read my mind.

"I read the card while you were sleeping, in the hospital." So maybe she read the card and *not* my mind, "You know me, I'm very curious and I thought it was weird that your boss would send you something so…big." Mami waves her hands in the air.

"Yes, that was him." I smile and I look down. I do remember that bouquet. It *was* over the top.

Mami smiles.

I'm startled by the sound of my phone notification.

I pull the phone out of my purse. It's Christine.

You ok?

Christine must know that Brent called Justin. I answer her quickly.

Yes

She responds seconds later.

Call me when you have a chance.

I hear Dad walking in with Matthew and quickly start to get his things together.

"Thank you, Mami" I go into the kitchen and give her a kiss. She is still cooking.

"Bye Bye, Laurita." She kisses my cheek, "Will you be here tomorrow?" she asks me.

"Yes, Mami." I smile. "Of course. I never miss Family Day."

"Why don't you bring your *friend,* Eric?" She smiles at me. Mami wants me to be *more* than just friends with Eric, she'll try anything.

"I don't know," I tell her, actually entertaining the thought of inviting Eric, "maybe." I smile a mischievous smile at her and walk out.

I leave her house wondering if Eric would even want to come to Family Day. I don't know if he wants to be exposed to my whole family like that. Besides, Eric has a new girlfriend and after Justin's reaction last night, I don't know if I want to rock the boat.

Since when do we let some guy tell us what to do, Laura? I think to myself and my devious smile is back.

Why do my thoughts always seem to lead me into trouble? And when did I become devious?

I text Eric before driving off.

My mother would like to invite you for dinner Sunday

I smile at the thought of Eric coming to Family Day. He really made an impression on my mom. Obviously.

Somewhere in the back of my mind, I can't help but want for him to say yes to me and keep him away from little *Miss Assistant DA.*

He and I had a great time last night. AND didn't I hear Eric say, 'I love you'. Geez, how could I forget that?

Are you forgetting about Justin, Laura? I hear my conscience say somewhere in the back of my mind.

"Yes, Yes, I know, I'm with Justin," I say out loud to my conscience.

I start to drive away, as I dial Christine's number.

"Hey, Lori," Christine answers quickly after one ring.

"Hey, what's going on?" I ask her wondering what is so urgent that she needs to talk to me right away.

"Lori, Brent called Justin last night and he told him that Eric was with you." She starts to say, almost as if she is warning me.

"Chris, it's too late." I stop her "Justin was at my house when I got home." I tell her and I hear her take a deep, loud breath on the line.

"Oh, Shit, What did you do?" She asks me, as usual, holding nothing back.

"I had nothing to hide, Chris. I wasn't worried about it." I tell her plainly. I leave out Justin's jealous rampage. Christine doesn't need to know about that.

"Shit, I would be. If you heard what Brent told him." Christine sounds upset. "We sort of got into a fight about it afterward." I'm curious now as to what was said.

"Really, was it *that* bad?" I want to know. It might explain why Justin was so upset.

"Well, Brent told him that he confronted you all about the rumors and that you got fidgety. Like in an 'oh, no, you caught me' kind of way. He said that the whole night, you and Eric just laughed and stared into each other's eyes and that after seeing it for himself, he was convinced that the two of you have something going on." Christine sounds upset just telling the story. I hear what Christine is saying and I keep thinking to myself, Mami said she saw how Eric and I look at each other. Now Brent is saying he saw something. Am *I* the only one who doesn't see this *thing* that everyone else does?

"Lori, are you there?" Chris says on the other line. I snap out of it.

"Wow, Chris, I'm sorry, but why is your boyfriend such a 'Chatty Cathy'?" I mean, really, was the gossip that good he just had to call him that night.

"No, see, this whole time I'm thinking that Brent doesn't know about you dating Justin, I mean, I *never told him.* The whole *'swear on the bible thing'* you made me do. Then I wondered why he would call him just to tell him about you and Eric." She stops and takes a breath "Well it turns out that he did know!" She yells at me thru the phone. "Apparently, Mr. Perfect, tells his friends but you're not allowed to tell yours." She says rather disgusted. "Brent thought you were cheating on Justin and had to call him."

This explains why Justin was so upset. I am so glad Eric did not walk me to the door last night. It could have been much worse.

"Chris, I'm driving. Let me call you later." I tell her as my mind is lost again in thought. I can't talk about this right now. It isn't making any sense to me.

"Ok, Sweetie, but tell me did everything go ok with Justin?" she asks before we hang up.

"Oh," I pause, Again, Christine doesn't need the details of our disagreement last night. "Yea, we're fine. I just told him that Eric and I went as friends. It was no big deal." I don't want a lecture about jealous men or for Christine to start judging him based on one incident.

"I'll talk to you later then." She says

"Ok, bye." I hit end call.

Obviously, I am distraught at all this drama. I have always stuck by my rules for a reason. To avoid drama.

I hear my notification sound and look down.

It's a text message from Eric.

Sure. Time?

Ay, Laurita, you're playing with fire. I think to myself. But there it is again, my evil, little wicked smile. Who knew that I had it in me?

As I drive up to my house, I see something at my door. I take Matthew out of his car seat and quickly make my way up the walkway.

It's a bouquet. I place them on the table and walk over to lay Matthew down in his playpen.

Who could have sent me flowers? It's a beautiful bouquet with Roses and Daisies, my favorites. I grab the card, admiring them.

Just because I love you.

Justin

I smile to myself thinking what a wonderful boyfriend I have. I stand there admiring their beauty, and I'm taken away to the last three months with Justin. He's been perfect. Everything I've always wanted in a man, in a boyfriend. I take the vase into the kitchen to put ice in it. Mami has always told me ice keeps the flowers fresh.

My phone starts to ring, and I frantically run back to my purse to get it. I'm fumbling through everything in my purse and I end up missing the call. I'm still having a hard time getting it out of my purse when it starts ringing again.

Finally, I'm able to get my phone out.

"Hello?" I answer knowing the call is from Justin.

"Hey, why aren't you answering your phone?" He answers right away without saying hello.

I laugh, "Well, hello to you, too, and Thank you for the flowers," I tell him not answering his question.

"Oh, did you like them?" He asks me, his voice is changed now.

More sincere.

"Yes, my favorite. Thank you." I'm smiling from ear to ear.

 I quickly call Christine and she agrees to babysit. She and Brent made up after their fight last night, but she does not want to go out, so she was more than happy to babysit for me.

I quickly erase the text messages between Eric and me, remembering Justin going thru my phone last night. This is the first time I feel like I have to watch what I do. I feel a little weird about it.

The little voice in my head goes off again.

Really, Laura, what are you afraid of? A man? Maybe, we need to re-examine this relationship.

"Shut up," I tell myself out loud.

Now it's Mami's voice.

'The two of you aren't fooling anyone saying you are just friends.'

The cheesy grin is back on my face thinking about Eric. He's dating his attorney girlfriend. We really are *just friends.* In my mind, I am taken back to that day in his office. When I felt Eric's lips against mine. I still get chills when I think about it.

"Stop it, Laura," I say out loud to myself again. We are both in committed relationships now.

And Mami? Ay, Mami. She doesn't know about Justin. She has no idea what she is talking about. I have feelings for Justin, I think I love Justin. He's everything a girl could want. I'd be crazy to let him go.

Chapter 18

Who do you think you're fooling?

I'm getting ready for my date with Justin when Christine arrives, letting herself in.

"Hey, La La, I'm here!" She yells as she walks in making her way to my room.

"I'm in here! Matthew is here with me." I yell back from my room. I'm still wearing sweats and a tank top, doing my hair.

"Hello, Pumpkin." She says to me as she walks in and she quickly takes a seat on my bed.

"Brent might come over later to watch a movie if that's ok with you?" she asks me not really concerned about my answer because she's going to do whatever she wants anyway.

"Of course, I don't mind." I smile at her, "Just don't do it on my bed!" I say looking over at her now in a playful tone, I laugh loudly.

Christine throws a pillow at me. "Lori!" she's laughing loudly now, too. "that's gross! We can wait until we get back to my place, we're not humping each other like rabbits all the time!" She says thru her laughter.

The doorbell rings at eight on the dot.

Lucky for Christine, Matthew is already asleep.

"Thank you, Chris. I'll see you in a little while. There's wine in the fridge, help yourself." I tell her knowing she will anyway.

I answer the door and to my surprise, it is both Justin and Brent at the door. I look over at Brent and I can't help but make a face. I'm still upset with him over his little call last night.

"Hello, Miss Laura," Brent says as he walks in. "I guess now you know the cat is out of the bag." He smiles looking over at me. I manage a half-smile, looking over at Justin. Christine is at Brent's side now. "I've known about you and Justin for a while now." His East Texas accent is very heavy.

I smile and walk over to Justin leaning over to kiss him.

"Are you ready, Sweetie?" I say trying to get out sooner than later.

"Sure," Justin looks over at Brent and Christine, "We'll see you all later." He smiles and winks at Christine. Christine's smile is wide, she looks so happy with Brent.

Justin, of course, opens the passenger door for me waiting as I get in. He closes the door and gets into the driver's seat starting the Tahoe. He starts to pull out of the driveway when he looks over at me.

"You don't have to be rude to Brent, you know? It isn't his fault you showed up with Eric last night." I look over at Justin surprised.

"I…" I stop myself. This doesn't even deserve an answer, I think to myself.

We pull up to the restaurant and Justin sits there for a moment looking out into the night. He looks over at me, his gorgeous eyes staring at me, right thru me.

"Lori, I'm so sorry." He tells me. His voice is low. "The thought of you with Eric makes me crazy, that's all." He pulls my arm towards him, kissing my hand. I turn to look at him.

"Justin, I promise, nothing is going on between Eric and me. Our relationship is strictly plutonic. It's never been anything more, " I tell him, smiling, lying just a little but only because I'm trying to get him to understand. "C'mon, let's go in. I'm famished." I smile at him lovingly. He kisses my hand again and gets out of the Tahoe, coming over to open the door for me.

The restaurant is beautiful, Justin has told me this restaurant was voted one of the ten best in San Antonio and I can see why.

"Lori, I know your birthday is not for another two months, but I got you something," Justin says as he reaches into his pocket. Oh, my God. He pulls out a long box from his pocket. A black box and I am floored.

"Justin," I say surprised, in a whisper. I can't believe this. I open the box and see a stunning, diamond bracelet. I put my hand to my mouth, I am literally shocked and for once, speechless. I sit there admiring the beauty of this bracelet for about a minute before I speak.

"I can't accept this, Justin," I tell him looking over at him. "This is too much." My expression is serious, concerned. I have never received a gift so extravagant and feel a little uncomfortable taking it.

"Lori, let me do this for you," He sits at the edge of his seat, taking the bracelet in his hands and placing it on my wrist. "I want you to know what you mean to me." He says smiling, staring into my eyes. I smile back and he kisses me gently on the lips.

"Thank you," I whisper, admiring the bracelet. I am astounded at the breathtaking beauty of this bracelet. I have never owned *anything* like this before. This bracelet is probably worth more than my car, I chuckle to myself.

I look over at Justin. Perfect Justin. He must love me. He wouldn't buy this for just anyone, right?

Ay, Laurita, do you love him? I ask myself. I don't know if I do. My feelings are mixed. I'm not sure why. I definitely have feelings for Justin, strong feelings.

But do I love him? I don't know. Maybe?

We get back to my house, Christine clearly surprised at the bling around my wrist. She and Brent leave quickly, probably because they can't wait to get to be alone.

Quickly, Justin and I make our way to the bedroom. The heat between us is stronger than ever. Clothes flying everywhere once again. The intensity of this moment takes me away. Maybe I *am* in love with this man. I think to myself.

****

As I lie there, once again weak from our lovemaking, my mind wanders. I lift my arm above me admiring my gift. I am still in awe at the beauty of this jewelry hanging on my wrist. It is exceptionally expensive, and I can't even begin to imagine the cost.

"Hey, what are you thinking about?" Justin says as he comes up next to me hugging me, his body still warm, his lips gently kissing my temples.

"I am just in awe, Justin." I say to him, in a low voice, "I have never received a gift so," my words escape me, "so beautiful." I say for lack of a better word.

"It comes straight from the heart, Lori." He says in a whisper, he moves to position his body over me " because I Love you." He smooths my hair and I smile saying nothing back. His eyes looking straight into mine. He kisses me again.

"Me, too," I say to him softly. I can't bring myself to say the words. I see the look in his eyes. This man is truly in love with me. He kisses me again, then lies back down next to me.

"Good night, Lori," he says holding me, "Go to sleep now." He tells me his eyes closing.

I lie there for a minute thinking about tonight. I look at the bracelet one more time. I sit up to take it off and put it away. I pick up my phone to look at the time. It's only one o'clock.

I hear Mami's voice in the back of my head as I put away my gift.

'Laurita, a man who gives you expensive gifts always expects something in return.'

I turn to see Justin lying in my bed. This would definitely fall under the definition of an expensive gift. I place it in my drawer for safe keeping and walk back to my bed. Well, Mami, I'm already sleeping with him, what more would he want?

Lying back in bed, my thoughts go back to my perfect boyfriend.

Perfect Justin.

Today, I smile as I fall asleep.

****

Justin leaves early, around six. He tells me had a prior engagement with his family. I can't help but wonder when we will finally tell everyone about us, including our families!

I get an early start cleaning the house. Today is also Family Day, not to mention, I am going with Eric. I feel the nerves in my stomach. It's almost like I'm scared? Excited? I'm not sure. I smile to myself. Again, this little devilish smile rears itself once again. I'm starting to wonder if it was a good idea to invite Eric. I know I am supposed to be more committed to Justin, but I think some part of me still wants Eric.

Ay, Laurita, you are absolutely evil. I tell myself thinking about the repercussions if Justin were to find out about me spending time with Eric today.

Eric shows up early, and he looks gorgeous, as always. I just hope he's ready to meet my family, my brothers especially. I laugh to myself. I should say a little prayer for him. Maybe even throw one in for myself.

Mami asked me to go to church with her this morning but she called me at the last minute and there was no way I would be able to get ready on time.

So, I ask her to pray for me. I should have asked her to pray for Eric, too.

"Are you ready for this?" I tell Eric as we walk out the door. Eric looks good, he's wearing jeans and a plain blue shirt.

"I'm good" Eric says with confidence. "are you ready?" he asks me looking at me as if he's trying to read my mind. "I mean, are you ready to introduce me to the whole family?" his eyes have a look of curiosity now.

"Sure, I just hope you can handle it." I laugh nervously. I just realized that Eric will be the first guy since Jake that I take home and Jake never came over for Family Day.

He really looks good, though. Gosh, he can make a plain shirt look sexy. It's no wonder little Miss Assistant DA likes him, I think sarcastically in my head. I can't help but feel the pinch of jealousy. Stop it, Laura! You're with Justin, remember!

"Well, I have to warn you, my brothers aren't the easiest to get along with when you first meet them, ok? And my Dad. My Dad is a quiet man. Our relationship has not been the same since I had Matthew." Eric looks over at me, a surprised look on his face. "You have no idea how deep the Machismo can go," I say to him.

"So, Alex is your older brother and Manny is your younger brother," Eric says as if he's been studying for a test. "Manny is married to Janet and Alex is married to Gracie."

"Yes," I tell him. "And Gracie is pregnant, and Manny and Janet have two boys."

"Ok, and your Mom's name is Estella and your dad's name is Roberto." I smile at him. He's going to be fine. Except when my brothers give him the third degree.

We walk up the familiar walk to my parents' house. I almost want to pray before going in. I have never brought a guy over for Family Day. Not even Jake. He never wanted to come. I am so nervous. My stomach is in knots.

I open the door and walk in, we are quickly greeted by my nephews running down the hallway. Janet is closely behind. Only, this time, Janet stops when she sees Eric.

"Oh, Laura, you brought someone." Janet is shocked that someone is with me and clearly even more shocked at how good-looking he is. I think I see drool coming out of her mouth.

"Janet this is Eric, Eric this is my Sister-in-Law Janet." I introduce them.

Eric puts out his hand. "Nice to meet you."

They shake hands and Janet doesn't say a word, she just smiles.

"C'mon, Eric, let me introduce you to everyone else." I take his hand into the living room where my older brothers Alex and Manny are deep in conversation about cars, I think. Only they both stop when they see Eric.

"Lori?" Alex looks at me like I just committed a crime.

"Hi, Alex," I walk over and hug and kiss him.

"Hi, Manny" Manny hugs me but doesn't take his eyes off of Eric. This is where my brothers try to be intimidating.

"Alex, Manny, this is my friend Eric, Eric these are my brothers Alex and Manny" They are both still sitting there staring as if they are sizing Eric up.

Eric walks over to shake their hand, but they just keep staring.

"Hey, C'mon, guys, don't be rude!" I yell at them.

And they both put out their hands to shake. My brothers like to try to intimidate anyone I go out with, it's been that way since I was in high school.

"So, Eric, what do you do?" Alex is the first one to talk, wasting no time to find out about my new *friend.*

"I work with Laura at Black Gold?" Alex turns to look at me, a look that I haven't figured out yet on his face.

"Oh, really? What do you do there? You look too clean-cut to be a driver or field worker." Manny says mockingly, smiling, proud of his observation. My father and mother are now in the living room and I would like to introduce Eric to my father.

"I'm Superintendent," Eric starts to say, and I see my brother's expression of surprise, "I handle a lot of the business accounts," Eric tells him modestly. My brothers don't know that Eric's last name is Johnson, as in son of Patrick T. Johnson, Texas Oil Tycoon, and Millionaire.

Manny and Alex both look at each other when they hear this, I think they are both stunned. I guess they didn't expect that. Imagine if they knew he owned part of the company?!

"Eric, I would like you to meet my Dad, Daddy this is Eric." My Dad quickly puts out his hand and Eric firmly grips my father's hand and shakes it.

"Good Handshake." My father says in a deep voice. "You can always tell a man by his handshake."

"Nice to meet you, Sir." Eric smiles at him.

Eric looks over at my mother and he quickly makes his way over to her.

"Mrs. Sanchez, so happy to see you again." My mom is smiling ear to ear. I see my brothers watching him as if they don't understand what is going on.

"Hey, Bro, you want a beer?" Alex asks Eric pointing at his beer.

"Sure," Eric answers and he looks over at me, "Lori, can I get you one, too?"

"Yes, Please," I tell him. God knows I need one. Eric steps outside with both Alex and Manny. Alex returns with a beer for me but quickly goes back outside with my brothers.

Here we go. I just hope they go easy on him. Eric comes from a different culture, he's not used to *our* ways.

I walk into the kitchen with my mother and sit at one of the bar stools.

Mami is, as always, cooking. It looks like she's making rice and beans. She smiles and looks over at me.

"Lori, I ran into a friend of yours from high school. " My Mom says and I look at her curiously. "The boy you used to tutor, that played football." She has to be talking about Justin. He was the only football player I ever tutored in high school.

"Justin Porter?" I tell her as I look outside, Eric is talking with Alex and Manny, He still looks like he's in one piece.

"Yes," Mami says with a smile on her face, "Justin. He was such a nice boy. I saw him at church." I didn't know Justin went to Church, I think to myself. Mami goes on. "He was with his family. He just moved here from Austin not too long ago. They still live only a couple of streets down from here." Mami points outside the house. My eyes are wide. Did she say, family? My heart is racing, I hope she means his mother and father because I won't be able to handle it if Justin has a *family*.

"He has a family?" I ask her and I feel my stomach start to hurt. I'm afraid of the answer. Mami doesn't know about Justin and me. Maybe this is why Justin has been so preoccupied

"No, Laurita, his mother, and father. Justin is still a bachelor." Leave it to Mami to throw that in. She smiles looking outside at Eric. "If you weren't already taken, I might call his mom to set you up." I almost want to laugh. Oh, Mami, if you only knew. I can't take anymore. I hate lying to her.

"Mami, I told you Eric and I are just friends." My smile is big and

Mami laughs.

"Si, I know you *said* that, and you keep on saying it." She hits me with her kitchen towel, "but do you even believe it?" Mami is joking with me and she has no idea what she is talking about. I am with Justin and if she knew that, she would stop with this thing about Eric.

I turn around and walk outside. I should check on Eric in case he needs help with my brothers.

I sit at the picnic table. Eric hands me another beer. The three of them are now deep in conversation about the new Camaro, it seems.

"Hey," Eric sits next to me and leans in. "I don't want to speak too soon but I think your brothers like me" He smiles a playful, youthful smile and he looks cute. I manage to smile back but my mind is preoccupied. It's somewhere else. I want to tell my mom about Justin. I hate keeping secrets from her.

"Eric, are you ok out here?" I ask him as I get up again, "I have to go in for just a minute," He looks over at me, his beautiful smile dances in my head.

"I'm fine." He says. "Your brothers are great." He gets up as I get up from the table. Ever the gentleman, My Eric. I think to myself.

I walk back into the kitchen and see Mami by the stove.

"Mami, can I talk to you about something?" I tell her, my voice is nervous.

"What's wrong, Laurita?" she sees that I am uneasy.

"Mami, I already knew that Justin was in town." I start to tell her, and she furrows her brow. She is confused. "He is one of my bosses. He owns part of my company. Remember, I told you we were getting new partners?" I ask her, I'm speaking quickly now.

"Yes, I remember… that was him?" she looks at me still puzzled. "So, you already knew he was back in town, why didn't you tell me that when I told you that story just now?" she asks me look-ing more confused than ever.

I look outside at Eric, he's laughing and talking with Alex and Manny. He is really having such a good time. Mami looks outside, looking at Eric as well.

"Mami, the truth is, I've been dating Justin for almost four months now." I finally come clean. I'm looking down, I can't look her straight in the eye.

"Laura, what?" she is truly surprised. "How did I not know this?" she asks me.

"Mami, Justin, and I, we work together, and I told you about my rules and we," I stop and look at her, I'm not sure if she is happy or mad or what, "we don't want to tell anyone until we know this is going somewhere," I tell her slowly.

"Laura, I – I am very surprised. Does Eric know you are dating Justin?" she points outside, "That poor guy is chasing you and you are dating someone else!" She makes an apologetic face star-ing over at Eric.

"No, Mami, it isn't like that. Eric knows." I tell her and she looks even more befuddled. "Mami, Eric owns part of the company, too," I tell her, and she starts to back up, looking for a chair to sit down.

I think this is too much information for my mother. She doesn't understand my life, my way of living my life and now she is sit-ting here probably on the verge of a heart attack. She starts to fan herself with her hand.

"Laurita, you are playing with fire, Mija." She says to me and I chuckle because I remember saying the same thing to myself not too long ago.

"Mami, you can't tell anyone about Justin. It has to stay a secret." I beg her, looking into her eyes, "I just couldn't keep it from *you* anymore." I look at her, I'm standing next to her and she puts an arm around my waist.

"Laurita, you are braver than me. When I was younger, I couldn't even imagine being in a situation like yours." She laughs a little, "I will keep your secret, but you need to stop playing games with these boys, Laurita." She scolds me, her voice a little louder. "Make up your mind already!" and like that my mom goes back to cooking.

"Ay, Mami, I told you. Eric and I are just friends." I get up and this time it's my mom who is rolling her eyes. What is that all about?

I'm not sure what she meant about playing games and making up my mind, but I'm glad I finally got that out. I hate keeping secrets from Mami.

I make my way back outside and find my seat next to Eric. Eric quickly moves in closer to me, a huge smile on his face. He's enjoying himself, the conversation, and his arm quickly finds its way around me. I don't pull away. I see Mami watching us from inside.

Yes, Mami, I see what you mean. I say to myself.

"Dinner is ready," Mami calls from the door, and we all walk inside taking our seats at the table.

****

The drive home from Family Day is quiet. Eric is smiling almost as if he is reminiscing tonight's events. I am going over my conversation with Mami. She knows me, just like Christine knows me, it seems everyone knows about my feelings for Eric *except* me.

I turn to look at Eric again, "Eric, I hope you had a good time tonight." I say to him trying to break the silence between us.

He glances over at me, the beautiful smile still on his face, "Lori, it was great. Your family is awesome." He turns back looking out to the road. "Hey, we aren't going to drive up to a Black Tahoe on your driveway again, are we?" he asks me, teasingly.

I smile, nervously, the thought hadn't occurred to me, but now it is definitely a possibility.

"Who knows, Eric." I laugh. "Justin gets so jealous when I'm around you," I admit to him looking down. He's turning into my street and we both look quickly down the street to my house.

When we see that there is no Black Tahoe in the driveway, we turn to look at each other and laugh. "Well, I guess tonight is a *'No Drama'* night," Eric says pulling into the driveway. "I'll get Matthew from the back," He tells me.

I jump out of the Tahoe, fumbling in my purse looking for my keys. I open the door and Eric follows me in with a sleeping Matthew in his arms.

"I'm going to put this little guy in his crib." He tells me as he makes his way to Matthew's room. Sometimes Eric surprises me with the things he does.

"Can I fix you a drink?" I ask him as he disappears into the hallway.

"Sure," he whispers loudly back at me.

I make my way to the kitchen, grabbing two glasses, ice and the Jack Daniels Eric left the last time he was here. I look over to my table and see my flowers, still beautiful, and vibrant adorning my table. Eric walks back into the living area.

"Wow, that's a bouquet," Eric says nodding over at my flowers. I smile at him. "From your Mr. Perfect, no doubt?" he tells me as he takes his seat at the bar.

"Yes," I tell him handing him his Jack and Coke. " but that's nothing compared to the roses you sent when Matthew was born, Eric!" I say not even thinking about the words that I am saying. Why am I making Justin's gift seem like nothing compared to Eric's?

Eric takes a drink and smiles. "I wanted to go to the hospital." His eyes dazed, he is remembering, "but I didn't want to intrude." I walk over and sit next to him at the bar.

"Hmmm, I'm not sure I would have liked for you to see me like that." I'm remembering now the day Matthew was born. A smile on my face.

"I'm sure you were beautiful, as always," Eric says, his eyes watching me with adoration. The sparkle in his eyes, and the feel of his hand taking my hair and placing it gently behind my ear, takes me away, lost in my own head. The tension is building between the two of us, just as it used to. I've known Eric so long and he still has this effect on me. I try to change the subject, distract both of us.

"I haven't shown you the gift Justin gave me," I tell Eric, getting up from the stool. I start walking down to the bedroom.

I hear Eric's voice as I walk down the hall. "No, you didn't."

I walk into my bedroom, reaching into my drawer pulling out the Americus Diamond box. I run my hand over the top of the box, thinking of Justin.

He would be so upset if he knew Eric was here right now. I think to myself.

I walk back into the living area where Eric is waiting anxiously. I walk over and hand him the box.

"He gave it to me last night at dinner," I say smiling. "I tried telling him it was too much, but he wouldn't take it back," I'm looking at Eric and my hands are clenched. Why am I nervous?

Eric opens the box and looks at the beautiful, over-the-top, extravagant bracelet. I suddenly see a changed expression on Eric's face.

"Wow, Laura, this is…" he takes a breath, his mouth is open in awe, "this is really…" he stops at a loss for words, "expensive." He finally manages to say handing the box back to me. His expression is different. Eric's cheerful self from before is no longer evident. He is now serious, uninterested. He turns and takes another drink.

I take the box from him. I'm confused. "I'm – I'm going to put this away," I tell him walking back down the hallway to my bedroom. I am baffled by Eric's response to my gift. His expression changed so fast. What was that all about?

Walking back into the living area, I see Eric standing and pacing.

"Do you love him?" he asks me in a tone I really didn't recognize from him. "I mean, do you see yourself with him instead of me?" Eric is sounding panicked and anxious.

"Eric, why are you asking me this?" I don't know how to answer, and I don't like that he is putting me on the spot.

"Lori, he gave you that gift and that means he wants more from you" he's pacing quicker now, "he may even want marriage! Are you ready for that?!" he yells at me as he continues to pace.

"I-I don't.." he doesn't let me finish before he interrupts again.

"Is he going to keep your marriage a secret, too?" He stops to look at me and he grabs my face, "you deserve to be with someone who will show you off to the world." He leans his forehead on mine. He has me against the wall now "Who loves you with every fiber of his being." He's leaning against me

"Eric…" I close my eyes. I don't know what to say. "You are seeing someone else, too." I can't believe I just said that.

I hear Eric let out a slight laugh.

"So, we are both in the wrong here." He kisses me gently on the forehead and I feel his body gently pressed against me. "should I go?" he asks me as he starts to kiss me ever so gently on my neck and lips. I feel my body start to quiver. The tingling feelings shooting thru me once again.

"Eric?" I start to tell him, but he kisses me again, "Eric, we can't." I finally tell him. How can I tell him that I want *our* first time to be special and not like this. NOT while we are both dating someone else.

Laurita, a man will only go as far as you let him.

"Eric, we have to stop, really" I pull away from him. "We both have other commitments," I tell him.

Eric pulls away.

"Yea, how could I forget." He starts walking towards the door.

"Eric, I just don't want to make it more complicated than it already is." He is still walking, and he goes to open the door.

"No, Laura, you're right." He stops before walking out. "You have Justin and I have Jessica." I didn't know little Miss Assistant D.A. was named *Jessica,* "we should just concentrate on that instead of whatever this is between *US!*" He waves his arms motioning towards both of us.

Why is my stomach hurting? Why does the thought of Eric with *Jessica* bother me?

I'm standing by the door as Eric walks to his Tahoe. I want to run to him. I want to ask him not to go.

Why is this so hard?

He starts to leave, and I close the door.

I hear Mami's voice in the back of my head.

'Stop playing games with these boys, Laurita, make up your mind already.'

Ay, Mami, what have I gotten myself into?

My emotions are all over the place.

I don't know what happened to the Devious Laura, but she is no longer here.

Mami said I was brave, but I don't feel so brave anymore.

Chapter 19

Drama, Drama, Drama

I walk into the conference room for our morning staff meeting and the only one in the conference room is Eric. I take my seat, looking over at him nervously.

"Hi." He says looking over at me, no expression on his face.

"Good Morning. How is *Jessica*?" I smile at him sarcastically, looking down at my notepad, pretending to be getting ready for the meeting. I never take notes during meetings. I usually just scribble on my notepad. Before Eric can answer, Justin walks in.

"Good Morning, Beautiful," he says to me sitting next to me. I see Eric roll his eyes. Justin notices but ignores him. "I saw your mom yesterday; did she tell you?" Justin is facing me and suddenly Eric is listening intently to our conversation.

"Yes, she mentioned that she had seen you at Church with your parents," I tell him, and Eric furrows his eyebrows. Justin looks over at him curiously, when I see the strangest expression come over Eric's face. One that I have never seen before.

Eric suddenly sits back and says rather maliciously, but intentionally, "That's funny, I didn't hear your mom mention *anything* about Justin last night." My head hastily turns to look at Eric, my eyes bead looking at him, "She must have told you while I was outside with your brothers." Eric looks at me then back at Justin with an evil, hateful smile. There are no words for the feelings that are going on inside me right now. Eric has to know that I didn't tell Justin he was with me yesterday, this is why he is bringing it up now.

I turn back to look at Justin. He must be fuming right now! I'm almost afraid to look at him. I feel the nerves creating knots in my stomach. I turn to look at Justin who is looking at Eric, with no readable expression on his face. Eric is still smiling at him fiendishly. Oh, no, what have I done?

Evan walks into the conference room, interrupting, thankfully the death stare between Eric and Justin.

"Hey, Good Morning, Everyone," Evan says as he makes his way to his seat. I see Justin adjust his coat and say good morning. I am truly amazed at Justin's composure. He has said nothing. He turns over and looks at me and he smiles his cute smile. I smile at him nervously. I don't know if Justin is really upset and putting on an act, or if everything is ok.

My stomach is hurting, I feel the knots, and I cannot concentrate when the meeting finally gets underway. I haven't looked over at Eric since that last glance when he was looking at Justin so brutally.

I slowly, subtly turn my head in Eric's direction. His head is down. It seems that he is not concentrating on the meeting, either. He turns his head catching my gaze and I don't turn away. His eyes are sorry, I see it. But what's done is done, I think to myself still holding my stare. I hear Trace talking in the background when I hear the words *'meeting adjourned'*. I hear these two words, gather my things, and jet out of the conference room, speaking to no one. Not to Justin and definitely not to Eric. I walk hurriedly to my office, closing the door behind me.

Breathe, Laura, Breathe.

I'm standing behind my door hoping neither one of them follows me to my office. I wait about two minutes and finally make my way to my desk. I need air. I'm about to hyperventilate.

My hands are shaking, and I still feel the knots in my stomach.

I spend the rest of the day locked in my office, miraculously avoiding any confrontation with Justin or Eric.

You should have stuck to your rules, Laura! This is the kind of drama that you were trying to avoid.

****

I stop to pick up Matthew after work and I spend some time speaking with Ms. Marty, the lady who watches Matthew at his daycare. I don't want to be rude, but I can't wait to get out of there. I want to get home. Quick.

I drive up the familiar street to my house, when I notice the Black Tahoe parked in my driveway. My heart quickly starts to race. Oh, dear, is it Justin, or is it Eric? I think to myself. That's one thing about the oilfield, everyone drives the same type of vehicle.

Pulling up, I notice Justin sitting in the driver's seat. My stomach starts to hurt, along with my nervous shaking. I really don't like confrontations.

Justin gets out of his vehicle and he is waiting for me outside my door. I take a deep breath and wonder how this is going to go. I know Justin has a jealous streak and I just hope he has been able to calm down since this morning. Both he and Eric did not bother me at all at work, which surprised me, so maybe he isn't that mad.

I open the door to the car and make my way out.

"Hey, Babe," Justin tells me holding out his hand to help me out. "I thought I would stop by so we can talk," He says as I open up the back door. Before I can answer, he has taken the keys from my hand to open up the house. I have taken Matthew out of his car seat and I am holding him in my arms. One thing I notice about Justin, he never helps me with Matthew.

"Ok," I tell him as I walk up to the front door. I feel my heart pounding. I think it may come out of my chest. My nerves are abundant, and I wonder if Justin can tell.

We are both very quiet as we walk in, I quickly take Matthew and place him in his playpen. I walk over to the kitchen, so I can start making Matthew's dinner. For some strange reason, my appetite escapes me.

"Would you like something to drink?" I ask Justin without making eye contact, my nerves still wound up in a ball. My heart beating fast and loud.

"I'll take a water." He tells me flatly. He seems normal, I don't hear any kind of emotion in his voice so, maybe he isn't upset. I grab a water bottle from the refrigerator. When I close the door, I see the bottle of Jack Daniels on my countertop, taking me back to last night, when Eric was here. Everything was good until I showed him my gift, or he had to go with Jessica. I'm not sure which set him off.

Justin is sitting at the bar now. Obviously, he wants to talk to me or he wouldn't be here. He knows I was upset by the way I stormed out of the conference room. Both he and Eric saw it. I don't get mad very often, but when I do, watch out! I'm usually a very passive person.

"Lori, it was my fault," Justin finally says after what seems like forever. "I instigated Eric's reaction in the conference room." He says this in an apologetic tone. I'm puzzled at why Justin would think this is his fault. I look over at him and he truly looks sorry.

I am biting my thumbnail now, my nerves getting the best of me. I'm looking for the right words to say. As I stand there, Justin is watching, waiting for me to say something…anything.

"How do you think you instigated Eric's response?" I finally ask him, looking at him. "Aren't you upset that I spent time with Eric? That he was with me for Family Day?" I question him, I'm confused. How does Justin think this is *his* fault?

This is all my fault. I took Eric to Family Day with me. I kept it from Justin and gave Eric the fuel for his malicious words today in the conference room. I'm the one who has been playing games with the two of them, forcing them into this confrontation today. It really isn't your fault, Justin. This is ALL my fault! My internal struggle is strong and is causing a roller coaster of emotions.

I'm lost in my own head when Justin goes on.

"You made it clear that you didn't want our relationship to cross over into work. And I went in there, clearly trying to make sure Eric understood that you were dating *me*." Justin says and he looks straight at me now, "I guess he put me in my place, heh?" My expression is blank. I know what Justin is trying to say.

"Justin, I *am* dating you." I tell him softly, "Eric and I, we're…" Justin cuts me off.

"just friends. Yes, the two of you keep saying that. I know." He says, looking down now. "Lori, I love you," Justin says, and he walks over to me standing in front of me. He places his hands on my waist, "I can't share you with anyone else."

"You're not, Justin." I say quickly, "Eric is seeing someone else, he isn't even a factor." I sound convinced, but deep inside I'm not even sure I've convinced myself. I hug Justin trying to ease his doubts. Trying to ease my own doubts.

"Can we please keep the drama out of work?" I tell him, in a stern slightly sarcastic voice.

"Yes, Lori, I promise." He smiles his movie star smile. I look at Justin and I think how lucky I am to have him. He is a catch, after all. He leans up to kiss me gently on the lips. "Well, I'll leave you to make dinner for Matthew, I have some business I need to take care of," he says as he gets up to make his way to the door. He looks over at me, winks, and walks out.

I take a deep breath. That actually went better than I thought. I'm still not feeling better, though. I think somewhere deep down inside, I was hoping that it was Eric sitting in my driveway when I pulled up. I feel my heart physically hurt. Why am I feeling like this now? I'm with Justin. Is it because of *Jessica*? The thought of her with Eric makes me upset, I feel the pinch of jealousy.

What did you expect, Laura? He couldn't wait forever.

I'm feeding Matthew, watching the six o'clock news when I see a story about a recent murder case. The Assistant District Attorney trying the case is Jessica Stromberg. I wonder if this is Eric's Jessica. She looks young and actually, the report speaks about the public's concern that her lack of experience may hurt the case.

She's pretty, I guess. Blond, tall, and slender.

Who am I kidding? She could be a model. Of course, she would be dating Eric Johnson, it makes more sense than Eric Johnson dating Laura Who? I think to myself. I change the channel. The green monster is rearing his ugly face.

****

I keep half-heartedly expecting my doorbell to ring, hoping that it is Eric. He'll come in, we'll talk, laugh and everything will be ok. But three nights have passed since that day in the conference room and Eric has yet to speak a word to me. Thank God tomorrow is Friday, the weekend will give me a chance to regroup. Get away from work for a while.

Matthew is fussy tonight. It takes me almost forever to get him to sleep. It's almost 10 pm when my doorbell rings. My heart sinks. Justin had a late meeting and is probably still there, so, that means it could only be one other person.

It has to be Eric; I think to myself. Almost excited. Happy that we are finally going to put this behind us.

I walk over quickly to the door, swinging it open without looking out the peep hole.

Oh no, this can't be happening again.

"What are *you* doing here?" I feel sick to my stomach. My disappointment raging.

I can hear Mami in the back of my head.

'Laurita, love doesn't know any of your rules.'

I guess it didn't get the memo on timing, either. I can't believe this is happening again. I really should start using my peep hole more often.

"Jake, what are you doing here?" I repeat myself staring at the man that is standing there. He is staring at me as if in wonder or shock. I only hope he hasn't been drinking. I don't need another scene like that.

"Lori, I-I…" he stares at me again, "I just can't believe how beautiful you look." What? Jake only gives me compliments when, well, when he is trying to get me in bed, or we are already in bed. Never like this. He never just says it like this. "It's like, I don't know, you look good, you know?" Well, doesn't he have a way with words? I say to myself. I raise my eyebrow at him curiously.

"You still haven't answered my question. Why are you here?" For once, Jake standing here in front of me does not have me all 'hot and bothered'. No butterflies in my stomach, no overactive hormones, nothing. I'm proud of myself. I glare at him, my eyes leaving no question of his unwelcome presence.

"I wanted to see Matthew…" He smiles. At ten o'clock at night, I think to myself. You're crazy, Jake.

"Right now? Do you know what time it is?" I look at him, the anger building up inside of me. He smiles again, almost amused at my edginess.

Oh no, Jake, not this time. Your smile is not going to work here! I smile back coyly still holding the door.

"And you, of course. I wanted to talk with you." He goes on. "Did your brother tell you that I work with him?" He's trying to make small talk.

"Look, Jake, I don't have a problem with you visiting your son," I don't release my stare. "But if you are, it needs to be scheduled." Matthew starts to cry again in the background. Obviously, he has heard us talking loudly. Jake immediately tries to walk in the door. I put my hand on his shoulder to stop him. "AND, you need to be a constant. Not just someone who pops in every once in a while." Jake looks at me and smiles.

"I plan on it." He walks in and heads over to Matthew's room. I'm left holding the door, not knowing if I want to run Jake out of my house. I never said he could come in and I'm still not sure I want him here.

"Jake, seriously, you need to call if you want to see him," I tell him as I walk into Matthew's room. He is holding him now trying to get him to go back to sleep. I'm standing over him with my arms crossed. "right now, is not a good time." I'm tapping my foot on the ground.

"You can't tell me you were going somewhere dressed like that." He says pointing at my clothes. "That's your 'stay at home' clothes," I see him make a gesture as if an idea just went off in his head, "Unless… someone is coming over?" Oh, whatever, Jake, that's beside the point! I think to myself. I'm still standing there with my arms crossed giving him nothing.

"I'm not on *your* schedule, Jake. Please, you need to leave." I point at the door. "Next time, call before you come over." Jake isn't moving. Matthew surprisingly goes back to sleep and Jake places him back into his bed.

He makes his way back into the living area, I chase quickly behind. He pulls out a chair at the table and sits down.

"Uh, did you not hear me?" I am bewildered. Didn't I just ask him to leave?

"Lori, Lori, calm down. You always get all crazy when something is outside your plans or your *rules*." Jake puts up his hands mimicking quotation marks when he says the word 'rules'. "You always drove me crazy with that." He laughs, looking over at me. "C'mon, sit down with me. We haven't talked in a while." He points at a chair on the table. I don't want to talk to him. Every time we talk, we end up sleeping together and after a couple of weeks, I'm left holding a baby, broke with a broken heart.

What is your game, Jake Lakewood? I stare at him trying not to let my guard down.

"You *can* sit down, Lori," he says sarcastically, "I don't bite." I make my way and pull out a chair and sit down. He turns around to look at me. "Well, not in this situation, anyway." He smiles his rugged smile. He's trying to be coy, and flirt with me. He's testing the waters. Well, not this time, Jake. I'm seeing someone else and he is a great guy, one who won't leave me with a note on the nightstand or pregnant and alone. One who fits the very description of the perfect boyfriend. These thoughts race thru my head while Jake's hazel eyes are burning thru me, sending familiar sensations thru me.

Jake is still amazingly handsome. His hazel eyes reminded me of a better time. Still, the effect that Jake once had on me is gone. I am not the giddy schoolgirl anymore and Jake has noticed. I can't sit here, I'm restless. I get up and head for the kitchen.

"Would you like a glass of water?" I ask him as I look thru the refrigerator. I think I need something stronger, but I can't lower my inhibitions.

"Um, No, I'm fine, thanks." Jake gets up and heads for the bar. He sits across from me. "Laura, I need to tell you something, if you would just stop running away from me and hear me out." He looks at me with sincerity and I can't help but finally agree.

"What is it?" I look at him. After everything he has done to me, after all of it, at the end of the day, he is still Matthew's father, I need to remember that. I come around and sit next to him. I take a deep breath, "Ok, you have my attention."

"I want to apologize," He says, and I look into his eyes, I can always tell how sincere Jake is by looking into his eyes. "I wasn't the man that I should have been for you or Matthew. You loved me and I took advantage of that," so far, he seems to be speaking from the heart. "I regret treating you the way that I did. I just hope that you will find it in your heart to someday forgive me."

I wonder if Jake means forgiving him in the sense that 'hey, everything is ok, and we can be friends' or if he means 'hey, let's get back together' kind of forgiving. I look at him confused.

"I know now what I have lost," he continues, and he looks down, "I know now that I am in love with you, Lori." He has said it before, but for some reason, it sounds different today. "I didn't understand what that meant before, to be in love," he is still looking down, "but I do now, and I know that I am in love with you." He looks at me and I see it. In his eyes, he is telling the truth.

I think of the night Eric was here. His words to me that Jake will one day realize what he has right in front of him, but it will be too late. Is that today?

"Jake," He stops me before I can say anything else.

"We can be a family, Lori." He says to me. "I know I fucked up. I want to make it right. I want to be Matthew's Daddy, and I want to be the person that makes you smile like whoever it is that is making you smile right now." He looks over at the door and turns back grabbing my hands. "You don't have to say anything, right now. Just think about it." He stands up and is composing himself.

I am sitting there speechless.

"I will leave you to think about it. Think about Matthew." He tells me as he points over to Matthew's room. He walks over to the door and looks back at me.

"Please, Lori, tell me you will think about it?" He looks sincere and I see the begging in his eyes. I see the honesty. "I love you, Lori." He whispers. Suddenly, feelings are rushing back. I don't understand. How can this be happening to me?

He leaves me there holding pieces of a heart that I thought didn't exist anymore. I feel a tear in my eye. I'm beyond confused. Jake usually comes over and tries to sleep with me, thinking that he can make everything better that way. He seemed so sincere this time. Like he's had an epiphany. My head is spinning.

I want Matthew to have his Daddy. I don't want to be the reason that he doesn't, I have to, at least, give it a chance, don't I? I go into deep thought. Thinking about Justin, but for some reason, it isn't Justin that I'm worried about. It's Eric. If Eric knew that I was entertaining the thought of ever taking Jake back, he might truly never talk to me again. My internal struggle is running deep, I can't do this alone. Christine is out of town again, I need to talk to Eric.

I pick up my cell phone from the counter without a second thought, quickly texting Eric.

I need you. Jake came by.

I sit on the couch waiting for a response. Maybe I'm expecting too much. Eric might still be upset with me. Maybe, he's out with Jessica.

Who knows? Not to mention, that it's almost midnight.

I wait almost ten minutes, without a response. I *do* expect too much. I think to myself. I start turning off the lights and make my way to my bedroom. I feel emotional. For the last couple of years, it seems Eric has been there when I needed him. Always.

Without question. Have I lost him?

I lay down to sleep feeling sad and alone. My eyes are heavy now.

I'm startled by my phone notification.

I look at my text messages.

I'm standing outside your door.

It's Eric. My heart starts to race. I struggle to get out of bed, almost running towards the front door.

I stop for a second trying to compose myself, I open the door. Eric is standing there. His gorgeous green eyes are staring right at me. He's got one hand on each side of the door frame, leaning gently in. His face is serious, with no smile.

"Hey," he says in a low, soft voice. He makes his way in and I quickly go in to hug him. He holds me tight, hugging me, kissing the top of my head. The familiarity of Eric's arms holding me, makes me feel safe. My protector. My Eric.

"Lori, let me first apologize about the conference room," Eric starts to say, but I stop him.

"No, Eric, No," I don't understand why I am so emotional, but I feel my eyes getting teary, "you don't need to apologize. That was my fault. I did that. I did that to both of you. I'm so sorry." I say in a frantic, anxious voice. "And then Jake showed up today," I stop and look up at Eric, "the only person I wanted to talk to was you." Eric grabs my hand and leads me over to the couch.

"What happened, Lori?" Eric's voice, his smell, his presence, has already made me feel better, "Did he come by? Was he drunk? Did he hurt you?" He starts asking questions.

"He came by and he was surprisingly sincere." I start to tell him. I smile at Eric, I am so glad he is here, this has to mean he still cares for me. "One of these days was today," I tell him as I start my story.

Eric looks worried. He doesn't say a word. He just sits there listening, taking in every word. I sit closer to him, I want him to know.

"You remember that night? You said, One day he was going to realize what was right in front of him, but it was going to be too late." Eric looks over at me. He is still looking at me, a querying look on his face.

"And is it too late, Lori?" He looks over at me, moving the hair from my face and placing it behind my ear.

"I think so," I look up at him. "For a second, I entertained the idea of us getting back together, for Matthew's sake," I am looking down as I tell Eric this part of the story, "but then, I realized, it *is* too late." I look up at Eric now, my voice is shaky "My heart belongs to someone else." As I say this, Eric looks down and away.

No, my heart is crying out. I belong to you, Eric. I want to tell him. But before my heart finds the words, Eric turns to look at me, he's saying something, my mind is trying to comprehend, make out the words.

"…Justin is a lucky man." I hear him say, but what really catches my attention is "Jessica and I are engaged." I almost fall over. Did I hear that correctly? They've only been dating for what? Two months, maybe? It wasn't that long ago, he was telling me that he loved *me*? What the? No! No!

"Wait, Eric, did you just say you're engaged?" I look over at him, the displeasure evident in my voice.

Eric takes a deep breath, looking over at me. "I – I asked her tonight." He says a hint of tension in his voice. "Well, I shouldn't say we are engaged, I asked, and she said she would think about it," he continues, "She feels we might be rushing things." He turns to look at me.

"Shhh, yea, you think?" I can't help myself, this bit of news is not what I expected to hear from Eric tonight. My demeanor is completely changed.

"Well, hey, you are with Mr. Perfect now, and after that bracelet, I'm almost positive the ring isn't too far behind," he looks over at me, Eric's attitude reciprocates mine.

That doesn't mean you go out and ask your girlfriend of two months to marry you, Eric! I scream inside my head.

Why do I keep these things locked away? Why can't I just tell him how I feel.

"Eric, you really should think about it." I lay on the couch, placing my head on his lap. "Sometimes, you think you know what you want," I feel Eric's hand going thru my hair now, "and you act on that, but what you really want is something else." I don't turn to look at him. I'm speaking in code.

Why don't you just come right out and say it, Laura?

In the back of my mind, I think of Justin. He doesn't deserve this. I care about him. He's everything a woman would want, could wish for. He's the Perfect Boyfriend. I take a deep breath. I feel Eric's hand caressing my arm now.

I don't remember falling asleep, but I feel the familiar arms carrying me to my bed. Eric was here when I was a mess after my breakup with Jake. He stayed with me. He's always been here for me.

I feel him place me gently into my bed, placing the covers over me.

"Laura, I'm leaving now." He whispers. Holding the cover over my arm. I place my hand over his. Justin, Laura. Remember, Justin.

"Good night," I say to him, wishing he wouldn't go.

"Good night." He says leaning over and kissing me on the cheek.

"Thank you, Eric" I whisper as he leaves my side

****

. . . .

Chapter 20

No More Lies

I knock gently on Justin's door, he is sitting at his desk, talking on the phone. He waves me in. I close the door behind me and take a seat across from him. It's Friday and I want to catch him before he leaves.

He finishes his call and looks over at me.

"Good Afternoon, Beautiful." He says quickly, "I'm sorry I haven't been able to speak with you all day, but I've been really busy." He looks busy. Black Gold has almost doubled its client base since PSM Corp. came on.

"Don't worry about it." I say comfortingly, "I've been busy myself." I really have. This is the first break I've had to come by to talk to him. "I was thinking about tonight," I ask him, wondering if he's already made plans. "Have you made reservations for us, yet?"

Justin tilts his head looking at me curiously. I have never taken the lead on any of our dates. Justin always makes the arrangements.

"I just thought you could come over instead of us going out. We can stay in tonight" I tell him, looking at him sitting there, his award-winning smile comes across his face. I sense a bit of reluctance.

"I would love that." He says, his voice trying to sound excited, "What time?" he asks me. Justin doesn't like swaying from the norm.

"I will have my mom pick up Matthew at seven, so, how about our regular time… eight?" I say, tilting my head at him.

"I'll be there." He says quickly. He stands up from his chair and comes around his desk. He hugs and kisses me before I leave.

I walk out into the hallway and see Michael watching me. Great. Another rumor is sure to start. I think to myself. I put my head down and walk back to my office.

I need to mentally prepare myself for tonight. This may be one of the hardest things I have ever had to do.

****

"I'm sorry, Justin." My voice is shaky. Justin is looking at me, speechless. I have obviously caught him off-guard. "I just don't think it's going to work between us." I slide the box over to him, the box holding the overly extravagant bracelet he bought for me.

"Lori, I bought this for you." He puts his hand over the box, stopping me from sliding it over to him. "Keep it." His voice is low, still in shock.

"No, Justin," I tell him again. "It isn't right. It's too much." I pick up the box this time and place it in front of him.

"Lori, maybe things are just moving too fast for you." Justin looks over at me. His ever-so-polished look of a salesman ready to pitch, as always, "Things got out of hand, I promised you no drama and I didn't deliver." He grabs my hands. "For that, I'm sorry. I can see why you want to run." Is that really why? I ask myself. Has he really figured it out?

I mean, the fiasco in the conference room was a bit much to handle, I admit. I have always lived by a certain set of rules and breaking my rule about dating a co-worker has been the single most stressor in my life so far.

'Love doesn't know about your rules, Laurita'

There's Mami again. Ay, Mami, you don't understand.

I start shaking my head, taking myself out of my own mind.

"No, Justin, you're right, of course, the drama has really been stressing me out," I admit to him. "Since the day you walked into our office, my stomach has been tied in knots!" This is not a lie. I feel that transition day was a turning point. I have not relaxed one day since then. "It's been a lot to handle, and maybe it is part of the reason," I look down. Who am I kidding? It *is* a big part of my reason for doing this. It's work, it's you and Eric under the same roof, competing it seems and me trying to pretend everything is ok and nothing is going on. I roll my eyes and Justin squeezes my hand, he wants in on my thoughts. "I'm sorry, Justin, I just can't do it anymore." I laugh slightly, "I feel like I'm on one of my Mom's telenovelas, and that's *not* a good thing." I assure him.

Justin's face is pale now. He did not expect to hear me tell him this today. He was expecting a nice, homemade dinner. He tries one more time.

"Lori, what if we tell everyone that we are no longer seeing each other, Eric, the partners, and just take it day by day." He's pulling at strings. "I love you, Lori." He whispers, I see the longing in his eyes and my heart weakens.

"Justin, I can't promise you anything," I say knowing I am only doing this to appease Justin and keep from hurting his feelings any further. "But you really have to take this back." I push the jewelry box closer to him, he closes his eyes, frustrated with me, it seems, and takes the box.

"Ok," he says reluctantly. He gets up and walks to the door.

Before he leaves, he pulls me in, holding me close and tight. I feel him, smell him. I feel the emotion start to well in my heart. I do care for Justin deeply and this is hurting me, but maybe I am just not *ready* for this. He hesitantly releases me from his hold, opening the door and making his exit. I stand there for a moment, listening as I hear the sound of his vehicle leaving my driveway. I feel the sorrow fill my heart. Letting him go wasn't something I anticipated to be this difficult. The confusion is mounting and the knots in my stomach are fierce. I need Christine.

With just a call, she is on her way.

****

"Hello, Pumpkin, how are you?" Christine says as she walks in. She's holding a bag of what looks like four bottles of wine.

"Chris, I feel like Shit," I tell her, still feeling an awful pain in my stomach for breaking it off with Justin.

"Oh, Sweetie, Everything that ends, usually ends badly." I look at her my expression confused, almost upset.

"That really doesn't make me feel better, Chris." She smiles her, *sorry I have no filter* smile and hands me a glass of wine.

"So, tell me, how did you do it?" she says leaning over on the counter, I'm sitting at the bar. "Did you just come out and say, 'Hey, it's over, get to steppin', Dude' or were you your usual nice self and say a, 'It's not you, It's me' kind of thing." Christine really gets straight to the point. She knows me better than that, though, I could never talk to anyone so bluntly.

"Chris, it wasn't easy. I do care about him, you know?" My eyes are serious, and I see Christine trying to be sympathetic.

"I know you care about him, Laura," she says, "but I also know you weren't *in* love with him." She looks at me, taking another drink of her wine, certainty in her stare. "every time you spoke about him, I didn't hear the emotion, you know. It was…" she shrugs her shoulders, raising her hands, "well, it was kind of boring for lack of a better word."

"What? Justin was a sweetheart. He did everything the Perfect Boyfriend should do." I fight back, looking at her now, she raises her eyebrows at me as she listens, "He was…Perfect." I say the word 'Perfect' again. And she throws her hands in the air, rolling her eyes.

"That's just it, Lori!" her voice a little higher now, "where's the excitement?! Where's the fun?!" she yells asking me, looking at me waiting for answers.

"We had fun," I tell her, trying to ramble a memory.

"The two of you had a schedule. That's what you had. Every Friday night at eight. Dinner, drinks then maybe, if you're lucky, sex." My eyes grow wider. Geez, again, leave it to her to put it so bluntly. "Does the guy ever do anything spur of the moment? Has he ever just come over to hang out with you? Take you and Matthew anywhere together?" I shrug my shoulders. She's right. Justin is very schedule-oriented. In our whole time together, we only went out one Saturday and that was only because he canceled on Friday. I look at Christine sadly, shaking my head, no, he never did anything like that.

"I'm not saying you *didn't* have feelings for him, Lori, I'm sure you did and I'm sure you probably even *love* him in your own way. But in the end, that's why you just did what you did." She leans in towards me, her hands waving in the air "because you aren't *in love* with him."

She takes our empty wine glasses and serves some more.

"C'mon, let's go to Benny's. I could use a Margarita." She says enthusiastically. Normally, Benny's would sound great, but today I'm just not feeling it.

"No, Chris, I don't want to go out tonight. I'm not in the mood to be around a bunch of people." I tell her taking my wine glass and chugging my wine in one drink.

I am absorbing all the information Christine just fed me. Have I been trying to love Justin because he fits the model of the perfect boyfriend? Is that the only reason?

"Ok, then," Christine says slowly. "More wine?" she says sarcastically taking my glass and filling it up again.

"Chris, I didn't tell you that Jake stopped by the other day." Christine's eyes get wide, her face gets red. Christine secretly has a Jake button, when pressed, her anger boils. She really cannot stand him.

"Shit, I hope you told him to go to hell." She quickly says taking a drink, her irritation at the thought of him coming over her.

"He actually came to apologize," I tell her, "He confessed his love for me." And for some reason, I start to laugh. "Eric said he would someday realize it." I'm smiling now. "and he said it would be too late."

Christine's face quickly changes, her eyes sparkle devilishly, a mischievous smile now on her face. "Eric, huh?" the corner of her mouth turns up, "Now, there's the man you should be wasting your time with!" she exclaims.

My face suddenly pales, my eyes fill with gloom.

"Chris, he's getting married," I tell her, I feel the physical pain in my heart once again.

Chris quickly walks over, hugs me tight.

"Oh, Shit, Lori," she says as she's holding me, my tears are starting to fall. "You're all messed up." She stands there comforting me.

All I can think is that she has no idea.

"Gee, thanks for that newsflash." My mind is racing. How did I ever get in this mess?

I'm a good girl. I followed the rules.

Chapter 21

Life's Curve Balls

Sitting here at my desk, a week later, I still don't feel any better about breaking up with Justin.

Work must be good; I haven't seen much of any of the partners in the office all week. They have been out in the field, barely checking in with Corey. I'm not complaining, it has made this week a little bit easier, although, my curiosity over Eric's impending engagement is killing me. I am wondering if little Miss Assistant Da, will become Mrs. Eric Johnson.

"Miss S, you have a call on line 1" Casey comes over the speaker.

"Thank you, Casey," I tell her.

"Laura Sanchez" I answer line 1.

"Lori!" It's my brother Alex, he is yelling, and I can barely make out what he is saying, "Lori, there's been an accident!" I sit at the edge of my chair. "Manny was in an accident at work." He continues. He's yelling, out of breath. "There was an explosion at the disposal."

"What?!" I start to shake. "Is he ok? Where is he?" I feel my stomach start to hurt, a lump in my throat.

"They're taking him to SAMMC, right now. I'm taking Mom and Dad." He tells me frantically.

"I'll meet you there!" I say in a panic myself and hang up the phone.

Oh, dear God, please let my brother be ok. I pray silently as I gather my purse and search for my keys

I call Christine and ask her to please pick up Matthew from day-care. She unquestionably says yes.

My hands are shaking, and I have knots in my stomach.

I dial Casey, "Casey, I have to leave. There's been an accident and I have to meet my family at the hospital." I tell her, my voice sounding clearly distraught.

"Ok, Miss S, I hope everything turns out ok." She says and I hang up the phone. I quickly leave my office and practically run out to the parking lot to my car. My nerves almost getting the best of me.

In the back of my mind, I keep thinking about Jake. He works with Manny. What if he was hurt in the explosion, too?

The thought makes my stomach hurt more.

I take out my phone and text him.

Are you ok?

I quickly get in my car and race out of the parking lot. On my way out, I see the familiar Black Tahoe turning into the parking lot. I am too worried to notice who is driving.

I race over to SAMMC (San Antonio Military Medical Center). This is where most trauma victims are brought. I walk in and quickly find my family in the waiting room.

Mami is holding her bible, her eyes red from crying, Janet is sitting next to her, in a much worse condition. I can't even imagine what she must be feeling. My Dad is sitting on the other side of

Mami, holding her hand. His head is down as if he is praying. My brother Alex is pacing up and down in the hallway. I walk up to him first.

"Alex, what is going on?" I ask him as I hug him, he holds me tight. He is understandably emotional, as we all are.

"Lori, it's bad. They've been talking about the explosion all over the news. It's really bad." He says, he wants to cry. This makes me even more emotional. Alex has always been the strong one. Even growing up, it was Manny who was the 'Cry Baby', Alex is the big brother.

"Has anyone come out to talk to you all?" I ask him, I want to know what they know. I want to know my brother's condition.

"No, we only know that he's here. We got a call from his work, and when we got here the nurse said he is here but that's it. No one has come out to talk to us." I don't like this. How long do we have to wait to find out how he is doing?

I pull my cell phone out of my purse, I still have not gotten a response from Jake. My heart hurts. The knots in my stomach are making me sick and my whole body is shaking.

I walk over and say hello to my mom and Janet. Janet is barely hanging on, the not knowing is driving her crazy. I stand there hugging Janet trying to console her, but I don't know what I can say at a time like this. She sits back down. She is weak from crying. My Dad stays in his seat. He doesn't get up and I want to hug him, too. I know he must be worried, just like the rest of us. I bend down and hug him, kissing his cheek in the process, "Hi, Dad." I tell him. He doesn't respond or reciprocate.

I take a seat, checking my cell phone again, still no response from Jake. I try calling him, but his phone goes straight to voice mail.

This doesn't make me feel any better.

It's been over an hour and no one has come out to give us any information on Manny. I decide to ask at the nurse's station.

I get up and make my way up to the desk. I'm scared, shaking, my heart is pounding.

"Excuse me," I say to the nurse at the desk.

"How can I help you?" The nurse's voice is cold, rushed.

"Can you give me information on a patient, Manuel Sanchez? He was in the …um…explosion at Republic." I ask her.

She goes thru some paperwork on her desk. "What was the name again?" she asks me.

"Manuel Sanchez" I repeat.

"Are you related to him?" She looks at me, she sounds unemotional, detached. I could never be a nurse. To be cold and disconnected like that, I just could not do it.

"He's my brother," I tell her.

"I can have someone come out and update you on his condition." She tells me, her voice is indifferent, still unemotional. There is no way I can get any kind of read from her.

"Thank you," I tell her. I wonder if Jake is on one of those lists. I want to ask, but I'm afraid to know.

I stand there for a moment. I'm contemplating whether or not I should ask about Jake. But I'm afraid to know.

I walk back quickly letting Mami know that someone should talk to us soon.

I'm sitting here thinking about the possibility that Jake might have been hurt or worse. The thought hurts me, worries me. Emotionally and physically. I silently say a little prayer,

"Please, Lord, let Jake be ok. Let Matthew keep his Daddy. Please." I want to promise that I will do anything if God will just keep Jake with us. I have this overwhelming sense in my heart that something is wrong. I want to cry, and I look over at my parents. My Dad is looking at me now, studying me it seems.

"Laurita, what's wrong?" he asks me as I sit there, clenching my hands and the obvious look of worry on my face. "Did they tell you something about Manny?"

I look over at my Dad, he is worried, too and my face can't be making things any easier. There is a seat between us and I think of moving over. I wish I could just go over and hug him, find comfort with my Daddy

 "No, Dad. It's not Manny." I'm trying to contain my emotions. "I'm worried about Jake." I finally say, my voice cracking in the process, a tear escaping down my cheek. "I don't know if he was there, too," I tell him, no longer able to contain my feelings. "I texted him and he has not responded, and when I call him it goes straight to voicemail." I'm crying now, and my whole family is listening to my emotional rant.

I look up, everyone is looking at me unsure of their feelings maybe? I see mixed feelings in all of their eyes. Mami is the only one who looks at me with understanding. She gets up and comes over to sit next to me, putting her arm around me.

"Ay, Laurita, let's say a little prayer for him, ok?" She puts my head on her shoulder. I hear her whisper a prayer, but I do not understand the words. My heart is racing, hurting.

"Family of Manuel Sanchez." I finally hear in the distance. I sit up and Mami quickly let's go.

We all stand up and walk over to the female doctor. A good-looking woman, young. She is smiling. I hope it's good news. I really am worried about Manny, too.

Janet stands in front, Mami and Dad right next to her. "Yes. We are the family of Manuel Sanchez." She tells the doctor as she holds my mother's hand tightly.

"I'm Dr. Davis. I've been assisting the physician attending to Mr. Sanchez." I hear optimism in her voice. "Luckily, Mr. Sanchez was on the outside perimeter of the blast." She starts to tell us. My brother is alive. I see Janet's grip on my mother's hand loosen as she takes a deep breath. She is relieved to hear that my brother is alive, "He has suffered some broken bones, from the debris, but amazingly, he has no burns to his body." She smiles widely now. "And although he has some recovery ahead of him, it looks like he is going to be alright." Janet hugs Mami tightly, she is so happy. She is crying from the release of emotion.

"When can we see him?" My brother Alex asks Dr. Davis.

"We are moving him to the ICU as a precaution until his blood pressure is stabilized," She smiles again. "For now, I can allow one person at a time in with him." Janet moves forward. "Once he is moved upstairs, he can have regular visitors." She puts her arm around Janet and starts to lead her.

"Ay, Gracias a Dios!" Mami cries out and she throws her arms around my Dad. I smile as I see them holding each other. Alex and Gracie are in a tight embrace as well. Everyone is so relieved to hear that Manny is going to be ok.

I look up at the TV and see the Breaking News Story about the blast being covered. I take my seat and listen intently. I am listening for the names or numbers of the victims. I have to get up and walk closer to the TV, I cannot hear from my seat.

According to the news report, there are two dead at the scene and three transported to SAMMC. Manny is one of the injured obviously. This is not calming my nerves. I pull my phone out of my purse again. Dialing Jake's number one more time.

Nothing. Straight to voicemail once again.

I'm shaking, and I have a lump in my throat. The feeling of not knowing whether Jake was hurt in the blast is driving me crazy, but I do not dare to ask at the nurse's station if they have any information on him.

I hear my cell phone ringing and quickly look down hoping it is Jake.

I look at it sadly, It isn't Jake, It's Eric.

I answer reluctantly, "Hello?"

"Laura, Casey said you had a family emergency and I saw the news, is Manny ok?" Eric asks quickly. Normally, I would be happy to hear from Eric but right now, it's Jake I want to hear from.

"Yes, he is going to be ok," I tell him flatly and very short.

"Are you ok? Do you need anything?" He asks me, my mind still preoccupied thinking about my Baby's Daddy.

"No, Eric, I'm fine. Thanks for calling." I see a familiar face walking into the ER. "Eric, I have to go. I will call you later." I do not wait for a response and hang up the phone right away. I quickly get up and walk quickly towards the nurse's station.

As I walk up I hear him ask the nurse behind the desk. "I was told my brother was here, he was in the accident at Republic Disposal." These words go thru me. Jake *is* here. I feel the emotion start to intensify. "His name is Jake Lakewood."

I walk up, grabbing his arm, "Bob?" I am looking at Jake's brother with tears in my eyes.

"Laura, do you know anything about Jake?" He asks me right away seeing the tears in my eyes.

"No, I didn't know he was here," I tell him, the emotion overwhelming now. "I'm here because my brother was involved, too" I start to cry. The nurse is looking at both of us.

"I'm sorry what did you say his name was?" Bob turns around to look at her.

"Jake Lakewood." Bob turns to look at me, "I got a call from Jake's work saying he was brought here." He looks worried, almost as if he wants to cry as well. I lean in to hug him. God knows we both need a hug right now.

"After our mom died, we only have each other, you know?" He

says to me as he returns my hug.

"Sir, someone will come out to speak with you." The nurse interrupts our conversation, her cold, emotionless voice giving no sign, no hint as to what might await us when the doctor comes out.

Bob nods his head and he starts to walk towards the chairs in the waiting area. I follow behind. I don't know Bob very well. I've only seen him a handful of times and each time it has been at a bar, running into him while Jake and I were out and about. He never came over to visit, has never met Matthew and I don't even know if he is married.

"Bob, my family is over here if you would like to sit with us." I point towards the row of chairs by my Family. Bob quickly turns to make his way over to the chairs.

"Is your brother ok?" Bob asks me. He's nervous, but he's trying to be nice.

"They just came out and told us that he's going to be ok," I tell him. He is trying to smile, but I understand his reluctance, he's thinking about Jake.

"Mami, Dad, this is Bob, Jake's brother," I say as we walk up to Mami and Dad. Mami's face drops, suddenly realizing the only conclusion to this scenario. Jake *is* here. Bob shakes their hands without saying a word. Alex and Gracie are nowhere to be found.

We are about to sit down when I hear someone at the double doors, yelling. "Is there someone here for Jake Lakewood?" It's a female voice and Bob and I quickly walk over to her. She's a nurse, I think, she's wearing what looks like a nurse's uniform to me.

"Are you here for Jake Lakewood?" She says to both of us as we stand there in front of her, looking at her. Both of us seem to be at a loss for words.

"Yes," I finally say to her. Bob is still standing there unable to speak.

"Follow me." She says. Another detached, unemotional nurse. I could never work in the healthcare field and have to be able to keep my emotions under control. It would be too much for me.

She takes us into another waiting room. "The doctor will be out to speak with you in just a minute," she tells us leaving us in this waiting room by ourselves.

I turn to look at Bob, he is distraught and starts to pace. I'm worried now. This waiting room is small, out of the way. There is no one else here. Why would they come to get us only to bring us into another waiting room?

I see a doctor coming towards us. His face is not so cold and distant. A look in his eye that tells me it isn't good news. He is not so comfortable with what he is about to tell us.

I suddenly feel chills come over my body. His words are fuzzy.

****

Chapter 22

Letting Go

Imagine every feeling of sadness or loss that you have ever experienced. You take all of them, put them together, multiply it by one thousand and you still do not have the emotion that envelopes your whole being when you have lost someone that you love. Everything they have ever done to you suddenly seems small and unimportant. You hang on to every happy moment, every smile. Every memory.

Jake's last words to me, confessing his love to me, was, I believe fate allowing him to say goodbye. Making it right between the mother of his child and him.

I hear Mami's voice again.

'Everything happens for a reason, Laurita'

I have been on auto-pilot since, throwing myself into my work and giving Matthew all of my time and attention.

I feel the stares from both Justin and Eric during our staff meetings and around the office. Occasionally a call or text comes in. If it is not business-related, I cut it short or do not respond. I don't even answer my front door anymore unless I'm expecting someone.

Depression? Maybe, but everyone grieves in their own way. This has been my way for the last four weeks.

Black Gold is expanding. Two new locations in Carrizo Springs and Pleasanton. It's actually pretty exciting. Our fleet is almost tripling in size and on the Drilling side, we have work scheduled for the next two months.

I have to start hiring personnel for the two new locations. We will have a small administrative staff at each location.

I make my way into the conference room for our Friday Morning Staff Meeting. I don't arrive early anymore just to avoid conversations with anyone. I usually get there just as the meeting is going to start. I take my typical seat in the back. The partners all sit in front, Corey and I stick to the back.

"Laura can you please sit up here." Trace tells me as I walk in. I don't understand why I need to sit up front, but I do as I'm told. It looks like we have a power point presentation today.

I see Justin and Eric walk in. Eric's smile tells me something is up. Justin, too, flashes his movie star smile. Everyone is smiling at me. Why is everyone smiling at me?

Trace closes the door to begin our meeting.

"Laura, the partners, and I have been discussing your role here at Black Gold." Trace starts to say and again everyone is looking at me. I sit up a little straighter in my seat. I definitely did not expect to be the first subject of today's meeting. "With the two new locations, we feel your position needs to be upgraded to match your responsibilities." Trace smiles at me. Am I getting a raise? I manage to smile. I haven't smiled in so long.

"We have decided to upgrade your position to Executive Officer in Charge of Administration." My mouth drops. I can honestly say, I am quite surprised. Just yesterday I applied for an Office Manager position with another company. In one of my moments, thinking it's best I just get away from here. Now, I'm being *promoted?* I am in shock.

"Actually, everyone's title is going to change. This office is going to become our Main Headquarters. You will have administrative staff at each of the two offices. You will be in charge of them, hiring, firing, etc. We'll continue to handle the operations." Trace sounds really happy to be telling me this. I am happy as well. It's been weeks since happiness has shown on my face, I'm having a hard time showing my emotions.

Everyone has their eyes on me. It almost seems like they're waiting for a response. I turn to look at Trace. "Do you need an answer from me?" I ask him, putting my hand to my chest and for some reason, everyone starts laughing. I didn't know I was funny.

Trace answers, still with a smile on his face. "Well, we would like to know if you accept the position?" he says.

"Oh," when he said they were upgrading my position I didn't think I had a choice. "Yes, sure. Thank you." I say thinking about my application to the other company.

"You won't be Office Manager anymore," Justin says from the back. "You will have two Office Managers at each of your locations." This is big. I will no longer be a Manager, but instead will be one of the Officers? I smile.

"Ok, I'm sure I can do it. I appreciate your confidence in me. Thank you." Trace continues with his power point presentation. It speaks of the changes; title changes, new buildings, and hiring initiatives. I notice Corey's new title is Regional Manager over Operations.

The meeting lasts a bit longer than usual, but I am truly excited about the direction Black Gold is headed.

I am ready to get up and go when I notice Trent walking towards me.

"Laura, can you stay behind, I would like to talk with you a moment." I sit back down. Everyone is congratulating me as they walk out, and I smile. I'm trying to be happy. I am happy.

It's just Trace and myself in the conference room. Maybe he needs to go over my added responsibilities.

"Laura, as the officer over finance, we decided I would be the one to speak with you about salary." Oh, that's what this is about. My $48k a year is already a blessing, I can't imagine what they have in mind.

I see Trace writing something down on a sticky. He then hands it over to me. "This is what we had in mind. Is this ok with you?" I look down at the sticky and I blink my eyes twice to make sure I didn't look at it wrong.

"Trace, this is more than I could have ever imagined," I tell him looking at the $75,000 number he has written on the little yellow paper.

"Well, your salary should match your responsibilities," He says in a stern voice. "You have and continue to do a lot for Black Gold and we feel this is the right decision." I am so grateful and feel guilty again for applying for another job. What was I thinking?

"Thank you," I tell him, at a loss for any other words.

I gather my things and head back to my office. I see, out of the corner of my eye, Eric and Justin still standing in the hallway.

"Congratulations, Lori," Justin says as he leans in to hug me.

"Thank you," I told him giving him a one-arm hug. I see Eric watching us. He's smiling, but I see the jealousy in his eyes. He doesn't know that Justin and I are no longer seeing each other. At least, I never told him.

"You deserve it, Lori," Eric says as I walk away from Justin. He doesn't lean in for a hug, but he does put his arm around me as we walk. "I wish you would start smiling again." He whispers, looking down at me as we come to the front of my office. "Really." He says as I walk in. I turn around, leaving my door open for the first time in a long time, and smile back at Eric. He quickly reciprocates.

Life doesn't stop, and it's about time I join it again.

****

I promised Christine I would go to Benny's with her tonight. Our long, overdue Friday night, Girls night out.

Mami is almost too happy to babysit. I drop off Matthew and I see the smile on her face.

"Enjoy yourself, Laurita," she tells me as I walk out the door. I haven't heard Mami *ever* tell me to enjoy myself on one of my Girls Night Out with Christine. I know she is probably just glad I am out of the house.

"Thanks, Mami," I kiss her cheek and start to make my way to the door. In the corner of my eye, I see my Dad. He is standing now, up from his recliner. This surprises me because, at this time of night, nothing can get Dad away from his recliner and TV. I see him walking towards me and suddenly he is standing right in front of me by the door.

"Dad?" I'm looking at him puzzled. In an even more surprising move, my Dad stretches his arms out to me, as if he's asking for a hug. I move in to hug him. I haven't been hugged by my Dad in what seems like forever.

"I'm glad to see that you are doing better, Laurita." He says to me in a deep, low voice. And just like that he lets go, composing himself and walking back to his TV and recliner. I feel emotional. Happiness and sadness are all wrapped up in one.

What a way to start my night.

****

I pull up to Benny's and it is in full swing, already packed.

"You're here to have fun, Laura," I tell myself out loud before going in.

I walk in making my way to our usual table. I see Christine, she is waiting, a Margarita for me already on the table.

Christine is smiling when she sees me, her ever so contagious smile. I can't help but feel happy.

"OH MY GOD!!" Christine sees me and she is getting up and coming over to hug me.

"Hi, Chris," I tell her forcing a smile on my face.

"Lori, I'm so glad you are here!" Christine does seem very happy.

"I'm glad, too, Chris. I was getting cabin fever." I tell her, I'm ready for today. I need a drink.

That first sip of Benny's famous Margarita is the best I've ever tasted. It could be that I haven't had a Margarita in a while, but it really tastes good.

"You look happy, Chris." She quickly locks a smile on her face from ear to ear.

I smile back at her. I can do this. It's been too long.

"I guess you are still seeing Brent?" I ask her, I see the glow on Christine's face. She is different, she's happy.

"Yes! How did you know?" Her eyes are sparkling at the mention of his name.

"I see it on your face, you look happy." I smile and take another drink. These Margaritas are really going down well. I believe my best friend has ordered mine with a double shot once again. "I guess it's getting serious, then?"

"Oh, Lori, who would have thought that I'd finally get serious about someone, right?" She's beaming. "Brent and I are going out of town tomorrow, just to spend the night at a little cabin he found in the Hill Country." In forever, I have never heard Christine talk like this. About anyone.

"How about you?" Christine looks over at me. "Have you talked to Eric or Justin?" the smile on my face drops and I finish what is left of my Margarita. Christine is studying me, her smile not so wide.

"I need another Margarita, you?" I ask her, trying to avoid her question. Christine is not buying it.

"I guess that's a no!" She yells at me. She calls over the waitress, ordering two more drinks. "You can't avoid them forever, Lori." She tells me as the waitress leaves the table with our order.

"I talked to them today…sort of," I take a drink thinking of Justin's hug and the smiles between Eric and me.

I look over at Christine, "I've applied for an Office Manager Position with a different company." The stunned look on Christine's face makes me almost want to laugh.

"What?!" She holds my arm, "You love working at Black Gold!" She yells at me.

I try to smile, but she is right. I do love working at Black Gold.

"I just applied, Chris, it doesn't mean I'm going to get the position," I tell her sarcastically.

"You're running away, Lori," she fights back. She points her finger at me, almost upset. "You're running away."

I smile at her, "Whatever." I take a drink of my Margarita, scanning the bar now. It's a packed house.

I do notice a familiar face at the bar.

"Chris, look!" I turn to her pulling on her arm. "That's Eric's fiancée!" I point at *Jessica* who is standing by the bar with what looks like other attorney types.

"She's the blonde," I tell Christine and we both stare for a moment when suddenly an unfamiliar face walks up to her and plants a very long, sensuous kiss on her lips.

"Oh, Shit!" I say as I turn back in my chair.

"I guess she's not with Eric anymore," Christine says laughing hysterically and I start laughing along with her. I really missed Christine.

"What are you going to do if they want to hire you, Lori?" She asks me, a little more serious now. "You know you bring a lot to the table. They'd be stupid not to give you, at least, an interview."

"Chris, I don't think…" I'm really feeling these Margaritas. I'm trying to tell her about my promotion, but she doesn't let me finish.

"Eric will probably get his Daddy to buy that company just to stay next to you." She says, trying to be serious but smiling. I tilt my head but we both start laughing once again.

I look down and see my telephone notification go off. I pick up my cell phone and see that I received a text message from Eric.

"Geez, I swear that man knows when we are talking about him!" I say to Christine as I swipe the screen to read my message.

I really love your smile.

I look up from my phone and start to look around. He has to be here. He wouldn't have sent this text if he wasn't here.

Christine sees the look on my face. "What's wrong, Babe?" she says, looking around puzzled and unsure what she is looking for.

"He's here, Chris," I tell her. I think I'm having an anxiety attack. I can't breathe.

Breathe, Laura, Breathe.

"Where?" she's looking around when I see her stop and sit back. I hear Eric's voice.

"Hi," He hugs Christine first, probably trying to figure out my mood. I'm looking down, shaking, unsure of my feelings right now.

"Hey, Lori, in case you didn't notice, we have a guest at our table!"

Christine yells at me from across the table.

Pull it together, Laura!

I finally look up, making eye contact with Eric. He is handsome as always, the beautiful eyes, perfect hair, and a beautiful smile. The smile I have always loved. Suddenly, I feel weird.

"Isn't that your fiancée over there?" I ask him pointing at *Jessica* over at the bar. Eric doesn't take his eyes off of me. I smile at him.

He places his hand under my chin, with his thumb running across my bottom lip.

"I really missed that smile, Lori." I bite my bottom lip, I missed him, too. "and I'm sure you've noticed, she is with someone else now." He says smugly, smiling again that sincere, beautiful smile. "What about you? Where's Mr. Perfect?" he says, and I look down. Again, Eric understands my unspoken words. His wicked smile came over his face again.

"Would you all like to join us, we have a table going in the back." He says looking at both of us. I look at Christine. Before I can say no, she says yes, and we are both up and following Eric to the back. The back room is usually reserved for exclusive guests and private parties. I guess Evan and Eric can come in here and just get the room when they want to. As we walk in, I see *Mona* sitting in a corner with some guy, deep into a make out session. Geez, get a room. I guess she wastes no time.

I see Evan, he is in the middle of the room, sitting at a table sur-rounded by mostly women but I see a couple of men there, too. Probably there to pick up Evan's scraps. I chuckle a little inside. I missed going out. It's so much fun to watch people.

Eric walks up behind Evan and whispers something in his ear. He quickly turns around and comes over to hug me.

"Laura! Great to have you here! Whatever you want, you just ask, ok?" He's drunk, I can tell. "It's good you're here. Eric is a mess without you, you know?" He smiles again and just like that, he goes back to his table.

Eric takes my hand and shows us to an empty table. He leaves us there and goes to the bar. As he is getting the drinks, I look over at Christine. I didn't notice the cheesy smile on her face until now.

"What?" I ask her, looking at her with a crazy expression.

"I don't know if you've noticed, but you haven't stopped smiling since we got up from our table over there." She says pointing in the direction of the door. She starts fumbling thru her purse, taking out her cell phone. "I'm calling Brent. If your boyfriend is here, I want my boyfriend here." She says as she starts to text on her phone.

"He's not my boyfriend, Chris," I say, throwing the small napkin that is on the table at her.
"Whatever." She says putting up her hand as she stays glued to her phone.

Eric comes back with our drinks and he takes his seat next to me.

Brent must have been waiting for Christine's call because he shows up only twenty minutes after she calls.

"Lori, we'll be back. We're going to go dance" I hear Christine say over the music and I smile as she leaves the table.

"I'm glad to see you out tonight," Eric says, sitting there with his beautiful smile. "I've been bored following Evan around everywhere." I turn to look at Evan and laugh.

I smile at Eric and say nothing.

"So, you and Justin. Is that over?" Eric asks trying to verify his earlier guess.

"Yes, actually, it's been a while. Since before that last night you came over to my house." Eric tilts his head, "you know, the day you told me you had asked Jessica to marry you?" I smile the sarcastic smile I have learned so well.

"That was just a big mistake, Lori," Eric says. "I did it for all the wrong reasons and she called me on it." He says looking at me now, studying me. "I didn't even have a ring when I asked her. It was just dumb." He says taking a drink from his glass.

"Well, we all have our moments, I guess." I look at him and smile. I know I've had my moments where I think I know it all and then something happens to let me know just how wrong I am.

I see Christine coming back over to our table.

"We're gonna get outta here." She says, looking down at me. I mouth 'ok' and lean in to hug her.

"Have a safe drive home," I tell her whispering in her ear.

"Are you ok here?" she asks me, a look of concern on her face.

"Oh, yea, I'm fine." I look at her seriously, "It's Eric, Chris. I'm good." And I make a goofy face at her and she smiles.

"Eric, always a pleasure." Christine walks over and hugs him, saying something in his ear. These two *still* have something going on that they haven't told me.

"Don't worry, Chris, I'll take care of her." He says as she straightens back up. I smile.

My two best friends. My Protectors.

I see Brent at the door and Christine quickly takes his hand and they are off.

I turn around and I'm met by the beautiful sparkle of Eric's green eyes and an award-winning smile. I can't help but smile.

"I missed your smile, Lori." He says again. Eric's voice sings in my ears. I never realized how much I missed hearing his voice.

"I missed you, too." I finally say to him. "It's been too long." I take a drink of my new Jack and Coke that he has brought to the table for me.

"Yes, it has. How is your brother doing?" He asks me. I notice that Eric is wearing jeans and a tee-shirt and, as always, he looks good.

"Manny is good. He's home now, Thank God." I tell him, trying to concentrate on our conversation but for some reason, I am now looking at Eric's lips. They look so…sexy. "He's on crutches now, but he's, at least, getting around on his own." Oh, my, it really is getting hot in here.

We both sit there for a moment staring into each other's eyes. So many things were left unsaid the last time we spoke.

"Evan really looks like he's enjoying himself," I say looking over at Evan's table in the middle of the room. Trying to distract both of us. Eric smiles shaking his head.

"Yea, Evan knows how to party." He looks around the room and takes a drink of his Jack and Coke.

"Mona has found a new victim," I tell him laughing, pointing to the corner.

"I only hope you didn't think I messed around with that?" Eric says laughing. "She's not my type. I don't do the bar rat thing." He looks over at me.

"Oh, really?" I say jokingly. "I know all about your long list of girl-friends, Eric." I'm pointing into his chest.

"It's a distinguished list." He says trying to keep a straight face.

We both look at each other and start to laugh. It's almost midnight now and I think it's time for me to go.

"Eric, I really think I should get going." I look at Eric and his expression changes suddenly. He sits up straighter in his seat.

Eric doesn't question me, "Lori, let me take you home." He says quickly. I smile at him. Of course, My Protector.

"I have my car, Eric. I can't leave it here." I tell him taking out my keys.

"Well, I'll follow you home then. Make sure you get there ok." He says as he gets up. "Wait here a second." He walks over to Evan and whispers something in Evan's ear. Evan turns to me and waves goodbye. I wave at him and smile.

"Ok, let's go." Eric puts his hand on my back in the small of my waist. It sends what feels like a jolt of electricity thru me when I feel his touch. Oh, Dear.

As I drive home, I see the Black Chevy Tahoe following me close behind. I feel like I have Secret Service following me home. As I pull into my driveway, I feel the door to my car open slowly. Eric is already standing there holding out his hand, waiting for me to get out.

I reach for his hand and climb out.

"Thank you for following me home." His sparkling green eyes are looking at me, straight thru me. Eric is standing right behind me when I feel his hand in mine, taking my keys from my hand. He opens the front door, letting himself in.

"Do you have anything to drink?" he asks me. I give him a crazy look as if I can't believe he would ask me that. I point to the kitchen. He walks over to the kitchen taking out some glasses from the cabinet. I walk over and take a seat at the bar and watch him. He makes himself at home, wandering around my kitchen effortlessly, without question as to where things are kept. I place my chin down on my hands on the counter as I watch him.

He finds the bottle of Jack Daniels he left on his last visit. "Ah, yes, Jack and Coke?" he asks me? The smile I love back on his face.

"Yes, thank you," I say as he starts to pour our drinks. He comes around and sits down next to me on the bar. He's suddenly looking at me seriously, with curiosity in his eyes.

"Lori, I got a peculiar call today." He starts to tell me. He's staring into my eyes and I'm almost lost in the moment. "It was from Rambler Oil Services." My eyes suddenly get wider. I know where this is going. "They wanted to know why you were leaving, said you applied for a position with their company." I look down. I can't believe they called before I even had an interview.

"What did you say to them?" I ask him without a hint of concern or worry.

"I told them you wanted more money and that you were worth it." He smiles at me. "I told them that unless they were willing to give you more than we were, you weren't going anywhere." I look down, feeling Eric's hand on my chin pulling my face back up so our eyes meet. "Don't do that."

"Don't do what?" I ask him. Is he telling me not to leave the company?

"You always put your head down as if you are ashamed or shy." He starts to say, "I know you are one of the strongest women I know, Lori. You should not hide this beautiful face or ever be ashamed of what you are. You are the reason I want to be a better man."

My heart completely melts.

For so long, I stayed with Justin because he fit the model of the 'Perfect Boyfriend', everything a woman would want. But not once in the whole time that I was with him, did he ever make me feel the way Eric makes me feel. Much less, did he ever make my heart melt.

"I don't want to leave Black Gold, Eric," I tell him almost looking down again. "I love my job. And now with this promotion, I would be stupid to leave." I close my eyes instead and start to fidget with my hands now. "I just didn't want to cause any more problems," I tell him as I open my eyes. Eric moves the hair out of my face, placing it behind my ear.

"C'mon," He motions to me, taking my glass. "Let's move over to the couch." I follow him obediently.

"Now, we aren't' going to watch some chick flick, ok?" he laughs a little as he says this. "We need a new movie." I smile at him. "Nothing mushy. Do you have any manly movies in your house?" I have to think. What's a 'manly' movie?

"I have Super Hero Movies," I tell him with a gleaming smile, the thought of those *manly* Super Heroes always makes me smile. Eric is not buying it.

"Uh, anything else?" he says playfully.

Suddenly, it hits me.

"Oh, yea!" I get up and take out a DVD my brother Alex gave me. "You know Alex is a police officer, right? Well, he gave me this movie." I hand over the DVD to Eric. "He said he really liked it."

"Ok, now that's a guy movie," Eric says as he pops it into the DVD player.

I sit there with Eric, snuggled up against him. I like the movie even if it is a 'guy movie' about law enforcement. Eric seems to like it, too. It feels good just sitting here with him. I don't feel pressured but with Eric, I've never felt pressured.

The movie is intense. I guess I should have read more about what it was about.

I wipe the tears from my eyes. Eric is watching me; he turns on the couch facing me now.

"Is that what Alex does?" he says trying to get my mind off of anything I might be thinking about, I'm sure.

"Well, it's San Antonio, not L.A," I tell him laughing. "I mean, it can get bad here but not *that* bad." I sit up and look over at him. "He has some stories, though. He can tell you some next time you see him." I look over at him and see a smile ease across his face.

"Maybe at the next Family Day," Eric says searching in my eyes for an answer.

I lean back on the couch. "I haven't been to Family Day in over a month," I tell him taking a deep breath, thinking about it.

"Well, as your friend, I can help you get back into the routine." I grin at him, a flirty smile. "I mean… however, I can help you, I'm here for you." He says playfully.

"That would be nice." I'm looking at Eric, remembering Mami's quote about Love being patient. Eric has been more than patient. I've been thru almost the unimaginable and Eric is still here. I smile at him again. "Four o'clock? You can pick us up." I tell him.

"You bet. I'll be here." Eric gets up from his seat. "I will leave you now." He takes our glasses to the counter. I get up wondering, wishing Eric would stay, but I'm too weak to make a move myself.

"Ok." I walk him to the door. Before he walks out, he pulls me in for a hug, holding me like he used to, kissing the top of my head. I feel one of his hands come between us pushing my face up towards his, and I feel his lips against mine. A small, gentle kiss that leaves me wanting more. He lets go of my waist and makes his way out the door.

"Good night, Lori." He whispers, only I can barely hear him over my pounding heart.

"Good night," I tell him softly.

I hear Mami in my head again.

'Find a nice boy who will respect you, Laurita.'

I think I have, Mami.

****

Chapter 23

Family Day - Round 2

Eric has arrived almost an hour early for family day. I'm still getting ready and he is in the living room with Matthew. I hear him talking with Matthew, whose vocabulary is now much more advanced. He can say a couple of complete sentences and phrases. He is already completely potty trained which has made my life so much easier, even though I started potty training late. According to Ms. Marty.

"Hey, do you need me to get a bag ready for Matthew?" Eric asks at my door as I'm still trying to get into a simple pair of jeans and a tee-shirt.

"Um, Yes, If you don't mind. Just a change of clothes and undies, please." I yell thru the door.

"You got it." He says. I really love that Eric is so at ease with Matthew. I hear giggles as I'm getting ready and it makes me smile. Eric always knows how to make Matthew giggle.

I climb into the passenger seat of the Tahoe and Eric straps Matthew into his car seat in the back.

"So, is there any new information I need to know before we get there?" Eric asks as he starts pulling out of the driveway.

"Well, my Dad has softened up a little with me," I tell him. "You know since Jake died." I look at Matthew. "He actually hugs me now," I say happily. My Dad is finally over the whole single mother thing. Maybe because I really have no choice anymore as far as Matthew's father is concerned, anyway.

Eric smiles. "I bet that makes you happy." He says looking over at me. "I mean, that your Dad has softened up a bit…" he fumbles over his words. "Not about Jake. Seriously, Lori, I didn't mean.." He's being really apologetic.

"It's ok, Eric." I reassure him. "my mind didn't even go there. I knew what you meant." I tell him. "but yea I did miss it. My Dad hugging me, I mean." I try to change the subject " and Alex and Gracie might be off again." I tell him. Even with Gracie towards the end of her pregnancy, those two cannot stop fighting. "Janet and Manny are pregnant." I laugh. "I guess his injuries weren't that bad, huh?" I look over at Eric who is now smiling wide.

"Really? Pregnant?" I'm shaking my head. "Wow, that's great. Do they know what they're having yet?" He asks me.

"No, I haven't seen them in a while, but they might already know." We're driving up to Mami's house now.

I get out of the Tahoe and take a deep breath. I see Eric carrying Matthew as he puts his hand out for mine.

"C'mon, you ready?" he tells me.

I look at Eric, taking his hand, he's carrying Matthew. This is where you need to be, Laura. I think to myself silently. This is where you should have been all along. I hold his hand a little tighter now.

I see the front door open. Alex comes running out.

"Hey! Little Sis!" He runs over and hugs me. "We've missed you. We were already gonna do an intervention." He laughs. "Hey,

Eric, how are you, Man?" He shakes Eric's hand.

"Hey, How's it going?" Eric answers Alex.

"Let me take my nephew. I haven't seen him in a while!" Alex says taking Matthew into the house. I hold Eric closer now as we make our way in.

We walk into the living room, and I see Manny, still in crutches and a pregnant Janet, Gracie is on the other side of the couch. Dad is sitting on his recliner, but when he sees me he quickly gets up.

Everyone greets Eric, glad to see him again, giving us both hugs. I'm sure they are wondering what exactly our relationship is. Daddy comes up to us next.

"Hello, Eric." My dad puts out his hand and Eric shakes his hand.

"Hello, Sir," Eric says to my Dad who is now looking at me.

"Laurita, you look more and more like your mother every day." My dad says as I see a look in his eyes that I missed so much. "Eric I hope you know exactly what you have here," Dad says taking my hand. "Laurita is my little angel and she has a heart of gold." I feel a little embarrassed at Dad's words.

"Sir, I have always known Lori is an angel. I just hope you're ok with me taking care of her now." I turn to look at Eric, his eyes are sparkling, and his smile is sincere.

My Dad is obviously also shocked at Eric's response and he turns to look at him.

"Well, as long as she'll have you." My Dad says seriously and we all stand there staring at each other.

I see Mami walk into the room.

"Hi, Mami." I walk over and hug her tight.

"Hi, Laurita. I see you smiling again. That's good." She says. Eric is still talking with my Dad but I'm not sure about what. "And I see why you are smiling," Mami says as she points at Eric. I smile back at her.

"Mom," I start to tell her, but she cuts me off.

"Don't tell me the two of you are still telling that silly story that you are just friends." She says almost a hint of frustration in her voice. "He looks even worse than the last time I saw him, Laurita! He's in love." She says lifting her hand over at Eric. "There are two things that a man cannot hide: that he is drunk and that he is in love," Mami says repeating another quote she has heard.

I giggle just a little and look over at Mami. All the times she has been in my head, Mami always has something to say. No matter what, I have always listened.

"Hello, Mrs. Sanchez." Eric comes over to say hello. She smiles taking his hand.

"Eric, please tell me that you will start making Sunday, Family Day with us?" She tells him smiling at him. I see what Mami is trying to do.

"Well, of course, Mrs. Sanchez, as long as your daughter can stand me, I will be here." He says smiling over at me and winking.

"C'mon, Eric, let's get something to drink," I tell him taking his hand and leading him to the yard.

Eric hands me a beer and we both take a seat at the picnic table.

"You're beautiful, Lori," Eric says as we sit there. I look over and smile at him. "No, I mean it. Everything about you. Your personality, your eyes, your laugh, your smile…" He pauses for a moment and smiles even wider "your rules." He takes his hand and places it under my chin. His eyes locked with mine. My whole body longing for him to kiss me.

"I just thought I was being smart that's all," I tell him, as we sit there staring into each other's eyes.

"Love doesn't know your rules, Laura." He says as he kisses me finally taking me out of my misery. I feel his lips press firmly against mine, leaving no doubt in my mind that I want anything else.

And somewhere in the back of my mind, I hear Mami.

'Love doesn't know anything about your rules, Laurita'

It seems Eric and Mami think the same. Eric loves me and I love him. I know that now.

****

"Thank you, Eric," I say, my cheeks still blushed, and my smile locked on my face. I absolutely had a great time at Family Day.

"No problem." He says looking over at me on the passenger side of his vehicle. He is still holding my hand. "Let me help you with Matthew. Poor Baby is done." I look back at Matthew, who is now sleeping in his car seat. He had a good time, too.

I walk up to the front door, Eric meeting me there with Matthew in his arms. I look up at him and smile.

We walk in and he immediately takes Matthew into his room, placing him gently into his bed. I'm watching him, studying him. He kisses Matthew on the forehead as he pulls the covers over him.

I can't be this blind. How didn't I see this before?

I walk into the living area with Eric closely behind. He walks into the kitchen, taking out a bottle of wine. He does things here without a thought. I walk over to the couch, lighting a candle and taking a seat.

Eric walks over, holding our wine.

"Eric, I need you to know something," I tell him as he takes his seat facing me. "I love you." I close my eyes. I don't want to look down. "I love you for being there for me through everything, I love you for being you. I just want you to know that…" I put my hands in the air. "That I love you." I laugh just a little. Giggling like a little girl deep down inside.

"Why, Miss Sanchez, are you telling me that you might be ready to…" he looks over at me curiously, "break your rules?" I am laughing out loud now. Blushing, feeling happy.

"Well, my Mom and you made it clear to me." I look at him seriously, "Love doesn't know any rules." Suddenly, Eric is close, I feel his lips on mine. We are kissing and I feel his body. His hands caressing my legs and finding their resting spot on my waist. His kiss is deep, long, sensuous, and full. I'm lost in the moment. I feel a tingling sensation throughout my body. Little bolts of electricity running thru me with every touch of his hands. I feel Eric breathing heavily, he's kissing my neck and holding me close. I have waited for this moment for so long.

"It's always been you, Lori," Eric says to me in a whisper. "Since the day that I met you, my heart is yours." My heart melts once again.

How is it that Eric knew from day one, and I've been oblivious until now?

"I love you, too, Lori, I've waited so long to find the right time to tell you." He says his voice is low and he is breathing hard.

"Eric," I say to him as he kisses me again, my heart is racing, and I feel the rush. He makes eye contact with me. His green eyes burning through mine.

"Yes," I say. He's looking at me now kissing my lips gently, questioning my words.

"Yes?" he repeats as his hands are caressing my back and going thru my hair.

"I'm ready to break my rules," I tell him, and he looks back up at me. The smile on his face is loving, mischievous, and playful. He lifts me from my seat, carrying me to the bedroom. I'm more than lost in this moment. I'm cherishing this moment.

Feeling his body on mine, finally. It feels as if it should have always been.

Why have you been wasting your time, Laura, when he's been here all along?

Eric knows who I am, what I need, and he has never asked for too much.

The night is perfect, and I know now where I need to be.

Lost in Eric Johnson's arms.

****

Chapter 24

Everything Happens for a Reason

Our staff meeting this morning feels a little different. Eric walks in, he's smiling. I wonder why? I think to myself sarcastically, knowing the answer to that question. Justin walks in next, I look up and catch his gaze. His eyes are full of questions, but I see a slight smile on his face.

"Good morning, Lori." He says as he takes his seat in front of me. "It's good to see you smile again." He looks over at Eric and tilts his head at him as if he is acknowledging defeat? I don't understand.

Justin turns his chair, he's looking at me now. "I was visiting my parents' house last night and passed by your Mom's house." I look at him, wondering where this conversation is going. "I just want you to be happy, Lori." He whispers as others start to shuffle into the conference room.

I look at Justin, confused and a bit sad. "Justin, what do you mean?" I whisper back. Deep down inside I know exactly what he means.

"I saw Eric's Tahoe, Lori." He says still whispering and he turns to listen to the meeting that has just begun.

During the meeting, I look at Eric and I see the cheesy smile on his face. He looks over at me and I know he is not listening. My phone notification goes off.

Eric is texting me from across the table.

You are beautiful

I smile over in his direction, pointing at Trace, mouthing the words 'pay attention' and Eric smiles. I don't think I've ever seen him this happy.

As the meeting ends, I can't help but feel that I, too, have not paid attention to this meeting. I make my way back to my office. As I walk in, I hear Justin's voice.

"Lori, I just want you to know, there are no hard feelings. I understand." He says. I look at him. I didn't mean to lead him on. I do care about him.

"Justin, I want you to know that there really was nothing going on before," I tell him, trying to reassure him.

Justin looks over at me and smiles, "Well, you're the only one who didn't see it, Lori. The rest of us always knew." He walks out of my office and I'm left there standing. Eric made it that noticeable and I still never *noticed?*

"Miss S, these are for you." Casey walks into my office with a beautiful bouquet of Red Roses. This time I count them, it's two dozen. I take the card and read it.

Just because I love you and always have.

Eric

I am on cloud nine. Only in my wildest dreams, could I have imagined being loved like this. This is what love feels like. I think to myself as I feel the butterflies in my stomach again.

****

The office Christmas Party has turned into the party of the year. It started as just a dinner but now we have moved it up and are having it catered, in a dance hall and it went from being semi-formal to formal. I can't say that I'm not excited. On top of that, we are allowed to invite our families. No, we are encouraged to invite our families.

Eric and I have been seeing each other for about two weeks now. As a couple anyway and we think the Christmas Party will be a good time to let everyone know about our relationship.

Officially.

We both are fully aware of the gossip. We think showing up to the Christmas party together and letting everyone know that 'yes, we are a couple' might ease up on the gossip chain. Plus, it will let my family know as well. They still think we are just friends.

It's going to be interesting for sure. Christine will be there with Brent, so, it makes everything all the better. Everyone I love under one roof.

****

It's been so long since I've dressed up in a formal dress. I asked a neighbor to watch Matthew since my family will be at the Christmas party with us. She's in high school, the daughter of one of my neighbors. A good girl, just like I was in high school.

Eric is punctual as usual.

"Lori, you look beautiful." He says as I answer the door. I raise myself to reach him, to be able to kiss him on the lips.

"Are you ready for this?" I ask him. Knowing that showing up together is going to put all the gossip to rest.

"I'm ready." He says, taking my hand and leading me to the passenger side of his Tahoe.

We arrive at the dance hall and park. I notice that there are a lot of cars already there.

"I didn't think we were late," I tell Eric as I make my way out of the vehicle.

I notice my family is all here. I see both of my brother's vehicles and my parents' vehicles as well.

"We're not late, Baby, we're just in time," Eric says as I step out of the Tahoe.

We make our way into the hall when I notice Mr. Johnson is here.

"Eric, you didn't tell me your dad was going to be here." I look over at him nervously.

"I wasn't sure he would make it," Eric says with a smile on his face.

I quickly go over to greet him.

"Mr. Johnson, so glad to see you again." He is looking at me with a different look in his eye.

"Miss Sanchez, I hear you are the lady that has put a smile on my son's face." His voice is stern, but I see a smile coming over his face now. "I saw the look in his eye the first day he met you. I'm amazed it took this long for him to tell you." I'm overjoyed. I was afraid that Eric's father would not approve.

Eric and I walk into the hall, my arm in his, leaving no question as to our relationship. I feel the stares and hear the whispers in the background.

"All eyes are on you, Miss Sanchez." Eric leans over and whispers.

"Oh, no, Mr. Johnson, I believe, all eyes are on us." I smile back at him and he kisses my forehead.

In the distance, I see Casey, our receptionist, her eyes wide at what she just witnessed. She is sitting at a table with Michael. Michael turns and raises his glass as we pass their table.

"Hi, Mami, Dad," my parents rising now from their seats to greet us. I hug my mom tightly.

"It's about time, Laurita." She whispers in my ear. "You look beautiful, Mija."

I walk over to my Dad and kiss his cheek. "Eric is a good man," he starts to say, and he looks me straight in the eye. "Follow your heart, Laura."

My nerves keep my hands shaking as Eric pulls the chair out for me. I see Eric calling over his father and mother to our table.

"Mr. and Mrs. Sanchez, I would like to introduce you to my parents Patrick and Alicia Johnson." Our parents shake hands and exchange smiles.

The DJ is playing a lot of country music and I don't know how to dance country so, Eric and I have not danced much. Still, the conversation at our table has been great. I feel so at ease with Eric, his parents, my parents, my family.

I am lost in this moment when I feel Eric take my hand.

"I believe they are playing our song, Miss Sanchez." He says as he leads me to the dance floor.

It's a slow song, 'Amazed' by Lonestar.

Eric takes me in his arms, singing softly into my ear. We dance close, and probably slower than we should, but we are both cherishing the song, the time we have to hold each other close. I dance in his arms with my eyes closed.

I open my eyes, only to see that Justin is watching us. He smiles at me, a hint of disappointment in his expression.

Eric pulls me in tighter. "I love you, Lori." He whispers in my ear.

"I love you, too," I tell him.

I look over at Mr. Johnson and he is smiling. Obviously, he has approved of our relationship.

Why was I the only one who did not see this before? Eric suddenly kisses me, in front of everyone, a long, passionate, wonderful kiss. My heart is filled.

When I am with Eric, I am whole, my life makes sense. My rules do not apply. He is not perfect, but neither am I. We complete each other.

We spend our time looking for things, trying to fit people into what we think is the perfect person, boyfriend, girlfriend and sometimes we miss what is right in front of us.

www.ingramcontent.com/pod-product-compliance
Lightning Source LLC
Chambersburg PA
CBHW071308140726
47996CB00005B/1685